ZENA

THE HOUSEWIVES' DETECTIVE

ZENA

THE HOUSEWIVES' DETECTIVE

Lyndsay Bird

Matador
Unit E2 Airfield Business Park
Harrison Road, Market Harborough
Leicestershire LE16 7UL
Tel: 0116 279 2299
Email: books@troubador.co.uk
Web: www.troubador.co.uk/matador
Twitter: @matadorbooks

ISBN 978 1 80514 079 5

British Library Cataloguing in Publication Data.
A catalogue record for this book is available from the British Library.

Printed and bound in Great Britain by 4edge Limited
Typeset in 11pt Minion Pro by Troubador Publishing Ltd, Leicester, UK

Matador is an imprint of Troubador Publishing Ltd

For my dear friend Liz.

CONTENTS

PREFACE

Zena Scott Archer started her career as a private detective in post-war 1940s. As my second cousin once removed and a minor celebrity she was part of six decades of family history. Mysterious and striking, Zena and her stories featured throughout my life. She would pop up on television shows like *Cleudo*, *Crimewatch*, and *Wogan* only for me to exclaim – "Is that really Zena?" She also featured in many radio interviews including Woman's Hour, and her exploits were closely followed by *The Liverpool Echo*.

When Zena died in 2011 aged 90, I found the courage to contact her younger sister Marion. I wanted to write about Zena. An immediate invitation to stay at their smallholding in the wilds of Cumbria came by return mail. It is entirely thanks to Marion that this novel came about. She gave me fat packets of handwritten diaries, newspaper articles, photographs, and taped interviews. Years of typing up diaries, interviewing colleagues and friends helped me to understand Zena's character: fascinating, complex, charming, and no-nonsense in her attitude to men and work.

This novel is a legacy to Zena. Inspired by real cases, it traces Zena's life from when she joined Scott's Detective Bureau in 1946 until 1953 when her father died. The novel complements Caitlin Davies' non-fiction book, 'Private Inquiries: The Secret History of Female Sleuths' (The History Press, 2023) which includes Zena as one of the leading private investigators 'on the world stage'.

Lyndsay Bird

JOINING THE BUREAU

November 1946. Liverpool. A crow lay stiff in the snow. Black belly up. Small boys swarmed bombed-out buildings, searching for treasure. Scraps of shrapnel drew cries of excitement as they vied for abandoned trinkets from hollowed houses. It was not only London that suffered the Blitz.

Zena perched on one of three oak desks in her father's office and looked down onto Cook Street. She watched the boys scatter snowballs and tried to shut out the endless ringing of the office telephone. Her fingernail, painted vermilion, traced snow-spattered rivulets down the window as she waited. What could he want? He had summoned her with no clue as to why. She looked at her watch. Her boss at the Kardomah Café would kill her if she was late. She tapped her foot in annoyance. How much longer? She looked down at her shoes and admired the red ox-blood ankle straps. A good buy.

Zena was about to rap the desk to attract attention, when she heard her father's voice rasping from behind a wall of rusting filing cabinets. His cubbyhole-cum office.

'What about the Mitchell case?' Syd demanded. 'You've

been on it for weeks. Time is money, Joe, time is money. C'mon, fella. You need to get your skates on. How far have you got?'

It was all very well her father saying 'time is money', but Zena knew that if she was not back in the office soon, it could be time finished for her.

'It's been a tough one, boss. Couldn't track down his business partner for love nor money. I've been to all his usual haunts,' Joe answered.

'Down the tic tac, you mean. Bet you've been putting a bob or two on them nags,' Syd said. Even his wheeze sounded cross.

'Ah, now then, hold your horses, Syd. Ha ha, get it? Hold your horses? There's no harm in that, seeing as I'm there, like.'

'Not funny, Joe, not funny at all. We've a deadline. Mitchell's on my case night and day. He's lost thousands. You need to crack on. Here, give me the file and let me take a butcher's.' Syd's cockney rhyming slang hadn't been dulled by his years in Liverpool.

Zena heard him take a deep pull on his permanent Craven A. She peered around the cabinets to catch her father's eye. He hadn't registered her presence. Joe and Syd were sitting heads bent. Her father in his patched leather armchair, grey suit hugging his bulk. Joe in a hard-backed wooden chair opposite. Their cigarettes almost touched as they pored over the case file. Zena rapped on the filing cabinet, and her father waved her away. Not a dismissal, merely a sign to 'Wait.'

Zena looked around at the fug of her father's office: case files piled everywhere, the pall of smoke from Syd's ashtray, phone never answered, and always one or two of the detectives lounging around, smoking and drinking tea. Or worse. Yet the cases rolled in, missing persons, divorce, libel, domestic violence. *Scott's Detective Bureau* was busier than ever.

Zena had never seen her father so happy. Since leaving the Met's Flying Squad, Detective Sergeant Sydney J. Scott had come a long way from chasing jewel thieves through the streets of London. A chance encounter on a train led to his move to Liverpool, family in tow, and his own business.

Zena was glad of the move. It meant that she and Dave had somewhere to stay when he came back shattered from India after the war. Sharing with Nana, her parents and teenage sister Marion sometimes palled, but Zena was thankful that she and Dave had the back room to themselves. The war left Dave needing peace from the squawks of Nana's demands, and shouts from Zena's mother Madge.

Zena was jerked from reverie by her father's bark. She'd been summoned.

'Zena!'

'Morning, Dad. Sounds like you were giving Joe a bit of a ticking off. Can't he handle the case then?'

'None of your business, my girl.'

'What *is* my business then Dad? Why did you call me in? Do you know what it took for me to beg that creep to give me an hour off for lunch?'

'That's why I called you in, love. You've been bleating on about how much you hate working for Croft.'

'I can't argue with that.'

'Well now's your chance to get away. Come work for me.'

'Work for you? As a private detective?' Zena rather fancied herself as Miss Marple. Her mother Madge was less keen on the private detective business, and certainly would not approve of Zena becoming one.

'Ha ha. Nice one. No, of course not. You a private detective? I'd be a laughing stock.'

'I don't see why,' Zena said, annoyed that her father might think her incapable of anything, let alone being a detective.

'*I* do. It's no profession for a woman. I need someone to help type up the reports.'

'Reports? Another typing job?'

'Yes I can't keep up and now Gracie's left to get married, I've no one to help. You can be my secretary.'

'A secretary?' Zena was disappointed not to be thought of as a detective, but Dave would be pleased to see her leave the café.

'Yes, why not? Come on, you and me. Same office. Keep it in the family. What d'you say?'

'I don't know Dad. It wouldn't be much different from working at the Kardomah.' She hated working at the Kardomah Café typing up orders and invoices, but it paid well, and for the most part she worked regular hours.

'Of course it would be different my girl. *I'd* be your boss.' Syd coughed a laugh.

'Ha. Are you sure that would be a good thing?'

'Very funny. Come on love. I'll pay you a bob a week extra. How about that?'

'Oh, OK then,' Zena sighed, 'but temporarily, to help you out. Only until I find a more suitable job.'

4

'You won't regret it love.'

'I better not.' Zena glared at her father. 'You'll need to keep those detectives in line if I'm to be sitting here typing up dirty laundry.'

'They'll be grand. You'll see,' Syd said.

*

Back at the Kardomah Café, Zena stared into Croft's mud-brown eyes.

'What…What an earth…?' Croft said, his face reddening in apoplectic rage.

'Yes, I am leaving Mr Croft.'

'You can't. Absolutely not. You owe me a week's notice.'

'No, Mr Croft. Today will be my last day. I have worked overtime and weekends for no pay, typing up your invoices and getting orders out on time.'

'That was of your own accord. It's not my fault you couldn't keep up.'

'I beg your pardon? Of my own accord you say?'

'Definitely!' Croft's eyes narrowed slightly in doubt.

'I won't go into the appalling way you manage things here Mr Croft. I could easily report you to the owner.'

'What…What…you wouldn't dare.'

'I would dare Mr Croft and I owe you nothing. You, however, owe me wages for this week.'

'You…You…bloody…' He stopped short; coffee stained spittle foamed his mouth. 'OK you've had it. You will leave this instant, young lady. Pack your things and go. And if I see you, or that skinny wretch of a husband of yours, I'll set the dogs on you both.' Turning on his heel, he slammed the heavy wooden door as he marched out.

'Just you try!' Zena shouted after him.

Zena's heart quickened as she packed her box, desperate to leave. She placed her things in the box one at a time: the photo of her and Dave on their wedding day in May 1941, the china cup and saucer in 'Old Country Rose' her grandmother had given her, a wooden letter rack with the silver letter knife from her parents for her 21st birthday, and her prized Remington Deluxe portable. Although it didn't feel very portable when she lugged the box downstairs. Croft held the door, furious. She glared at him as she neared the exit.

'Don't treat your next secretary as badly as you did me, Mr Croft, and you might be able to keep her,' Zena shouted as she strode out, head high.

*

It was Zena's first day at Scott's and Syd's bulk pushed behind her, hurrying her out of the front door of Ripon Road.

'Come on. We'll miss the train.' Syd slammed the gate behind him.

'Can't we go in the car?'

The previous summer Syd had bought their neighbour's old Austin A10 to help with the business. Stan had put a raggedy sign in the back window saying *For Sale 15 Guineas* and parked it outside on Ripon Road. Because it was Syd, he'd knocked off two guineas. A bargain.

'What, drive in this weather? In this old thing? Safer to get the train.'

'But this snow. It's playing havoc with my stilettos.'

'That's you being daft about your fashion. You should have worn more suitable shoes. Hurry now. We need to get a move on.'

The silent echo of snow-filled streets was soft and heavy. Zena took Syd's arm, glad of its heft.

The doors of the garages on Leasowe Road were pillowed in white, their grime erased. In a moment of giddiness, Zena threw a crunch of snow at her father, laughing at the spray of white on his heavy black overcoat. He coughed something back at her, as he heaved open the station door.

'What was that Dad?' she said, laughing back at him as the train steamed into Wallasey station. She climbed into the freezing compartment. The heavy bang of the latch jarred behind her, as she sat down next to the soot-stained window.

'I said, the cleaning bill for my coat will come out of your first week's wages,' he barked, wheezing into the seat opposite. Zena half believed him, until he scratched the jemmy scar on his chin. A legacy of his criminal catching days in London. Zena didn't need to be a detective to know he scratched it only when he lied.

*

It was not long before Zena became as bored of the leering detectives as she had been of Croft. On her third day, she came in wearing her mink coat with a white fur tippet. Charlie and Joe whistled and teased.

'Are you sure you want to go out with your fella tonight? I bet I could show you a better time,' Joe said, blowing her a kiss. His face creased into a gap-toothed smile.

'Yeah, you need a real man to show you how to have a good time,' Charlie said. He looked her up and down, his heavy-lidded eyes daring her.

'In your dreams, boys, in your dreams,' she laughed, turning her back. Not worth the fight.

As Zena took up one of the files to be typed, she looked across at Joe. Spread-eagled over his chair, his paunch hung heavy over his brown checked trousers. A grease spot stained his tie. His desk was piled with papers covered in dust, tea stains, and ash. It was clear the report she held was Joe's. She could hardly read the blotched and scruffy handwriting. Worse still, it had no description of the person being observed, nor the house where he ended up.

Dickson Case, Wednesday October 30th, 1946: Subject was of average height and build. Followed him to house on Stanley Street.

Such lack of detail. Zena needed more. What was the subject wearing? How old was he? What was his hair and eye colour? What was the house like? Well-kept or dirty? Who opened the door? There was nothing in Joe's scanty report to give clues as to what the subject was up to. The wife would scarcely recognise that it was her husband they were following.

'Joe,' Zena said, looking up. 'Do you have a minute?'

Joe looked over at her and exhaled a lungful of smoke. He raised a bushy eyebrow in query.

'I can't tell anything from your report. What was the house like? Was it a semi? A terrace? Any distinguishing features…?'

'Old. A big detached house,' Joe replied.

'What about the outside?' Zena refused to give up. 'Were there curtains in the windows? What did the front garden look like? Were there trees? Shrubs? A climbing rose…?'

Joe shrugged, blasé as usual. Zena knew the devil was in the detail: small clues that would give a better picture of who was living there. Maybe the mistress was married herself if she was living in such a big house. Zena finished typing up the report in despair. She handed it back to him with a look that shrivelled any attempt at jocularity. Joe thought he could get away with anything if he told a joke. Not this time.

She stormed into the cubbyhole, as fast as her tight button-down suit and high heels would allow. A drift of a dark curl loosened itself from the elegant chignon sitting high on her head. Hazel eyes flashing, she glared at her father.

'Dad, these reports are terrible. Have you seen them? How on earth do Joe and Charlie ever find, let alone catch anyone? You know I could do better!' She was sure that her attention to detail and tenacity would suit her for the role. No matter that it was considered no occupation for a woman. It had to be more interesting than endless typing.

'Oh you think so? You? Go into gangster hangouts… Where women aren't even allowed. Are you serious?'

'Come on, Dad. There are loads of other jobs than just those.'

'That's as maybe. But none you should be doing.'

'Please. Listen to me. I can do better than Joe. Look at him,' Zena said, peering over the cabinet at Joe, who was laughing at some joke Charlie had made.

'No, you stick to your typing and filing for now. You're good at that.'

Biting back a sharp retort that would have no traction, Zena said, 'You know there are a lot of women who phone up or come into the office. They take one look at Joe and Charlie and walk out again. They talk to me.'

'I don't care. No.'

'But it would bring you more business.' Zena hoped the enticement of more clients might work better than her plea.

'I said no, Zena. And I mean no. Leave it be.'

Zena went back to her desk and banged at the keys of her Remington.

That night in their bedroom, Zena protested to Dave.

'I don't understand him. It would be nothing for him to give me a case. I could do some of them standing on my head. Daddy must know that.'

'Now, love. Don't fret. Take it slowly. Try not to argue with him.'

'But what else can I do to convince him?'

'Look maybe he's right. Do you know any women detectives?' Dave paused and looked at Zena, who dropped her eyes. 'You see. None. Not a single woman in Liverpool is a private detective. That tells you something.'

'It means nothing. You know how hard women worked during the war. Women can do anything.' Zena was getting riled.

'Oh come on now love, I didn't mean it like that.'

'Really?'

'No of course not. But do you honestly want to take on all those ex-coppers your dad hires? Imagine what they'd think.'

'I don't care what they think,' Zena said. She didn't care a fig about anyone's opinion, let alone the men her father hired.

'Listen love if you're sure, just bide your time. Be patient. If it's meant to be and all that.' Dave tried to pull Zena towards him, but she jerked away. She knew she could do it. Why should she bide her time?

*

Some weeks later Zena walked along Cook Street, a freezing March wind behind her. She stopped and stared up at the smear of yellow in the windows of the third floor office. The light was on. She rubbed at one of the sooted plaques on the stone entrance until *Scott's Detective Bureau* appeared, etched in brass.

She pulled open the doors into the hallway. Pressing the enamelled button, she called the iron cage of a lift. It jammed with a clang on the first floor. There was nothing for it. With a sigh Zena ran up the curling sweep of the staircase. Her thighs burned by the third flight, and she fell, chest heaving, into the fug-heavy office.

'Good morning, Charlie. Dad busy?' Zena said.

'Morning, Zena. Glamorous as ever, I see.' Charlie grinned at Zena as she removed her white fur hat and muffler, and hung up her black wool overcoat. Zena glared back at him as she sorted through the reports to be typed on her desk. He thought he was God's gift. No point in complaining to her father. He'd tell her to get on with it. It went with the territory. Like his insistence that she couldn't be a detective.

'Zena!'

Zena jumped at her father's bellow. She was head down typing up one of Charlie's reports. Easier to read than Joe's but still without the essential detail. Syd's reports were the gold standard and nothing else came close. His neat handwritten reports contained precise details of his case: the client, the person he was investigating, the daily results, photographs and relevant documentation.

As Zena walked into his cubbyhole, Syd looked up at her quizzically. Zena hated that look. It brought a sense of foreboding. Her stomach lurched slightly.

'What is it, Dad? Is everything ok? Has something happened to Mummy? Marion?' Zena asked.

'No no…Nothing like that. Just sit down for a minute.'

'What is it Dad? Please you're scaring me.'

'Don't be daft. All it is…' Syd paused.

'All it is, what?' Zena said. She was impatient now instead of scared.

'It's the lass who caught Charlie and Joe out each time.'

'What lass, Dad? Who are you talking about?'

'The lass on the Mauretania. Divorce petition. You typed it up, remember? I can't remember her name.'

'The Elsie Williams case?'

'That's the one.'

'Yes, yes. I remember it. It was unusual as it's the husband who wants a divorce. Joe tried twice to serve the petition. That one?' Zena remembered the case well. The woman, Elsie Williams had committed adultery during the war and the husband came back from a tour of duty, to find her living with another man. The war caused so many marriages to break down and both women and men to stray. Zena remembered her own intense loneliness when Dave was in India. Who was she to judge?

'Yes, that's it,' Syd said. 'The court hearing is coming up and the lads have missed her every time. Her mates on the ship must have covered for her.'

Zena said nothing. Her father needed to think it was his idea to let her try. After what felt like hours, her father looked at her again with his hard-edged stare.

'I'll give you this one case. Only one, mind you. See how you get on.'

'You won't regret it, Dad. I know I can do it. I'll prove it to you, I promise.' She went to hug him, but he waved her away.

That evening at the Empire Theatre, Dave held down Zena's fidgeting hands. She could barely sit still. What with getting ready after work, she'd not had a minute to tell him her news. Her chance came during the interval.

'I know I can do it Dave. Typing up those dreadful reports isn't enough. I'll show Joe and Charlie. And Daddy.'

Dave smiled at her from behind his wire-rimmed glasses. She watched him smoke his pipe; not sure whether to be annoyed or pleased at his lack of reaction. Did he believe her or not? Did he think she could be a private detective, or that it was a madcap fantasy? He stayed silent. As her mother always said of him, "A man of few words."

'Dave?'

'What?'

'You know what.'

'What do you want me to say, Zena? That I think you'll make a great detective? Maybe you will. How would I know?'

'I just thought you might be pleased for me.'

'I am. I am if this is what you want. I just worry, that's all.'

'Worry about what?'

'That it'll change things. Change you.'

'Oh for goodness sake,' Zena said, exasperated.

'Look I'm happy for you, I am. You know I'll support you with whatever you want.'

Zena knew that Dave gave in to whatever she wanted, and she loved him for it. But she also wanted the affirmation that she was doing the right thing. She was cross that he couldn't or wouldn't give it to her.

At home in the quiet of their bedroom in Ripon Road, Zena tossed Dave's reaction around her brain. He had made her doubt herself. Was he indulging her? Could she do it? Was she always dissatisfied with her lot? Then she remembered Joe's terrible reports, and Charlie's smug self-assurance. 'I can, I can, I can,' she repeated to herself. She would prove them all wrong.

Zena Scott Archer, private detective. She had to admit it had a certain ring.

2

ZENA'S FIRST CASE

April 1947. The whip and clink of hawsers reverberated in the crisp spring air. Men in yellow oilskins tied down lifeboats; their smoky breath drifting as they shouted across the white tarpaulins. Zena gazed up at red and black funnels towering into grey, rain-threatened sky. The sudden slap of sea that echoed against the hull of the *RMS Mauretania* recalled the crack of champagne during the naming ceremony at Cammell Laird's yard in 1938. Requisitioned as a troop ship during the war, the Mauretania's bright colours had been concealed beneath gun metal paint.

Now, the lovely lady lay docked, proud and tall in her Cunard colours, ready to set sail on her second 'maiden' voyage to New York. Zena strode across the companionway in her tight black skirt, ignoring the pinch of her high-heeled shoes. A curl of excitement grew. Her first case. As she stood at the other end of the companionway, unsure of her next move, Zena's doubts returned. Could she do it? Only her father seemed to think she might. Dave...Dave veered neither for nor against. As ever straight down the line. He hadn't allayed her misgivings. Of course Charlie and Joe had sat tight lipped when they heard, willing her to fail.

Excitement was in danger of turning to fear. Zena repeated her father's instructions in her head, "Be bold, stare anyone down who questions you, but get out if it looks like trouble." She could do it. She knew she could.

Zena looked towards the upper deck, where white-uniformed crew were bringing up steamer chairs and blankets for the arriving passengers. They barely acknowledged her when Zena shouted up, 'Where's Elsie?' Call someone by their first name or nickname, and they are more likely to turn around. If they hear their surname, they're on guard. Her father's top tip.

'Down below,' a lanky lad called back. 'Should be in the Club Class dining saloon.'

Heading down the wide sweep of the staircase into the lounge below was like being on a Hollywood set. Zena felt like Hedy Lamarr, gliding down the curved steps, a white-gloved hand smoothing the polished oak rail. In the sumptuous Art-Deco entrance hall, the leather club chairs were buffed, and the plush red button-backed sofas spotless.

As she moved through the hall into the Cabin Class lounge, iridescent with chandeliers, Zena checked her lipstick in one of the bevelled mirrors. She smoothed down her skirt, brushed a fleck of ash from her jacket, and turned from side to side. Suitably official. She should have brought a clipboard. That would've clinched it.

'Can I help you?'

The rumble of a deep voice over Zena's left shoulder startled her. A man's reflection edged behind her. The captain. She stayed stock still, flashing him a look in the mirror as she took him in: greying temples, tight lips and straight back, his uniform a crisp black and gold. Zena felt her knees buckle, and her head swim. She must not give in. She swallowed the panic, and turned to face him.

'Yes please, if you wouldn't mind. I'm from Scott's funeral directors,' Zena said in a calm voice. She looked down as if in a moment of respect. She remembered her cover story with ease, but crossed her arms to hide her shaking hands. Good tactic. It looked more official.

'I'm here to see Elsie Williams. I was told she was in the Club Class dining saloon, but I seem to have got lost. Can you direct me?'

'Through there.' He pointed to the left and strode off in the opposite direction.

Zena breathed out, relieved she had not been frog-marched off the ship. Still shaking, Zena entered the elegant and formal dining room. It was vast and light. Stewardesses gossiped as they folded hard-edged linen napkins, and counted the heavy silver cutlery. There must have been over fifty tables covered in damask tablecloths. Zena pictured the guests coming down the staircase: men in dinner jackets and ladies in heavy sequinned ballgowns and elbow-length lace gloves. The glamour of the rich. Zena felt a sliver of envy. The war and the endless posters had instilled the ethic of 'make do and mend' in her and the nation. No glamorous new clothes for her. Her mink was a hand me down from Aunty Kath, and the fur tippet a wedding present from her parents.

Across the dining room, Zena spied a middle-aged woman – all pursed lips and dyed blonde curls. The woman was on edge, dancing from foot to foot. Zena watched as the woman checked the linen, running her finger down the folds.

'Elsie?' Zena said, her voice loud and firm.

The blonde head swung round.

'Mrs Elsie Williams?'

'Yeah! What d'you want?' Elsie's squawk pierced the room.

Zena took the divorce petition out of her bag and strode towards Elsie. The thick white petition in its red ribbon hovered over Elsie's wrist. Zena waited for Elsie to react. Nothing. Elsie stood rigid. Her wide-spaced blue eyes stared back at Zena.

Zena flinched as she felt a sharp slap on her wrist. Elsie knocked the petition out of Zena's hand, spun round and ran out of the dining room. Zena hadn't been prepared for that. Her father had assumed she would succeed, and so had she. Without thinking what might happen next, Zena picked up the petition and ran after Elsie. Through the back of the dining room and into the kitchen. Chefs and their underlings gawped at the two women who ran pell mell through their midst. Zena's brain whirled. How to stop Elsie? Zena could not bear to fail. She thought about tackling her to the ground, but realised her tight skirt would never allow such a manoeuvre.

Elsie ran up the back stairs towards the crew's quarters. Zena took off her stilettos. That at least she could do. She was closing in on Elsie.

'Elsie. Stop! Please. You will have to take it one day. If not from me, someone else will come, and they'll keep coming.'

'Why should I?' Elsie screamed back at Zena.

'It's the law.'

'The law? My arse the law. It's ok for him to have a floozy on the side even now, but me? No. No. Was I not allowed to find any comfort while he was away in the war?' Elsie stopped suddenly. She whirled round and faced Zena. A trickle of mascara slipped down her left cheek.

'Why stop the divorce though, if he has someone else?' Zena said. She barely missed a beat, the petition still in her hand.

'The kids. I know he'll try and take me kids.' Elsie's face crumpled. Zena reached into her handbag for a tissue.

'You could ask the court for joint custody. You're earning and you'd get the new family allowance. The courts usually favour the mother in custody cases.'

'I don't know. He always gets one over on me. Always has.'

Zena seized her chance. There was only one thing left to do.

'I'm sorry Elsie, I know this is hard,' Zena said as she edged forward.

'You've no idea, love. None whatsoever.'

'I know, and I am really very sorry. But I have to say this: Elsie Williams, you have been served,' Zena said holding out the petition a second time. Elsie stared down at Zena's hand. A multitude of thoughts raced through Zena's mind. What if Elsie still refused to accept it?

Zena coughed after waiting for what was probably less than a minute, but felt like an hour. She stared at Elsie, nodding towards the petition. With a resigned shrug, Elsie reached out her hand.

'You've done the right thing Elsie. I wish you luck at

the hearing,' Zena said. She whipped around and hurried off the cruise liner, legs and hands trembling. She'd done it! First time. It was hard on Elsie, and she felt sorry for her, but it was the law. It was not always fair. Zena couldn't wait to tell her father. Elated, she skipped back from Princes Dock, and almost tripping over her high heels, ran up the stairs of the Cook Street office. She burst through the glass panelled door, excited as a schoolgirl.

Joe and Charlie sat smoking, drinking tea and reading the daily papers. Charlie smirked at Joe, running his long fingers through his slick black hair. He leant back, his lankiness splayed across the chair, staring at Zena, daring her to speak. Joe's paunch pressed tight against the desk opposite Charlie. He ignored her entrance and turned the pages of the *Liverpool Echo* to the sports section. Zena rushed into her father's cubbyhole cum office, knowing Joe and Charlie would be listening. They would hate her success.

'You did it? Blow me!' Syd jumped up and gave Zena an uncharacteristically affectionate hug. 'No more money down the drain serving that petition. I'd say it's a winner all round. Well done, my girl, well done!'

'I followed your tip, Dad!'

'What tip was that then? I might need to remember it myself one day.'

'To call someone by their first name. It worked like a charm to get on the ship.'

'Works every time that one. Good job my girl, good job.'

'There were a couple of hairy moments, but in the end she accepted it. I told you I could do better than those layabouts out there.'

'Now, now, don't get above yourself. Those boys are OK. Beginner's luck is all.'

'I was good Dad,' Zena said.

'I'm sure you were this time. But there's a ton of reports for you to type up.'

Zena's heart sank, but she knew better than to argue.

'Let me work on another case, Dad. Please. Daddy, please? I can type up the reports at the same time.'

'No, not now, Zena. Now off you go like a good girl.'

'But…' Zena started and then stopped. No point. She cursed her father's stubbornness. Why couldn't he see what an asset she'd be?

Charlie looked over at Zena as she returned crestfallen to her desk. A sly grin twisted the corners of his lips. He whispered to Joe, loud enough for Zena to hear, 'Did you hear 'er? Another case my arse. This one was easy. Syd knows she'll never make a detective.'

Zena felt like slapping his face.

'Charlie, is this your report?' Zena held up a crumpled bit of paper. 'You need to write it out again. It's illegible.' She stared hard at him.

'OK, OK, Miss Hoity Toity. Don't get all arsy with me. You've been here five minutes and you think you can lord it over us.' Charlie's sneer spoiled his Cary Grant good looks.

'It's not lording it over you, Charlie. It's a fact. I can't read this report. Do you want me to give it to Syd in the state that it's in?'

'Daddy's little girl, eh?'

'Absolutely not! How dare you. I won that case fair and square.' Zena slammed out of the office. She had to admit that given what her father had just said, she may never get another case. Zena's mind whirled as she walked to the station. She was determined to win her father round and prove her worth.

3

THE HOUSE OF JOSEPH CASE

May 1947. It was less than a month after her first case when Zena first attended St. George's Hall Court. It was the divorce proceedings against Elsie Williams. The theatre of the court appealed to her, although the gowns and wigs seemed elaborate costumes for a simple case of adultery. Zena took in the pageantry of the stage, the oak panelled walls, and marbled columns. The high throne of the judge sat under the carved and painted royal justice crown. How many criminals must have faced that scene?

Zena felt sorry for Elsie who stood head down in front of the judge. Her thin, high voice a mere whisper as the judge boomed out a favourable verdict for Elsie's accusing husband. Elsie would get nothing. The scandal meant she also lost her job as stewardess on the Mauritania. No job meant no custody. What would become of her? Syd had told Zena not to get involved. 'Treat it as a job. Nothing else, my girl, and you'll be fine.' But Zena found it hard to watch Elsie crumble. She tried to imagine her own life with no support. No husband, job, and her children taken from her. She couldn't. She shook her head and left the court heavy of heart.

Back in the office Zena corrected the typed reports

and filed the invoices piling her desk. After the harshness of the verdict for Elsie, there was a mundane satisfaction in getting through the paperwork. Her desk was piled with papers labelled for filing: *Paid, Chase, Ongoing, Closed*. She filed the report of Elsie Williams under closed, and looked up as her father's bulk loomed behind her.

'I can't afford to hire another typist. If I give you another case, you'll have to type reports as well,' Syd said.

'Another case?' Zena's heart leapt. She would prove herself beyond doubt.

'Maybe. If you are sure you're up to it?' Syd said.

'Of course, Dad. Of course I am. You know I am. What's the case?'

'It's this fashion house. They've had a load of expensive gear nicked,' Syd continued. 'Seems to happen every time they have a fashion show for their private clients. They can't fathom how the stuff is going walkabout.'

'What would I need to do? Pose as a customer? I could pretend to buy some of the dresses.'

'Hold up, hold up. Let me explain.'

'Where is the fashion house?' Zena interjected. She had never been able to afford *haute couture*. She drifted into visions of tulle and lace trimmed dresses.

'Just stop. Now. Stop. And I'll tell you.' Syd's sharpness brought her back. 'It's already been decided what you'll do. Mrs Joseph has it all worked out.'

'Mrs Joseph? You mean Moira Joseph? *The* Moira Joseph?' Zena's heart raced. Moira Joseph. Liverpool's answer to Jeanne Lanvin. The House of Joseph. This was a dream job. Zena could barely concentrate on what her father was telling her.

'Yes. Now stop interrupting me and I'll tell you what's what. You'll be undercover. A model.'

'Gosh. Me a model? Me?' Zena's brain fizzed. Would she wear one of the House of Joseph dresses? It seemed like a dream.

'Shouldn't be too hard for you. Never known anyone love their clothes like you.'

'What would I need to do?'

'You need to find out what happens during the fashion shows. Who is stealing the dresses. If you do well, you might get to keep a dress.' Syd winked at her.

'You think they would give me a Moira Joseph dress?' The chance to keep such a luxury was tantalising. She'd saved hard for her leopard print grosgrain coat. It had cost her three pounds six shillings. She made most of her own clothes, or bought them off the peg in Henderson's sales. Even as a young girl Zena would run up skirts and blouses on her mother's Singer treadle machine. She loved the heavy see-saw push and whirr of the cast iron footplate, the spool of thread unwinding as it stitched. During the war, make do and mend was a necessity, but also a distraction from the gut wrenching fear of Dave serving in India.

Zena had already taken apart Dave's old Air Force overcoat and made it into a natty skirt and jacket. She'd added her own touches, blue pearled buttons, embroidered details on the pockets. It looked the business. But it would be wonderful to see something like Dior's New Look spring collection. One of the dresses had been on the front cover of the April edition of *Vogue*.

As Zena mused, the telephone rang and Syd snatched it up.

'She'll be over tomorrow, eight sharp,' Syd exhaled. It was the fashion house.

*

6 am next morning, and in her sleep-hazed fog Zena couldn't decide what to wear. Glamorous or utilitarian? Make-up heavy or light? Low chignon or high bun? She settled in the end for the simplest and quickest, and stifled a yawn as she headed for the door. She couldn't risk being late.

The rain was torrential, and Zena was drenched walking up the path. Her stockings were soaked, and she cursed the puddle forming in her high-heeled court shoes.

'Blast it!' she said, considering whether she should change her shoes, and hoping her father's car would start in such weather. Her parents would have something to say about rousing the household if it didn't. No matter that it was her father who was sending her on this job. She'd agreed with Syd she should go by car the first day. Better than the train on a day like this.

Zena had learned to drive during the war. She'd never regretted the trial of rabbit hop starts and screeching gear changes. She had become fast friends with the driving instructor's wife. Win was the best friend one could have. She was thoroughly dependable, witty and a fantastic hostess. Not only that, but she also matched Zena blouse for blouse in her love of clothes. Zena smiled at the thought of telling Win about being a model at the House of Joseph. Once the case was over of course. Her father had drummed it into her, "Never talk about cases out of the office. Never."

Scraping away the wet leaves clinging to the windscreen, Zena shivered as she climbed into the damp leather seat. The musty smell of old pipe smoke was not unpleasant. Zena wiped off the inside mist with her tan kidskin glove. No such thing as a heater. She pulled the starter lever and opened the choke. The engine coughed, spluttered and died. Blast. She tried again. Don't pull the choke too hard, or the engine would flood.

Another cough and the engine caught. Zena breathed a sigh of relief as she sat with her nose pressed over the steering wheel and inched her way forward. The stubby wipers struggled with the rain careening down the windscreen. Creeping out of Ripon Road, Zena settled her back into the curve of the seat. Chester and her pretend career as a model lay ahead, and as she drove Zena recalled some of the Moira Joseph creations she'd coveted: one a sleeveless, floor length gown in organza, another in brocade with a full underskirt of cream georgette.

The roads were empty, and as fast as the deluge had started, it stopped. With the sun coming out, the spray on the road produced a perfect multi-coloured arch, every colour candied, clear and bright. Zena recited the old mnemonic to herself, Richard Of York Gave Battle In Vain, as she drove through the rainbow towards Little Sutton. The shops on Whitby Road were about to open. She would arrive in Chester early. Better than late. She had a fear of being late and hated it in others.

Parked some way from the address she had been given, Zena could feel the pats of rain on her felt fedora as she walked towards the iconic Eastgate clock. It perched high on the ancient arch at the end of the road. She had time. She dived into the covered walkway of the Rows for shelter, and stopped to admire the gold bracelet in the window of the most expensive jewellers on Eastgate. Out of her league. The fashion house was on the level above.

Zena picked her way up the worn stone stairs, greasy with damp. She steadied herself against the half-timbered wall, and stumbled onto the galleried terrace, slipping on the last indented step. An Art Deco sign, *House of Joseph*, above an ancient oak door indicated that she was in the right place. She tugged at the heavy brass door-pull, and heard the jangle of bells echo in the hallway. Nothing. No footsteps, or voice calling for her to wait.

She listened at the door. Still nothing. Zena pulled harder on the bell. She was about to bang on the door, when it was opened by a slight, raven-haired woman. She wore a dark blue utility suit, cut to flatter her petite figure. Zena held out her hand, recognising the renowned Moira Joseph.

'Good morning, Mrs Joseph. My name is Zena Scott Archer. I believe you spoke to my father Sydney Scott, of Scott's Detective Bureau.'

A delicate butterfly hand laden with opal rings stretched out, took Zena's proffered hand in hers and held it with a firm grip. Piercing black eyes scrutinised Zena's anxious face under the feather tipped fedora; took in her navy-blue button-down jacket, the red camellia pinned to her lapel. She nodded as if to say, 'You'll do.'

'Come with me. And don't call me Mrs Joseph. Everyone calls me MJ.' Her bell-like voice matched her diminutive figure.

The drawing room of the fashion house was a temple of calm simplicity. Zena had expected it to be more Parisian with chandeliers and *chaise-longues*. MJ explained that this was where the regular clients would sit; in the green curve of the elegant Italian sofa, perhaps with their husband, or friend. They would pore over the fashion book, sketches of the house designs or the latest fashions from the Continent, drinking tea and nibbling *petits fours*. Part of the ritual. The models would come in wearing the choices the client had made. It was a different world.

'The girls won't be here until nine o'clock. We have time to talk. I'll explain everything.' MJ's fluting voice lifted high into the room.

'Thank you,' Zena said. 'The smallest detail will help.'

'Every month we have the mannequin parades. Our clients gather in the ballroom, as you'll see. The models wear my own designs along with other selected designers.'

'Where do your other designers come from?'

'I usually get the latest fashions brought over from Paris. They're very popular.'

'I can imagine. I've seen the Dior in Vogue. It was fabulous.'

'I'm glad you follow the fashions. It will help.'

'Tell me MJ, how many models do you employ?' Zena asked.

'Up to a dozen, but six are regular. The others we bring in for the day. It is quite an occasion as you'll see, my dear.' MJ frowned. 'But it's all going wrong.'

'My father told me dresses are going missing.'

'Yes. For the last six months. So many have been lost.

I can't bear it.' Her lip wobbled, tears poised to fall. 'Every month one or two dresses go missing. They're my life's work.'

'Do you have any idea who is stealing them? Any idea at all?'

'It must be one or more of the girls. But how? And why?'

'Hopefully we'll be able to find out. I promise I'll get to the bottom of it.' Zena wasn't sure how, but she knew she had to find the culprit.

'Why would they do this to me? What have I ever done to them? I've been nothing but a mother to those girls.'

'Thieves come in all disguises it seems.'

'But to betray me in this way. I just don't understand.' MJ wiped her eyes with a silk handkerchief, her initials monogrammed in grey.

'If you don't mind me asking, how much do the dresses cost?'

'A year's clothing rations and more. Most people wouldn't earn that in a year.' Zena could see how tempting that might be for a low-paid seamstress.

'Now to your role.' MJ returned to business. 'We have a big parade at the weekend for a group of ladies from Manchester,' MJ said.

'Parade?'

'Yes. A parade. We need all the models for the parades and it seems most of the dresses go missing then. All the comings and goings mean it's a muddle sometimes.'

'The thief is taking advantage of the chaos.'

'Yes, exactly. You'll need to keep your wits about you. You'll easily pass for one of the temp models we hire for these occasions.'

'I was wondering about that,' Zena said. Her mother had already questioned as to whether she'd pass as a model.

'You have the right figure for my latest creations: tall and slim, with good wide hips. Junoesque, one might say.'

Zena wasn't sure whether to be flattered or upset by such a description. She gathered what would be required of her as MJ continued to explain the daily routine and showed her into the ballroom.

The room had the Parisian look that Zena had first expected. A vast chandelier hung from the vaulted ceiling. On this dull May morning, its light cast shimmers onto the panes of the mullioned windows. High-backed chairs, *chaise-longues*, and deep sofas edged the room. Zena guessed that the elongated oak stage was the catwalk. It stretched out to the centre of the chestnut parquet. Would she look glamorous enough when it was her turn to walk along it? What dresses would she wear? Zena felt a flutter of excitement mixed with trepidation.

'Why don't you fire all the girls if you know one of them is stealing from you?' Zena asked as she stood admiring the scene.

'I know, I know. My husband asks me the same question. I can't. Most of them have been with me for years.'

'You must be losing hundreds.'

'Yes but these girls rely on me. I just don't understand it. You simply must find out who is doing this to me. Then I can fire her without getting rid of the rest.'

*

Precisely at nine o'clock, a gaggle of long-limbed, high-breasted girls poured into the dressing room. At twenty-six Zena did not feel like a girl. But she willed herself to get in role. Each model took her allotted place along the bank of mirrors and dressing tables. The dressers stood behind, holding out the gowns ready for them to slip into.

'You the new girl, then? What's your name?' asked a small, thin, pale dresser with deep red hair and startling blue eyes.

'Phillipa,' Zena said, using her middle name. 'What's yours?'

'Kitty,' replied the girl.

'MJ said you might be able to show me around, Kitty. Would that be OK with you?'

'I suppose,' Kitty said, her soft lisp barely audible above the chatter of the other girls.

They walked out of the dressing room into the hush of the narrow, darkened corridor. Heavy panelling lined the walls, an oppressive contrast to the lightness of the other rooms. Zena followed Kitty towards the arched window that cast a streak of damp daylight across the floor.

'How long have you been working here, Kitty? What's it like working with MJ? Do tell me all about it!'

'Oh Philippa, it's the best job in the world. Me da had died when I started here.' She accepted Zena's nod of sympathy and carried on. 'It were an accident. On the railway. Hit by one of the wagons he was. MJ gave me a chance. She saw me beggin' under the arches.' Kitty looked around to see if anyone was listening. 'You see, I'd just had a babby. I were only 16.'

'16? That's so young.'

'Yes,' Kitty looked down. 'Me boyfriend were older and

in the navy. Buggered off didn't he. They wanted to take it off me but I fought them I did. No way was I going to give up my baby. Not for nobody.'

'I'm so sorry Kitty. That's rotten.'

'Me ma said I could keep the babby and stay with her if I paid me way. Begging was the only way to keep me going. But it wasn't enough and my ma said she needed more.'

'That must have been very hard.'

'It was. I thought there might be just one way left for me. I'm sure you know what I mean?'

Zena nodded, shuddering at the thought.

'And then MJ came along,' Kitty continued. 'She saw me begging and got talking. She saved me. Gave me a job as a sweeper, and now look at me. A dresser!' Kitty beamed.

Kitty adored MJ and couldn't possibly be the thief. Zena did think, however, that she could be the perfect informer. Kitty led the way into a quiet, bright studio. Three artists sat at angled drawing boards, sketching the designs that MJ had pencilled in rough. Zena stopped at one of the boards.

'This is beautiful,' she said, admiring the delicate watercolour of a red flowing evening gown, lifted high at the waist. Ruched folds dripped down the front, pooling at the feet of the model.

MJ's pencil drawing sat alongside; a few notes added in her strong copperplate hand. *An elegant evening frock of red satin, ruched at front, and cut low at the back. A broad sash of pansy black ribbon, with bright appliqué red flowers.*

'It's amazing how you bring that simple drawing to life.

Sorry, do you mind me asking your name?' Zena stood over the artist, who shrunk further into her stool.

'D..D..Doris, miss,' the girl stammered. 'I went to Hull Sch...sch...school of Art.' She continued with her illustration, head bent.

Zena was entranced. The calm atmosphere and hushed tones of the studio were a serene contrast to the bustle of the dressing room.

'What's next, Kitty? I had no idea that there were so many levels to *haute couture*. It's fascinating.'

'It is, it is,' Kitty replied. 'I wish I could be in here instead of having to deal with them stuck-up models.'

'Oh dear, I thought you loved your job.'

'I do, honest I do. But sometimes them models -' She stopped herself short, narrowed her eyes, and carried on. 'Let's go to the cutting room. You'll like it in there.'

Zena made a mental note to quiz Kitty further. They walked through into the cutting room. This was where a team of seamstresses turned MJ's designs into exquisite gowns. As the seamstresses cut and stitched, a hum of chatter reached a crescendo of laughter as a raunchy anecdote from the night before was passed around.

In every room, Zena talked to the girls, finding out their names, whether they had a boyfriend, or were married, or lived at home. Small details which made her appear interested and friendly, but also gave her the background and history of all the girls working for MJ.

As she drove home to Ripon Road at the end of the day, Zena tried to list in her head all the information she'd learned. She would write it down when she got back. Doris was the stammering dowdy church mouse, drawing the most exquisite sketches. Mary the modish model from Manchester. Eleanor the elegant, who had rather a superior air. Zena got into the swing of the alliterations and giggled to herself as she recounted them: Lizzie the lazy dresser was lanky and loud, and Betty the blonde, blousy bustier maker wore too much make-up. They all appeared to be hard-working and dedicated to MJ. How would she uncover who was stealing?

Zena's eyes drooped over dinner, even though Woolton pie was one of her favourite meals. She was exhausted.

'So how was your day, my love? Those models treat you right, did they? What was the famous dressmaker like?' Syd placed his smouldering Craven A into the ashtray next to his plate and spooned in a mouthful of potatoes and cabbage. There was never any shortage of vegetables, despite the rationing. Wallasey was full of market gardens and the shops stocked plenty of potatoes, carrots, and greens.

'I'll tell you when I've finished the case Dad, not before,' Zena snapped back, annoyed her father had asked this over dinner. *He* was the one who told her never to discuss cases outside the office.

Syd raised his eyebrows and shot a smirk at Marion, who suppressed a conspiratorial giggle. Zena caught the look between them. Irritated, she slammed down her knife and fork and stormed off upstairs.

'Zena! Zena love. Come on. I was just asking,' Syd's voice called after her.

Zena heard her mother exclaiming so Zena could hear, 'Leave her be, Syd. There's no talking to her when she's in this mood.'

Zena wanted to go downstairs and reply to her

mother's taunt, but she was beyond tired. She crawled into a ball under the eiderdown.

Dave's soft tread on the stairs made Zena curl even tighter.

'Ah, come now, love, please don't take on so. You're tired.' Dave's voice soon soothed and calmed her as always. His arms were strong and heavy, as he spooned his legs into hers.

'One day,' she murmured, 'we'll get a place of our own. You and me.'

*

The next morning, Zena practised her modelling technique in front of Dave. He laughed in his gentle manner at her posing. MJ had shown her how: walk quickly, one leg crossed in front of the other, turn so each set of ladies can see the back of the dress, and don't flounce. Zena exaggerated the pose, pushed out her hips and swished one long leg in front of the other. She tripped over the rug, and fell deliberately into Dave's arms, laughing as he held her close.

Her buoyant mood of early morning dipped as she walked from the station along the canal to the House of Joseph. The reflection of City Road Bridge sank into the reeking cut. A Munch Scream of a hollow log floated underneath the bridge; its mouth twisted as it edged towards the scum of rotting debris. Zena regretted taking this route. The war had blighted many things, and the canal was another sullied casualty.

Zena arrived at the House of Joseph to the exclamatory

chatter of the girls. The latest designs from Paris had been delivered. Zena's heart lifted. Would MJ choose her to model a Dior? How exquisite the thought. She drifted into a reverie of dancing down the Champs-Élysées in a Dior; white jacket pinched at the waist and black skirt flowing outward.

As the girls prepared for the morning clients, Zena worried that her frame wasn't suited to the delicacy of some of the designs. Hoping her corset would pull her in tight, Zena looked in the mirror at Grumpy Grace, the dark-browed dresser. Grace showed no mercy. She squeezed Zena into a spring-green and white silk suit. It was an MJ exclusive, printed with delicate leaves edged in darker green.

'Ouch, Grace that pinched!' Zena said.

'Not surprising. You're too big. Why *did* MJ bring you in again?' Grace said. She narrowed her eyes and stared at Zena in the mirror.

Zena ignored her, got up, pulled on the elbow length white gloves lying on the table, and made her way to the door into the drawing room.

MJ opened the door to let Eleanor sweep back into the dressing room to change, and ushered Zena in. Zena walked tall into the room, the green and white skirt flowing behind her, the jacket elongated at the back, tucked and belted at the front. The suit was topped by a wide-brimmed hat in racing green, edged with peacock feathers. They echoed those on the hat of the glamorous woman perched in the curve of the Italian sofa. No utility suit for her. A shimmer of feathers peeked from the rim of the woman's pillbox hat. She lifted her head to look at Zena walking in, her beauty reflecting a life of sophistication and charm. Zena glided around the room, turning this way and that to show off the flow and style of the outfit from every angle. After a couple of minutes, MJ nodded for her to leave, and another model floated in.

Zena struggled with the speed of the quick change as she was immediately buttoned into a stunning black and white evening gown. The bow at the base of the long V in the back was nearly big enough to be called a bustle. This time it was Kitty who dressed her. Unlike Grumpy Grace she was all smiles and helpfulness. Holding out her arms, Zena waited for the soft lace gloves to slip over her hands. She lifted her head high as Kitty clipped on a black and white fascinator, then strode back into the drawing room.

After the last client of the day, Zena left for home, exhausted but elated at the success of her modelling debut. Perhaps if detective work palled this might be another profession. After her success with the Elsie Williams case, the snide comments from her male colleagues, especially Charlie, had worsened. Resentment hung in the air.

The railway station was deserted, as was the battered train. She could hear her mother's voice: "A lady must never travel alone." Zena rarely took advice, but she'd read of young women being molested in empty carriages. She was not about to fall victim. Walking up and down the narrow corridor, she found a carriage where a young woman and her two children were playing I Spy. The train lurched its way out of Chester. It was the slow one, stopping at every station, even Port Sunlight. Resigned, Zena sat back and recalled her day, jotting notes in her journal.

Wednesday 21st May, 1947: House of Joseph Case. Grace always dissatisfied and angry. Why? Observed her whisking away the dresses. All too quick. Frustrating I can't see who she passes them to. Need to quiz Kitty in the morning about Grace. Doris from the studio observed hanging around the dressing room where she had no business to be. Who was she waiting for? Eleanor's another one. Haughty girl overly concerned with appearance, although not all the time. She sometimes wears the strangest overcoat.

For once the family meal was lively, and Zena didn't feel like falling asleep at the table as she often did. Syd regaled everyone with stories of Joe's exploits tracking down an erring wife to a Cheshire hotel.

Syd could hardly contain himself, tears of laughter rolling into the deep creases of his cheeks. 'She ran outside and threw herself in the river. But the river was dry!' He took off his round spectacles, and wiped his eyes with a voluminous white handkerchief. 'Silly girl. It was all a bit of showmanship, but Joe had to pull her out of the mud. It'll cost him a new suit.'

Zena laughed along with the others at the image, not just of the woman lying legs up in the mud, but cack-handed Joe, struggling and slipping as he tried to pull her out.

*

Another dress had gone missing. MJ was furious that Zena was no nearer to catching the culprit.

'You seem to be enjoying modelling a bit too much young lady. Concentrate on finding the thief, not on how you look.'

'But MJ...I...' Zena tried to interrupt to defend herself, but MJ overrode her protestation.

'It was the black tulle this week and it was made to order. It was one of my best,' MJ said. Her snipe hit home. Zena couldn't help but admit that she did enjoy modelling. But it was unfair to say that she wasn't doing her job.

'Please MJ I'm trying. I know the tulle went missing, and I think I might have a lead,' Zena replied.

'What lead? Who? Who is it? Tell me. I want to know.' MJ glared at Zena.

'I can't be sure. I'd rather not accuse anyone right now. Please give me time MJ. I'm close. I'm sure of it.'

'You better tell me as soon as you know anything.'

'I will, I will. I promise.'

That lunchtime, the girls were smoking and chatting at the back of the building. In the corner of the yard, Zena noticed Grace hand over a large and heavy brown package to mousy Doris from the studio. They both looked round to see that no one was looking, and then Grace marched into the building. It was as Zena had suspected.

'Doris?' Zena touched Doris' arm, as she was about to leave the yard.

'Yes, m..m..miss?' Doris couldn't have looked more guilty.

'Looks like you've something heavy in that package.'

'Shhh. You m..m..mustn't say anything. Grace told me to say nothing to n...no one.'

'Why, what is it Doris? What's in the package?' Zena's

heart banged. It would be a coup if she solved the case this quickly.

'P…promise you won't tell, miss? I don't want to get Grace into trouble or nuffin.'

'Of course, Doris, your secret's safe with me.'

Doris opened a corner of the brown paper package to show Zena the contents.

'See, it's a right b..b…big 'un. Grace's dad breeds 'em. It's off the b..book like. She can't tell no one.'

'Goodness, it is big, isn't it? I hope your family enjoy eating it, Doris. I better get back to work.'

The chicken was huge – it was near enough the size of a turkey. Someone was in for a feast that night. Zena's head and heart dropped as she walked back to the dressing room. How had she got it so wrong?

As she headed to her dressing table, Zena started, hearing MJ's voice sharp behind her.

'Zena, I need to talk to you,' MJ said.

'Sorry MJ I'm only a few minutes late. I'm back from lunch.'

'It's not about lunch!' MJ snapped back.

The other girls fell silent and looked on in surprise. Zena raised her eyebrows and shrugged at them as she followed MJ into her cramped and overflowing office. It reflected nothing of the airiness and vaulted ceilings of the rest of the fashion house. A vast heavy metal desk was piled high with magazines, books and papers. The trestle table under the window stood alone as a clean space, graced by a neat row of pencils and a large sketch pad.

Motioning Zena to sit, MJ asked, 'Do you have any idea yet? Talk to me. I'm going out of my mind with worry.'

'I'm sorry, MJ. It's very hard to tell. Like I told you, I thought I had a lead today, and I followed someone. That's why I was late back from lunch. But it came to nothing.'

'Nothing? What do you mean nothing? Why didn't you catch them?'

'I would've told you in my next report, but I didn't think it worth mentioning now. It's very delicate. It's important I don't rouse suspicion. The girls need to trust me. I'm sure you understand.'

'I might understand, but are you making progress? It's frustrating. I need to know everything. Who are your suspects?'

'MJ I don't want to accuse anyone. I'm building up an idea of how, but it's not easy.'

'Of course, it's not easy. If it was easy, I'd have caught the girl myself. That's what I'm paying *you* for. I don't want to know how; I want to know who.'

'It's not so simple. I can assure you I'm doing all I can.' Zena tried to keep the ire out of her reply.

'That's as maybe but you need to stop keeping me in the dark, Zena. If you have a suspicion, voice it. Now, go back to the dressing room, and not a word to the girls.'

Flushed with annoyance at being told how to do her job, Zena returned to the dressing room. The girls looked at her and waited for a reaction, but stayed silent. They could tell that she'd been ticked off. Most of them had come under MJ's wrath at some point. Zena refused to tell MJ anything that she couldn't prove. She had an inkling as to how the dress might have been smuggled out. But not by whom. She needed to catch the girl in the act. After the false lead had come to nothing, there was one other girl she needed to keep a close eye on.

*

Saturday. It was the day of the grand fashion parade.

'Zena, I need you to come with me.' MJ's opal-laden hand waved across at Zena. The girls looked shocked. It was rare any of them were called in twice in one week.

'You've got no further, I see.' MJ's fluting voice was spiked with a hard edge.

'MJ, there is nothing I can prove. As I said before, I have a few suspicions. The girl I suspect needs to be caught in the act. How do you expect me to do that, given all the quick changes and chaos that goes on in the dressing room?'

'Don't get uppity with me, young lady. I am paying good money for your services. Or rather for your father's services. Maybe he would have been quicker at finding the thief than you.'

Zena was on the verge of exploding when her father's reminder came out loud and clear: "The client is always right. Never lose a case by getting angry, my girl. It'll get you nowhere but court."

'I'm sorry, MJ. Believe me, I'm as frustrated as you. I'm working very hard to find out who it is.'

'Seems you need to work a bit harder.'

'Like I said before, I can't accuse anyone until I have proof. Please forgive me for being rude. It won't happen again.'

'You see that it doesn't, young lady. It's the day of the Grand Parade today. You need to be on your toes.'

'I will be MJ, I can assure you,' Zena said, looking down at her feet.

'Good. We've a lot of clients, and many dresses to be modelled. If you need to catch a girl in the act, today's the day. Especially with the Dior dresses on show.'

'Dior? How marvellous.'

'Yes and I've heard from Audley Street in London that these dresses are stolen to order. Pay attention and catch that thief or I'll ask for you to be replaced.'

'Yes, MJ. I promise I will do my very best,' Zena said, biting her tongue.

The fashion house was fizzing with excitement. On high alert, Zena's heart thumped as the models were allocated their first set of outfits. She'd got a Dior! To wear such a dress. It felt like a dream. Zena wasn't sure she would be able to concentrate on being a model and keep an eye on her suspect.

Grace was Zena's dresser. Despite Zena's efforts to engage her in conversation, Grace's sour face scowled as she pushed Zena into the full-skirted black chiffon dress. It was tight in the waist, and Zena was scared that it might not fit. Grace undid the dress and pulled tighter on the corset. Zena gasped.

At last every small button was fastened and every eyelet hooked. It looked stunning. The long V at the front was set off by pearls, white elbow length gloves and high-heeled court shoes completed the look. Zena's hair was piled high into her classic chignon, her hazel eyes picked out with green eyeshadow, cheeks rouged and lips plumped with pearl lipstick. She looked every bit as elegant as the model she'd seen in *Vogue*. She couldn't help but give herself a little twirl in the mirror. Grace tutted and pushed her towards MJ's ante-room. Here she would be inspected by MJ and then announced to the audience. The other girls clapped, and Zena could see Kitty beaming at her in the mirror, struggling to get Eleanor into the electric blue silk, one of MJ's most beautiful creations.

Zena strode out onto the catwalk to a gasp. Had she popped a button? Then the applause began. Of course! Most of the women would never have seen the latest designs from Paris. In the days of clothes rationing, there had been nothing this extravagant. Zena twirled, arched her shoulders this way and that, swished the skirt to show its fullness. She walked back down the catwalk as the applause continued, and in the rush of the moment, turned back to the audience, grinned and curtseyed. The reaction was deafening. MJ would be cross with her for disobeying protocol, but who cared? She wasn't a real model.

Grace glanced up when Zena ran into the dressing room, flushed and breathless, one gloved hand at her throat. Grace unbuttoned the dress and whisked it off, passing it behind her. To whom, Zena could not tell; it was too swift and slick. Zena curved round to check in the mirror, but Grace stood stolid, hands on hips, blocking her view. This roused Zena's suspicions further. If Grace wasn't averse to selling black market chicken, maybe she had connections to get rid of stolen dresses. She needed to engage Grace in conversation.

'Did you hear them? They've never seen the like. I'm not sure if they thought it was too extravagant for these times. What do you think, Grace?'

Grace stayed silent, not acknowledging that Zena had spoken.

'You've been here a long time, haven't you, Grace? It must be exciting to work here. Being a dresser can't earn you much though, can it?'

'None of your business.'

'It's just that it seems a bit unfair to me. All those rich ladies paying so much for one dress, and all we get is a pittance. Don't you think so?' Zena saw Grace hesitate, about to answer. Then her mouth clamped shut, tight and cruel.

'Shut up, and put this on, you're up again after Eleanor.' Grace's rudeness and brusque manner was nothing new, but something in her hesitation roused Zena's suspicions. Grace yanked on the second outfit over Zena's head. It was one of MJ's creations, and although not as glamorous as the Dior, it flowed perfectly against Zena's figure. Grace pushed her towards the door.

*

Disentangled from the last dress of the day, Zena fell exhausted onto the dressing room sofa, dropped her head onto her hand and pretended to close her eyes. She was so tired it was barely a pretence. The other girls busied themselves to go home and the thrum of chatter was excited and happy. Everything appeared normal. Except through the slit of her eyes, Zena could see that Eleanor, tall, beautiful Eleanor with her angled cheekbones and cupid bow lips, was wearing her very long and very dowdy overcoat. The same one she had worn on a few previous occasions.

As Eleanor headed for the door, the coat opened an inch in the breeze, and Zena spied a tiny flash of blue silk. Could it be MJ's dress? Zena was unsure. If a dress was going to go missing, surely it would have been the Dior?

She waited until Eleanor left through the back door of the fashion house, grabbed her coat and bag, and readied her camera. She followed Eleanor into Godshall Lane. A rain-flushed sky pinked overhead in the spring air. All was quiet in the early evening dusk, except for the rapid chink of Eleanor's stilettos on the cobbles.

Zena glimpsed a shimmer of electric blue under the dun-coloured coat as Eleanor strode up ahead. She glanced back as she headed in the direction of the cathedral, as though she had heard Zena's softer footsteps. Heart pounding, Zena ducked behind one of the carved wooden pillars on St. Werburgh Street, back flush against the cool wood.

Creeping from her hiding place, she saw Eleanor turn right into Northgate Street. She pulled up short as a bear of a man lurched into her path. His heavy twill overcoat was half open. Tie askew, and hat tipped to one side, Zena could tell he was drunk. Impatient to get past him and follow her suspect, Zena tried to sidestep him, but he was having none of it.

'Good evening, young lady. Might I ask you the time?' he said, his whisky breath souring the air.

'It's six pm, sir,' Zena replied, trying to move past him. He blocked her path, arms wide, towering above even Zena's tall frame.

'Not so fast, my dear. No need to rush off, is there? The sun is over the yardarm and I'd like to treat you to a drink.'

'Excuse me, there is every need. I need to get home to my husband.'

'Your husband wouldn't mind you coming for a drink with me, I'm sure, young lady. Men of the world and all that?' He reached out and took a firm hold of Zena's elbow, trying to steer her in the opposite direction. Away from Northgate Street. Away from Eleanor.

Zena's panic turned to rage as a hot swell of anger rose to her face. She was not going to be thwarted. Not when she was this close. With a quick upward flip, she twisted her arm out from under the man's meaty hand. She kicked his shin hard and shouldered him into the wall, blessing her father's top safety tips. She ran. Heavy footsteps pounded behind her, but soon stopped. He was too drunk to follow her.

Zena ran down Northgate Street. Had she lost Eleanor? She almost missed her. Eleanor had crossed the street and was standing by the steps of the Town Hall. Zena ducked into the ancient arched doorway of the cathedral opposite and waited. Eleanor lit a cigarette and looked at her watch. The long overcoat opened wide at the front and the sweeping folds of MJ's beautiful silk dress shimmered under the streetlamp. Got her. Zena snapped photos quicky while there was light. A squeal of tyres interrupted her as an MG sports car screeched to a stop in front of the Town Hall. Eleanor opened her coat wide to show the driver her spoils. With a wide grin at his thumbs up, she jumped into the passenger seat. The car sped off. KXD 606, KXD 606. Zena repeated the number plate in her head.

A loose end nagged at Zena's brain on her way home. There must be an accomplice. Could it be Doris? Or a dresser perhaps? Grace most probably, but there was no proof.

*

'Eleanor? Are you sure?' MJ said the next day in disbelief. 'Eleanor? Who would have thought it?'

'What are you going to do, MJ? I didn't find her accomplice, but perhaps that's for the police to uncover?' Zena said.

'I'd rather not involve the police. Call her in. Call her in now. We'll confront her together.'

'Do you think that's wise, MJ? She could turn nasty.'

'No, call her in. I want to see her face up to this. You must be here, or she'll squirm her way out of it. She's a clever girl, that one.'

Returning to the dressing room, Zena called across to Eleanor who was peering into a mirror, examining her lipstick.

'Eleanor, MJ has asked to see you in her office, and she asked me to come too,' Zena said.

Eleanor swivelled round on her stool. Zena took in the green, almond shaped eyes, searching for a sign of panic or guilt. Nothing but arrogance stared back at her.

'She'll want to congratulate me on my success yesterday. Sometimes she gives me the dresses if it's been a successful night,' she said.

Her haughty voice grated, but Zena bit her lip and led the way to MJ's office.

'Wasn't it a triumph, MJ? Such a success. You must have had dozens of orders. I can't thank you enough for giving me the electric blue. I adore it!' Eleanor said. She stared at MJ, daring her to deny it.

Zena reeled in shock. MJ was sometimes forgetful. But surely she would remember that she had promised such a dress to Eleanor.

'Eleanor. You know this is not true. Please admit that you stole it. Phillipa saw you wearing it under your coat,' MJ said.

'Ha! I might have known Miss Nosey Parker would have seen something she thought she shouldn't. I didn't steal it. Come now, you must remember, MJ?'

'That's not true Eleanor. I didn't.'

'It is. Of course it is. You promised it to me when I first tried on the dress.'

'I don't remember that at all.'

'MJ, you must. You even made a few alterations. "It's yours," you said. It's your memory playing tricks again.'

MJ looked bemused, racking her brains. Zena watched fear and doubt flicker across her face.

'I saw you get into a car with a man. You showed him the dress. He gave you the thumbs up. It was as if you had done good work stealing it,' Zena said.

'You followed me? How dare you! You're worse than I thought,' Eleanor shouted.

'When I saw the dress under your coat, I thought I should see what you were up to. MJ told me in confidence that dresses were going missing. I was looking out for MJ.'

'Oh, looking out for MJ, were we?' Eleanor said. Her snide voice mimicked Zena's. 'Yes, I showed my chap the dress. Why wouldn't I? He said I looked a million dollars in it. I was over the moon that MJ had given it to me.'

'She didn't give it to you. MJ has told you that.' Zena was angry on MJ's behalf.

'Yes she did give it to me. And I've told *you*.' Her beautiful face sneered into an ugly caricature of itself.

'Enough both of you.'

'But MJ...' Zena exploded as Eleanor smirked at her, confident she could bamboozle MJ into believing her.

'Phillipa, please leave. I will sort this out from here,' MJ said. Zena was about to protest but was stopped by MJ's glare.

Zena left the House of Joseph with a heavy heart. Would Eleanor get the better of MJ? Convince her that it was her memory that was at fault? Zena knew full well that the crafty, clever girl had stolen that dress. She wished there was another way to prove it. But it was not her place to do more. Her report would be typed up and handed over to the House of Joseph. It was for MJ to decide what to do next. Zena was sad to leave the world of fashion, its glamour and excitement. She reminded herself that it was not a real job. She was only undercover.

She told Syd about her frustration when she handed over her report later that week. 'Listen, love,' he said, 'sometimes you'll never know. Get used to it. There are some clever cons out there. Remember, we are mere pebbles in a pool.'

Zena nodded. 'I suppose you're right, Dad. It's hard though. I'll know better next time.'

*

Several weeks later Syd shouted from the depths of his cubby-hole: 'Zena!'

'What is it, Dad? I'm in the middle of typing up a report.'

'There's a package from House of Joseph for you. And a letter for me.'

'Goodness, what's in this?' Zena looked at the huge square box, wrapped in brown paper and string. She opened the box and lifted out another package inside, wrapped in tissue paper printed with the MJ logo. Zena's heart pounded. She let out a gasp as she unfolded the tissue paper. She shook out the black chiffon dress. The Dior! Zena sat down in shock. She could hardly believe it. There had been nothing from MJ after she left, and now this.

'Seems she took a fancy to you after all. Take a butcher's at this,' Syd said, waving the letter at Zena. 'Moira Joseph called in the police after all.'

'What? She said she didn't want the police involved.'

'Seems she changed her mind. Based on your evidence, Eleanor Johnson owned up to stealing the dresses.'

'Goodness that sly girl. I never thought she would admit anything.'

'She blamed it all on her boyfriend. Said he coerced her. You did a good job there, love.'

'Someone else must have been involved. She couldn't have done it alone. Does MJ mention anyone else? Here, let me read it.' Zena snatched the letter from her father's hand, scanning MJ's beautiful copperplate hand.

Dear Mr Scott,

I enclose a gift for your daughter Zena, who was responsible for uncovering the culprit, or should I say culprits, stealing my merchandise. I trust she will like it.

You may be interested to hear that after much consideration, I took your daughter's advice, and let the police handle the matter. They got to the truth where I could not. Eleanor Johnson admitted stealing the dresses after she was presented with the evidence. She blamed her boyfriend for encouraging her. We will let the courts decide.

Please tell Zena that the accomplice dresser who helped Eleanor was Kitty Hardacre.

'Oh no. Not Kitty!' Zena blanched, and threw down the letter without finishing it. Not poor innocent Kitty. After everything MJ had done for her. Zena had been so sure it was Grace.

'Seems like Mrs Joseph was far too trusting of that young lass. It's always the innocent looking ones you have to watch,' Syd said, with a sharp breath as he took a drag from his cigarette. He eased the left side of his lower lip forward and let out a stream of smoke.

'But she was so plausible and friendly. Maybe she had no choice. She had a baby to look after,' Zena said, upset at being duped.

'It's like I said, love, there are some very clever and very charming cons out there.'

'Perhaps she was desperate for the money and Eleanor led her into it.'

'You may never know. Look don't let it get you down. Forget it and move on. Go on now and type up your report. It'll take your mind of it.' Her father was sympathetic. Up to a point.

Zena telephoned Win. Maybe she would have more

sympathy. Besides she wanted to tell her about the Dior. She'd be green. They met for lunch at the State Café as a treat.

'A Dior?' Win exclaimed.

'I know. I could hardly believe it when I opened the box,' Zena replied as she spooned a forkful of steak and kidney pudding.

'But why? Why would she give you such a dress?'

'Why not? I saved her hundreds in the end,' Zena shot back, miffed that Win thought she shouldn't have been given it. She was just jealous.

'I know, but still…'

'Anyway, forget the Dior, what should I do about Kitty?'

'Kitty?'

'You know, the young girl with the baby. I told you about her.'

'Oh yes, the accomplice.'

'That's her. I think she was bullied into it by that scheming whatsit Eleanor. But how do I find out?'

'There's only one way,' Win said. 'You'll have to speak to her.'

But when? How? Zena left the café with a heavy heart. That poor girl.

*

It was nearing mid-August when Zena received a summons to court. She broke the seal and opened the heavy envelope of the court summons with trepidation, not knowing whether she was being called to swear an affidavit, or heaven forbid, to be sued for libel against a client. The summons was to give evidence. The Moira Joseph case.

On Wednesday the 20th of August 1947, Zena took the train to Chester County Court. This was one court case she would not relish.

The Court House was cool compared to the summer heat outside. Zena shivered on the green leather bench outside Court No. 2. The barrister for the MJ case came by and told her that the case was delayed, and they would have to wait. Mr McKinnon was charming and immediately put Zena at ease. As they kicked their heels waiting for the case to begin, McKinnon entertained Zena with court stories.

'And then there was this time when I objected to the opposition's questioning of my client. The judge said he couldn't see what I could possibly object to in that question. I went into a huddle with my solicitor and eventually said, "I am sorry, your Honour, what I meant to say is that it's the next question I object to,"' McKinnon laughed at his own blunder. Zena liked him.

Half an hour later they were called in and Zena walked straight up to the stand. She took the bible in her left hand, waving away the card, saying, 'I know the oath.'

'Mrs Archer, please could you describe to us what you saw on the day in question. Your statement records that the accused stole an expensive dress from the Moira Joseph Fashion House in Chester,' Mr McKinnon began.

'Yes, that's correct. Scott's Detective Bureau had been engaged by Moira Joseph to identify who was stealing dresses. I posed as an undercover model and took part in the fashion parades. On the day in question, after the fashion parade had finished, we were about to leave when

I observed that Eleanor Johnson was wearing an unusually long overcoat.'

'Objection. Excuse me, m'lud, how can Mrs Archer know it was an *unusually* long overcoat?' The defence barrister glanced up from his notes as he made his objection in a bored monotone.

'Mrs Archer?' Judge Harvey asked Zena.

'Your Honour, I had noted the overcoat in my observations. Your Honour may not be aware, but the fashion today is for shorter coats and dresses. Eleanor Johnson was very conscious of the latest fashions, and I was surprised that she sometimes wore this long overcoat. I was suspicious of her and kept a close eye on her movements.'

'Thank you, Mrs Archer. Do please carry on.'

'Thank you, your Honour. On the day in question, I noticed an edge of bright blue underneath Miss Johnson's coat as we were about to leave. I decided to follow her. As she walked towards Chester Cathedral, I noticed the dress several times. I can confirm it was the dress from the Moira Joseph Fashion House. I then saw Miss Johnson outside the Town Hall open her coat, revealing the dress in full to a young man who had driven up in a red MG sports car. She got into the car and they drove off. I provided the registration number of the car to Moira Joseph in my report.'

'Mrs Archer, you are saying there can be no doubt that the dress you saw was the one that was modelled by Miss Johnson on the day in question.'

'Yes, that is the case.'

'Thank you, Mrs Archer. That will be all.'

Zena was pleased there had been no mention of Kitty. It was all over in ten minutes and Zena was free to go. The verdict and sentencing would be on another day. Zena waited outside the court room to see if Kitty would appear. After what Win had suggested, she wanted to corner Kitty and find out what had happened. She couldn't believe Kitty would have stolen from MJ unless she was forced into it. Not after everything that MJ had done for her. An hour later, the heavy wooden doors from Court No.2 opened.

'Kitty!' Zena called as a stream of people spilled out.

'Oh, it's you,' Kitty replied, looking hard at Zena, as if it was all Zena's fault that she was caught stealing.

Zena was about to turn on her heel but stood her ground.

'Please, Kitty, I only want to understand. What was it that Eleanor had over you? I know you couldn't have done this on your own. Please talk to me.'

Kitty's eyes welled up, and Zena took her arm. 'Come on, let's get a cup of tea somewhere.'

It all came out over tea and scones. How Kitty's mother had thrown her out. Her mother had a new boyfriend. She didn't want him to know she was old enough to have a grandchild. How vain and selfish. Zena urged Kitty to carry on.

'I was trying to rent a place on me own, but it weren't possible. It was too expensive and me mam wouldn't help.'

'I'm sorry to hear this Kitty. How did Eleanor come into the picture?'

'Eleanor, she were kind at first, said she'd lend me a few bob. Then when I couldn't pay it back, she got nasty.'

'That sounds like her.'

'I didn't want to do it, honest I didn't.'

'I believe you Kitty. It must have been tough with the baby all on your own.'

'It was awful. I tried to stop but she said she'd tell MJ it were me who was stealing.' Kitty broke into sobs. 'Who would believe me, Phillipa? No one. They'd take me babby away.'

As they left the tearoom, Zena pressed a half crown into Kitty's hand. Her eyes filled again. Poor Kitty.

When Zena returned to the office Charlie was there, all shiny suit and smarm. He sat legs wide on the chair at the detectives' desk, blocking Zena's way, smirking. His oiled hair matched his grin. Zena ignored him, took some headed paper and started writing a letter to MJ. Maybe it wouldn't work, but if MJ knew the circumstances of Kitty's downfall then she might not press for imprisonment. Zena shuddered at the thought of Kitty's boy without his mother. Maybe he'd be sent to an orphanage. Zena sealed and franked the envelope and went out to post it.

Two weeks later Zena received a reply from MJ. Eleanor had been sentenced to five years in Walton Gaol. Zena might have felt sorry for her, until she read on. It turned out that this was her third offence. She was already well known to the police in Manchester and was in cahoots with a lover who sold on the dresses to his fence in London. MJ also said that thanks to the letter Zena wrote, which was read out in court, Kitty was given a suspended sentence. Zena scanned what MJ had written: *'I'm glad. I know that deep down Kitty is a good girl. I've decided to give her another chance as a dresser. I've even found her a place to stay. It was the right thing to do.'* A better mother to Kitty than her own, Zena thought with relief. So many cases were short and sharp: get the job done, serve the injunction, swear a statement, and on to the next. This case and Kitty had got under Zena's skin, and she was pleased that it had ended in justice being well served.

'Dad? Dad!'

'What now? I'm busy. Another case has come in.'

'I just wanted to tell you about the House of Joseph case. I've had a letter from MJ. Kitty got off.'

'That's good news love, now let me get on. There might be another job you can do for me.'

'What's that Dad? Another undercover case?'

'Hold your horses. I said *might*. I'll let you know if I need you. It's only a small job.'

'I'm ready for anything Dad. Just give me a chance.'

THE CASE OF THE NAKED
SALESGIRL

November 1947. Her first day off in months. Zena couldn't remember a day like it. It was the Royal Wedding. Princess Elizabeth was about to marry Lieutenant Philip Mountbatten. Zena looked around at the family sat in the front room all in Sunday best. Nana in her wing-backed chair issuing orders for tea. Syd, Madge and Marion perched on the edge of the sofa. Zena sat with Dave, squeezed together on the armchair by the fire. For once, there were no arguments, or "discussions", as Syd would say. Just joy at the occasion. They listened to the radio updates, itchy footed, until it was time to go to the cinema and watch the wedding on the big screen.

'What do you think Princess Elizabeth will wear, Zena?' Madge asked. She was almost in tears at the thought of the young couple embarking on their new life together.

'I don't know, Mum. They say she used all her clothes rations. But maybe because we're all still rationing, she'll cut back. Keep it simple. Who knows?'

'I think she'll have a full train regardless,' replied

Madge. She looked around the room for confirmation. Only Marion nodded.

It was a mild November day. Zena held Dave's hand as they walked with the family to the Capitol cinema excited in anticipation of the occasion. The auditorium was already packed when they arrived, and the orchestra played patriotic tunes that roused the crowd. When the purple and gold velvet curtains opened, the orchestra started the National Anthem. Everyone stood and sang.

The voice of Anna Neagle on the British Pathé news rang out as the ceremony unfolded at Westminster Abbey.

'You are invited to the marriage of Her Royal Highness Princess Elizabeth Alexandra Mary daughter of their majesties the King and Queen to Lieutenant Philip Mountbatten at Westminster Abbey on Thursday 20th November 1947. This was the invitation to a few, but millions responded… Elizabeth a girl of 21 on this her wedding day…'

Zena cheered along with rest of the cinema, and the hundreds of thousands in the crowds lining the streets when they saw Princess Elizabeth walking out of the Abbey, radiant in her Norman Hartnell dress.

The street party in Ripon Road was in full swing when they got back. Those who'd listened on the wireless had already set up the tables. It felt like VE Day all over again. The whole street cheered and clapped as they cut the cake Zena had made, iced in the Union flag. The world after the war seemed one step closer to happiness on this day. The young couple had cast joy across the nation as they stood on the balcony of Buckingham Palace waving to the crowds.

Full of cake and champagne, Zena looked around at her family, at Dave, her own beloved husband, and smiled. Life was good. Christmas was around the corner and who cared if her father didn't give her the best cases. She would bite her tongue and take the next case without a murmur. What would be her next case? Zena's heart lurched in anticipation. Maybe something that would take her abroad?

*

Zena banged at the keys of her Remington. She was furious. Her father had put her on a store detection case. No exotic travel for her.

'But Daddy, please. It's nearly Christmas and I've not even had time to shop. I've already got too much on with all the writs and injunctions you've landed on me.'

'No time to shop? Are you serious? No time to shop indeed. I've heard all the excuses now. Charlie might say he's sprained his ankle, but is at the races. Or Joe pretends his mum is sick, and he's in the pub. But shopping. That's a new one alright. Am I paying you to shop?'

Zena had long forgotten her promise to take the next case without objection.

'Oh come now Dad, that's not fair. You know how hard I work. I'm asking you to ease up on me, that's all. Can't Joe or Charlie do it?'

'No. They can't. You are suited for this one. This is the life as a private eye and you know it. It's not all about the glamour of wearing *haute couture* you know,' Syd said.

'But it's not fair. They're lazing around the pair of them, and you're sending me out again.'

'That's enough,' Syd stared at her. 'L.J. Hart's are paying good money. Expensive clothes are going missing, and they need to find out who's nicking them. You can't pick and choose in this business. Look on the bright side. At least you won't be undercover for this one. You can fit it in around other cases. Pose as a customer and keep observations on staff. Simple.'

'L.J. Hart's? But they have a store detective, don't they?' L.J. Hart's was Zena's favourite high-end department store. These days she could spot the store detectives in any shop. The bureau and her father had trained her well.

'There *is* a store detective – Stan – but he's not been able to work out how the clothes are being stolen.'

'Stan? I know him. He's good. I don't understand why he hasn't caught the thief.'

'I know. He swears blind he's watched every customer and every girl working there. He's baffled,' Syd said, looking back at Zena as if waiting for another retort. There was none. She was intrigued.

The next day was a breezy, blue-skied December morning and Zena was glad of her hatpin as she strolled up the street outside L.J. Hart's. As she walked, she watched the salesgirls enter the building through the staff entrance. She needed an idea of their routines. Who was coming and going, when and how. She recalled Stan's instructions on the telephone.

'Remember. You're a customer. No interrogations. No heroics. If you catch anyone at it. You come to me. Understood?'

'Understood, Stan. I'll be very discreet. No one will know I'm here. Leave it with me. I'm sure I'll find out who it is.' Despite Charlie's jibes, Zena knew she was good at this job. She also knew how the shop operated from her many visits there as a customer.

As soon as the doors of the department store opened to the public, Zena walked into the high-ceilinged entrance. White marbled columns framed the entry. She looked up at the central chandelier, marvelling at how the ceiling took its weight. Under the thousand shards of light raining down from crystal drops, an enormous round velvet seat circled a blue-tinged pool. Blue and green mermaids were mosaiced in its base. Golden carp floated, mouths gaping, as if in awe of the two painted flamingos rising out of the water. Zena loved the flamboyance and had to tear herself away. She was on a job. Not shopping.

She made a quick tour around the building: accessories, shoes and perfume on the ground floor, ladies' fashions on the first and second floor, lingerie and menswear on the third. She knew the psychology of the layout, which anticipated that men might buy something for their wife or girlfriend on the way up, before buying anything for themselves. Storerooms were at the top. Goods were being stolen from all three floors. Zena had her work cut out. Heading for ladies' fashions, it was hard for her not to be distracted by the fabulous winter coats on offer in the sale. She was taken by a herringbone woollen trench coat. It had a pointed collar lined with dark grey felt, and two rows of buttons down the front. She slipped it on, buckled the thick belt, and checked herself in the wall mirror. It looked super.

'Can I help you, madam?' A clipped voice made Zena jump. She whipped around. An older woman eyed her with suspicion. The woman's grey hair was pulled tight into a low bun. She peered at Zena over the top of her browline glasses.

'Oh no, I'm browsing, but I do like the feel of this coat. Can you tell me why it's in the sale?'

'Can you see that slight gap there in the seam? We're not allowed to repair it, so it had to go in the sale.'

'Oh yes I see. That's an easy repair. Would it be OK to put the coat aside for me for a couple of days? I do like it very much.'

'Yes I often think that it's daft to give a discount like that for something so simple. But it's your gain.' The saleswoman smiled at Zena.

'It is indeed. But I'll need to check with my husband if he'll buy it for me,' Zena said. It was a good excuse to come back again. It wasn't even a ruse as she loved the coat. Perhaps Dave might buy it for her for Christmas.

'Of course, madam, I'll put it by for you until the end of the week. Ask for me, Ruby. I must say the coat does suit you.' Ruby wrapped the coat in tissue paper and slid it under the sales counter. As she did so, they chatted about the sales and the store, and Zena realised that trying on the coat was a good ruse. She could walk around the other departments and do the same. Shopping could be combined with work after all.

The next day, Zena arrived in time to watch the girls go in through the staff entrance before the store opened. One girl arrived in a taxi earlier than the others. A bit odd for a young woman on a shop girl's wages. A sugar daddy?

One of the rich customers? They would often buy their wife expensive gifts and clothing, thinking it might keep them sweet and off the scent. Foolish men. If anything was to arouse a wife's suspicions, it would be unexpected gifts.

When the store opened, Zena made her way up to the lingerie department. There was the girl from the taxi. She was working on her own. Very smartly dressed, Zena observed. Her sugar daddy must be rather generous. Zena browsed the lingerie and looked at a plain slip that would go under the red coat dress she was making. She'd bought the material at Birkenhead Market. The dress was nearly finished and Zena didn't want the bother of lining it.

Thinking ahead, Zena moved over towards the men's fashions to see if there was anything in the sales that might do for Dave for Christmas. She chose a rich plum cardigan. Dave's colour. It was reduced to half price because one of the buttons was loose. Another easy repair. As Zena paid, she chatted up the tall salesman dressed in a double-breasted blue pinstripe, sporting a wispy moustache.

'It's such a bargain. My husband will love this,' Zena said, handing over a ten-shilling note. 'So many of the clothes here are out of my reach. I would love a skirt like the assistant is wearing, over there, but it would cost me a week's wages.' Zena pointed to the taxi girl. 'Do you all get a big discount?'

'Oh, you mean Ivy? She says she saves every penny to buy nice clothes.'

'What to impress her boyfriend?'

'Ivy with a boyfriend? That's a laugh. Doubt she's ever had one.'

'But why wear such expensive and nice clothes then?' Zena said, puzzled.

'She says they make her feel more confident, like. To be able to talk to customers. She's that shy.'

Zena wasn't sure if she should believe him. She left the store. She would return later. Staying longer would arouse suspicion. After successfully serving three injunctions, Zena drove back to L.J. Hart's that evening. She decided to watch the girls as they went home. She brought her mother with her as a cover. Two women in a car was less suspicious than one alone. It was cold, but they had their crocheted war blankets. They had each completed a square per week while Dave was in India. With hot water bottles and a flask of tea, they soon got warm. As Zena watched, her hands strayed to touch the soft blue and red nubs on the blanket. Madge sat knitting up a dark green Christmas jumper for Syd. Zena's head dropped and whipped up again at a loud high-pitched laugh.

She watched as Ruby came out of the staff entrance. She was followed by a group of girls, laughing and blowing on their hands as they hit the cold air. Amongst them Zena noticed the girl from the lingerie department, her heavy overcoat swamping her tiny frame. The girl followed the rest to the bus stop, smoking and laughing. After the experience with the Moira Joseph case Zena found any unusual overcoat suspicious and took some photos of her and the other shop girls.

'OK, Mum, we can go home now,' she said. 'Maybe Marion has cooked something for us. She knows we're working.'

'About time. The hot water bottle's gone cold,' Madge

grumbled. 'I left Marion with clear instructions to turn on the pot roast and boil some potatoes. We'll see.'

When they got home, Marion had cooked the pot roast with mashed potatoes, along with boiled baby carrots from the market. She stood by the laid table waiting to dish up, as proud as punch.

Not a word. Madge said nothing. Marion sat down, cut to the quick, and ate her meal in silence.

Syd tried to jolly everyone along with some of his awful jokes.

'Listen to this. Woman says to a Scotsman, "Is anything worn under your kilt?" He replies, "No, madam, everything is in working order." Charlie told me that one!' Syd's laughter was infectious. Even Marion blushed a smile, and Madge giggled like a schoolgirl. Dave looked across at Zena and grinned. All was right again in the world.

Syd was on a roll. 'What about this one. The gynaecologist who decorated his house himself, and did it all through the letter box!' He could barely get the words out he was laughing so much.

'That's enough, Syd,' Madge glared.

'Oh, come on, Madge. It was a joke.' Syd was annoyed. The atmosphere soured. Syd brooded, Madge glared, and Marion cleared the dishes wraithlike, slipping between dining room and kitchen.

Dave and Zena looked at each other, and in one swift movement, retired to their back-sitting room.

Dave laughed as Zena told him about her day.

'Your mother as cover? She'd more likely blow *your* cover than give it!'

'Now that's not fair, Dave,' Zena retorted. It was one

thing for her to joke about her mother, but woe betide anyone else who did. 'She was in fact surprisingly good. She got into the spirit of it and was good company.'

'You said you'll use her again? Does *she* know that?'

'What has got into you? Why are you against Mum tonight? Has she said something?'

'No, no, of course not. Sorry, love, I didn't mean anything by it,' Dave said. He looked down at her with love, and Zena relented; happy to end what might have turned into an argument.

*

The next morning, Stan, the store detective at L.J. Hart's telephoned Scott's. 'How are you getting on Mrs Archer?' Stan's rough voice was hard to hear above the crackle of the party line.

"I can't prove anything yet Stan. But I do have my suspicions.'

'The clothes are still going missing, which means the thief hasn't clocked you yet.'

'I don't want my cover blown.'

'Have you identified her? I assume it is a woman?'

'No, not yet. I hope I'll have some hard evidence for you by the end of the week.'

Two days later, Zena reviewed her notes.

Wednesday December 17th, 1947: L.J. Hart case.
Lingerie girl arrived in taxi again. No sign of sugar daddy. I bought under-slip and chatted to her while paying. She is a small-framed girl, with mousey-

brown hair, and huge doe-like eyes. Fingernails bitten to the quick. Nervous. She returned home on the bus. No evidence of stealing and no other suspect.

Thursday December 18th, 1947: L.J. Hart case.
Same as yesterday and previous days. No sign of stealing, but why not go home in a taxi if sugar daddy is paying? Buses are full, and she needs to fight for a seat. Don't understand.

Back on duty at the department store next morning, Zena saw the lingerie girl arriving as usual, earlier than the other girls, in a taxi. Hurrying to follow her into the store, Zena ran to the staff entrance. A shout stopped her in her tracks.

'Stop right there!'

'Please sir,' Zena whispered in a small slight voice that belied her size. 'I'm a new girl, and I don't want to get into trouble for being late. Please let me through.'

'Where's your letter, young lady? All new girls get a letter.'

'Ah you see, Mr Hart plays golf with my dad, you see, so there was no letter as such. Mr Hart told me to come and see him this morning. That's why I'm running. I can't be late. Not for Mr Hart, now can I?'

That swung it. He let Zena through. She followed the lingerie girl who headed for the first floor. It was empty. The girl was wearing her usual oversized overcoat and carrying a large handbag on her shoulder. The girl skimmed around the women's fashion department, stuffing a few choice items into her bag. She then headed up to the lingerie department, where she added expensive underwear and silk stockings to her cache.

'Got you,' Zena said to herself. She hid behind one of the pillars separating the menswear department from the lingerie. She watched the girl head for the lavatories. An empty hush settled on the floor. Zena would have loved to have shopped here in such tranquillity. Instead, she crept into the white tiled lavatories. The girl was leaning against one of the square ceramic sinks, taking off her coat. Zena wasn't sure who was more surprised. The girl tried to cover herself. It was too late. Zena had seen everything. Or rather had seen nothing. The girl was stark naked, apart from her coat and shoes. No wonder she arrived in a taxi. She'd have been freezing on the bus.

Hanging from the lavatory door opposite was a complete set of clothes. Cashmere jumper, silk blouse and wool skirt, even down to expensive underwear and stockings. The brass neck of the girl. Zena couldn't believe it. The girl gaped and gawped, not knowing what to say or do.

'You had better put the clothes on at least. You don't want to be seen naked by all and sundry,' Zena said. The girl dressed, staring at Zena all the while, not saying a word. Zena accompanied her out of the lavatories.

'Young man,' Zena shouted across the floor, although the spiv salesman lining up the ties was not much younger than her own age of 26. 'Call Stan quick!'

The salesman wiped his hands through his Brylcreemed hair, and stared first at Zena and then at the lingerie girl in disbelief. He ran off to find Stan.

'Please, miss. Please don't turn me in. Let me go. Please. You can say I gave you the slip. I can't afford to buy clothes. Me mam will kill me when she finds out.'

'You earn money, you get a discount. You only have yourself to blame.'

'It's my boyfriend, miss. He likes me to dress well. He's proper posh, miss. I can't wear no cheap clobber when I meet him. Please, miss,' the girl sobbed.

'You should have thought of the consequences beforehand. I'm sorry, but I can't pretend you haven't been stealing.' Zena stared at the girl, not without sympathy. Her mascara dripped down her cheeks and her doe eyes were brimming.

In a sudden flurry, and to Zena's complete surprise, the girl twisted out of her hold. She ran through the menswear department, and dodged behind the racks of suits and headed pell mell for the stairs as Zena tried in vain to catch her. She recalled Stan's instruction. No heroics. It was not her job to be chasing criminals. Stan arrived panting from the lift.

'I'm so sorry, Stan. I tried to stop her, but she got away from me.'

'Don't worry, Mrs Archer. The doors are locked. She can't go far. Silly girl. I would never have guessed it was her. Thank you. Mr Hart will no doubt be in touch.'

'It's been a pleasure, Stan. A real pleasure.'

Back in the office, Zena recounted the story of the naked salesgirl to her father, knowing full well Charlie and Joe would be earwigging as well as sniggering.

'You see Dad, I'm getting rather good at this. You should give me some more difficult cases. Like the ones you give Charlie. Look at what a botch he made of tracking down those gangsters. That poor woman lost her heirlooms, and Charlie well, the least said.'

'I've told you Zena, there is no place for a woman getting mixed up with gangsters. It was a tough case and Charlie did his best. Now leave him be and get on with what you're good at. Finish off those reports on your desk.'

Exasperated, Zena left the office in a huff. On the way home she picked up a bottle of wine for Dave from The Telegraph Inn so they could celebrate her success. At least someone appreciated her talents. She was determined to prove to her father she was as capable as any man.

5

NEVER OFF DUTY

January 1948. Christmas had flashed by as quickly as the set of Twinkle electric lights they'd bought to decorate the tree. Zena and Dave went for their traditional New Year's Day walk. Zena tightened her herringbone trench coat against the whip of the sea air on New Brighton beach. Dave took the hint, and had gone to L.J. Hart's for the coat Zena had set by. Her favourite Christmas present.

As they came back indoors, ruddy-cheeked and delighted with themselves, Syd called to Zena, grave-faced and serious. While they were out, he had taken a phone call from a client. He wanted Zena to go and see him.

'What? You expect me to go out on New Year's Day?' Zena said, shocked.

'I've told you before, Zena, this is what being a private detective is about,' he said. 'There's no such thing as a holiday in this game, and the office is officially open.'

'Can I at least have my lunch first!' Zena said, put out, but not daring to contradict him. He was still drunk from the night before. He couldn't go. Zena ate the ham salad Madge had prepared in silence, head down, needles of annoyance pricking her thoughts. Pushing the dining room chair back, she stood up before everyone had finished, and said, 'I'm off then.'

The job wasn't that serious after all. Zena felt annoyed she'd been pulled out on New Year's Day as she listened to another client thinking he was God's gift.

'She has got to be seeing someone else. I'm going out of my mind here. I've given her everything. House, car, clothes. Now she won't see me except for two days a week. It's not enough. I want to know. What is she doing the other days? She says I should trust her. But I don't. Why should I? I'm keeping her. She should do what I say.'

The client reeked money and privilege. Zena bit her tongue and instead replied meekly, 'I will try and find out for you Mr Pearse. I'll get onto it right away.'

Zena felt sorry for the woman. A kept mistress in this case. Having a controlling bully in your life even part time was something she could barely imagine.

*

'Mum, do you want to come out on a job with me tomorrow?' Zena asked when she got back that evening.

'What is it? How long for? I might prefer to go to the market. I'm not sure, let me see tomorrow,' Madge replied.

Zena didn't believe her. She knew that her mother would come. Every time Zena went on a job alone, her mother was miffed at being left behind.

'Marion, how about you? Would you like to come with us on a job tomorrow?' Zena asked her sister.

Marion hesitated, and Zena could see that she was

unsure; if she said yes it might upset her mother, if she said no it would annoy Zena.

Madge rounded on her. 'Come on, girl, spit it out! You should come. It would do you good to get out,' she snapped.

'OK then, I'll come,' said Marion, although Zena could tell she wasn't keen. It would be handy for Zena if she came, as she could leave them both sitting in the car as lookouts while she scouted around. Her mother didn't like being in the car on her own for too long.

The next morning Zena was exasperated as Dave fretted about the new apprentice dispenser who was starting that day. Lazy Jimmy had been fired for stealing out of the till. Dave had caught him by using one of Zena's tricks. He'd put fuchsine on the notes; it was invisible but left red dye on the fingers of the thief. It couldn't be washed off. Jimmy was caught red-handed.

Zena watched Dave leave with a sense of guilty relief and curled deeper under the blankets. The acrid bitterness of semi-burnt toast floated up the stairs, but a few more minutes wouldn't hurt.

'Zena! Breakfast!' Madge's voice spurred Zena into action. She headed downstairs in her dressing gown to the kitchen. The January sun scattered like butterscotch across the floor, and Madge and Marion sat ready in their glad rags as though off on a church outing.

After breakfast they drove to the house of her client's mistress in Hoylake, Madge shouting directions.

'Turn right, Zena! No, don't go that way. Go on the Leasowe Road. We might get a view of the sea from there.'

They arrived at the house; a large, detached barn of

a place near the golf course. The irony amused Zena: she was being asked to track a woman whose wealthy married lover suspected her of cheating on him.

They sat in the car, watching from the side of the unpaved road. Madge chatted all the time, her needles clacking as fast as her tongue.

'I'm going to have a quick look around. Stay here and if anyone comes, say you're waiting for the breakdown service to come. Say the engine's overheated.'

'But it hasn't. Overheated I mean. You expect me to lie?' Madge glared at Zena.

'Look Mum, no one is likely to come, but you need to think of a cover story if someone asks you. Come on. You know the score after all these years married to Daddy.'

'You father never talks about his work.'

'Oh Mum, please!'

'OK Zena have it your way. But don't be long!'

Zena walked towards the entrance of the house. She saw a side gate to the left-hand side of the huge walled garden. It must be where the bins were brought out. Looking around, Zena turned the heavy round iron handle with a sharp twist. She nearly fell into the huge lawned garden bordered by trees and shrubs.

Zena jumped. There was a rustle among the dogwoods. A blackbird maybe. She stopped. Listened. All was quiet again. She skirted further around the edge of the walled garden, staying hidden behind the shrubs flanking the lawn. Twisting her binoculars to focus, Zena saw someone she assumed must be the mistress, talking in the kitchen. She needed a closer look. Maybe Pearse was right.

Zena inched round, careful to stay out of sight. She

stopped every few yards to follow the woman's movements. Zena let out a small shriek. Something wet touched her hand. Zean whipped around. Her coat pocket snagged the pyracantha; the sharp barbs stopped her flight. She couldn't afford to rip her new coat. She disentangled herself and edged out from the shrubbery towards the smooth safety of the wall. She felt her chignon loosen.

Holding her breath, Zena edged back around the wall towards the gate. Another rustle. Her skin flushed cold. Her heart lurched as she flattened herself against the wall. She couldn't be caught here. Whatever it was, they hadn't spotted her. If she stayed still enough, maybe it or he, would go away. There it was again. That wet bump on her hand. She yanked her hand back and looked down. Scared at what she might find.

She stopped herself from laughing out loud. A pair of deep brown eyes smiled up at her. The cocker spaniel nudged her hand again. She stroked the soft brown head, and breathed out with relief. The dog wriggled and wagged, and nudged her again for attention. Zena realised this could prove tricky. How to get rid of him. She picked up a stick and threw it hoping that it would distract him for long enough to make an escape. Bad move. He loved this game. He dropped the stick at her feet and looked up at her. When she didn't throw it again, he let out a sharp, eager bark. Zena heard the back door open. The mistress, Miss Evelyn Pritchard appeared. Her photograph didn't do her justice. She was beautiful. No wonder Pearse was jealous.

'Bruno! Come here boy. What are you up to? Bruno?'
'Go on Bruno, get lost!' Zena hissed at the dog. She

shooed him away. Bruno thought this was all part of the game. Barking at her, he jumped up. Another pair of stockings ruined. Zena cursed him.

'Bruno! Come on now. Leave the squirrels alone. Come on inside. Dinner time! Bruno!'

The dog left Zena without a backward glance and raced towards the house. Zena ran back along the wall, and through the gate with a sigh of relief.

When she returned to the car, Madge was boiling with rage. 'Where an earth have you been? I'm hungry, and I need the lavatory.'

'Are you ok, Zena? You look a bit dishevelled,' Marion piped up.

'I'm fine. It took longer than I thought that's all. We'll go now.' There was little point in explaining what had happened. Her mother would never believe her, or if she did, would say she had been stupid for nearly getting caught. Best sweeten the pill. Fish and chips and hot tea at the seafront café would do it. It warmed their spirits and dulled Zena's sense of failure.

*

'It's freezing, Zena! You expect me to go out in this?'

'Please, Mum. I can only catch this woman at night.'

'You owe me.'

'I know Mum, I know.'

Zena had uncovered that Evelyn Pritchard, the Hoylake mistress worked during the day. If she was up to anything it was probably at night. Zena's client visited his mistress twice a week, but he had convinced himself that on the other nights she got up to something with another man.

'She tells me she's visiting a sick friend in hospital,' he said, 'but I just don't believe her. No one is sick for that long in hospital.' He was as jealous as a husband.

As far as Zena had observed, Evelyn was telling the truth. She'd followed Evelyn for the past two weeks, and observed her visiting a woman with cancer at the Liverpool Royal Infirmary on Brownlow Street every Monday and Friday.

Zena wrapped her mother in a blanket with a hot water bottle, and packed a thermos and some cake. That might keep her quiet long enough for Zena to catch out the mistress. As they approached down the unmade road, the headlights of the car picked up the hollow luminescence of a rabbit's eyes. It stared momentarily and scurried into the hedgerow.

There were no street lights and the houses were enveloped in the deep blackness of a lingering winter. They could see a chink of light behind the curtains of Evelyn's house. A dark blue Morris Oxford was parked outside. Zena made a note of the number plate.

'Would you like a toffee, Zena?' Madge asked.

She appeared to be happier. Zena took one. A Mackintosh's deluxe. They sat in silence, watching and waiting. Madge chewed on the toffees. Zena tried to ignore the noise. Until she heard a splutter.

'Mum, Mum, are you OK?'

Madge gasped, and pointed to her throat. She spluttered again. She had taken a breath, and the toffee had gone down the wrong way. She wound down the window to get some air. Zena bashed her back, but the coughing got louder.

Eventually it subsided, and Madge got her breath back. She started to laugh, even more loudly than her cough. It was the kind of infectious laugh that comedians would love to have in their audience. Zena couldn't help but giggle herself, as Madge continued laughing, tears streaming down her face.

Lights flashed from inside the houses. Several people had opened their curtains to see what all the furore was about.

'Come on, Mum, we'd better go,' Zena said. 'We mustn't be seen.' She reversed the car back down the track like a Keystone Cop.

Madge couldn't stop herself from laughing again.

'Oh Zena, what a night! I haven't had so much fun since your father took me to see Arthur Askey!'

It was not until several months of observations that Zena had absolute proof that the mistress was not cheating on her client. If Evelyn was not visiting her sick friend, then her mother or sister visited her. For such a beautiful woman with an alternative lifestyle, she was in fact rather dull. Zena called her client.

'Mr Pearse, I can assure you that Miss Pritchard is *not* having relations with anyone else but you.'

'That can't be right, Mrs Archer.'

'It is, Mr Pearse, it is.'

'But she's been acting all weird.'

'It could be because she has a lot going on, with her sick friend, and her mother's visits.'

'Oh, that witch. She's had it in for me since Evelyn and I first got together.'

'That may be the case, Mr Pearse, but there's no evidence of anyone else visiting or of her having a lover.'

'Perhaps you haven't caught her at it, Mrs Archer. I want you to keep watching her. I'll pay you. I'll double your fee.'

'I'm sorry, Mr Pearse, but no. There is nothing to see. Please just accept it. You'll have my report, and it shows that Miss Pritchard is innocent of any wrongdoing.'

Except for having an affair with you, Zena almost said.

*

Zena was filing the Pearse report as closed when she overheard her father telling Charlie about an intriguing new case.

'It seems the local gaff lads at the New Brighton fair who are hired for a day or two are making a load of dosh on the side,' Syd explained.

'I've heard that story in the past. I could have a word with them. Stake 'em out?'

'Collins the owner lets some of their little scams go. He says it's not worth the trouble. Can't say I blame the lads, to be honest. He barely pays them.'

'I've heard that those lads don't get much for a day,' Charlie said. He looked squarely at Syd as if to say, "And that goes for me an' all."

'That's as maybe, but we've been asked to do a job. Collins says that during this tour, he's had too much of the profit creamed off. We've been asked to uncover which of the gaff lads are doing it.'

'No problem for me boss. I'll get the scammers.'

'We'll see Charlie. I might have another idea,' Syd said.

Zena listened waiting to hear the shout of her name, meaning she'd got the job. That would be one in the eye for Charlie. She waited. No shout came. Who *would* get the job? Not Joe. No. Joe at the funfair?

6

THE CASE OF THE FAIRGROUND
SWINDLE

June 1948. 'Not pigtails!' Zena said, staring aghast at her father's suggestion.

'You're still young and pretty enough to get away with it. Go on, love, you'll be grand. Can't think of any other way we'll catch the beggars.'

'But Dad,' Zena replied, 'Can't you send Charlie? He looks like he was born in a fairground.'

'They'd smell a rat,' Syd paused, and laughed, 'and you don't have enough hair on your chinny chin chin to be the bearded lady.'

'Oh God, Dad, the things you make me do,' Zena laughed back at him. Delighted to be given an interesting case, she didn't care what she had to wear.

'Bet you'll be great as a teenage schoolgirl. Look at you as a model. Disguise is the name of the game, love. Blend in with the crowd. No other way.'

'But surely no one will believe that I can be a schoolgirl. Look at me.'

Zena watched him almost concede as he looked at her statuesque figure.

'No. No. I still think it could work. A schoolgirl would be less conspicuous than Charlie roving around the fairground asking questions. I got the idea from the St. Trinian's comic strip. Have you seen it in *Lilliput Magazine?* It's hilarious. You'd pass as one of them gangling girls. Give it a go, love.'

Laughing, Zena came out of her father's cubbyhole and skirted round Charlie's desk, knocking off some of the piles of papers as she went. She ignored his angry shout and walked to her side of the desk, resisting the urge to laugh in his face. She was getting some good cases now. Syd trusted her.

*

The next afternoon, Marion giggled, and Nana snorted in derision. Zena walked into the kitchen in her disguise. She wore a schoolgirl's knee-length gabardine; her pigtails swung high, plaited with Dave's help earlier that morning. A straw boater completed the look.

'Are you saying I don't look like a teenager, Nana?' Zena laughed.

'Come here. I might be able to fix you.' Nana loosened Zena's striped tie, borrowed from Dave, and skewed it to one side. She pulled up Zena's skirt and pulled down her socks. 'There,' she said, cocking the straw boater to the left, and messing up the pigtails underneath. Without make-up, Zena could just pass muster as an older teenager.

Walking to New Brighton later that day – her disguise perfected – the lilac beauty of the sea asters edging the promenade caught Zena's eye. She stopped to admire their delicate petals clustered around the yellow buttoned centre. In the distance, the crowds piled into the fairground, ready for an afternoon of fun. Zena had loved the rides as a child. When they lived in London, she would pester her father to bring her to the Epsom fair in the autumn. She relished the toffee apples and candyfloss that made her teeth ache as she queued at the carousel for the galloping horses.

Entering the fair Zena's excitement built at the wheeze of the hurdy gurdy. She was unsure she looked like a fifteen-year-old schoolgirl, but she certainly felt like one. She decided on a tour of the fairground. She needed to try all the rides to find out which of the operators was swindling. Edging round the dozens of colourful stalls, she was jostled by the crowds and felt a tug on her pigtails.

She whipped around to see a mop-haired young lad, grinning sideways at her. He was leaning against the sign for the coconut shy. Zena scowled at him. She stuck her tongue out and tossed her pigtails behind her. She was enjoying her role. Pity she couldn't slap his face.

She marched off towards the darts stall. Three darts for thruppence. Zena scanned the prizes. The novelty Sairey Gamp teapot looked the best of a bad lot. But the hooked nose and gimlet eyes of the old lady face put her off. Too much like Nana.

Zena could not resist her favourite ride. The swingboats. She had loved them as a child, the whoosh up and clutch of the stomach as the swing came shuddering down. She had to have a go. Sixpence, like most of the rides. The burly operator's tattooed hand took her cash.

'Thank you,' Zena said. She spied him pocketing her sixpence without giving her a ticket.

'Off yer go, love – get in that one there.' He pointed to the heavy wooden boat painted in bright red and yellow.

The thrill of the ride banished all thoughts of whether the swingboat man was a swindler.

As she soared skywards, Zena felt as light as the lace of candy pink clouds drifting in the summer dusk. The ride was over all too soon, and Zena was about to have another go there and then. No. She stopped herself. She had a job to do. This was not a holiday. She noted to herself that this chap was one to watch.

Zena walked towards the queue outside a massive wooden drum. Crowds blocked her view, but she could hear the roar of the motorcycles on the legendary Wall of Death. Stick figures were perched high on the perimeter of the drum. Before the war Zena had stood up there, thrilled at the daredevils thundering round the circular wall, glued to the sides.

Zena watched the caller taking money from the punters: a squat, thick-set young man, sporting a pork pie hat. A shilling for the five-minute show. Zena calculated that they were taking a tidy sum each night and made a note to find out how much the lad paid to the owner.

Zena stopped for the day. She would come back tomorrow when it was less crowded. She already had a sense of all the rides and a couple of suspicions.

She still had the half-hour walk home to Ripon Road. As the tide was out, she walked via the beach. Untangling her pigtails and stuffing her straw boater into her bag, she pinned up her long dark hair into its chignon. She started to feel more like herself. Seaweed popped as she walked away from the sea wall towards the beach. Razor shells crackled underfoot, and a smoky dance of starlings circled the pier.

*

It was a cloudless blue sky the following afternoon when Zena returned to the fairground. She could hear the carousel in the distance. The Big Wheel looped round high and slow above the pier, its wooden boats swinging. What ride to try first?

The coconut mat scratched, and Zena was glad of her gaberdine tucked beneath her when she flew down the famous helter skelter – The Rocket. Before she knew it she was whooshed out of the exit, birth-like, onto a thick, soft mat. Breathless, and heart pounding, she laughed at the ground floor gaff lad and said, 'One more, please.'

This was another money spinner for the owner, Mr Collins. She observed the lad as he hustled customers through and up the stairs. There was a constant stream of people, one every couple of minutes. It would generate a huge turnover.

Heading back to the swingboats, Zena ducked behind the coconut shy for a quick puff of a cigarette. She'd picked up the habit from working in her father's office. They all smoked, and now so did she.

'Got you! I'll tell your da' on you.' A nasal, accented voice, made her jump. It was the mop-haired lad who had pulled her pigtails. Zena was not amused.

'Yeah, right, like you know who my dad is anyway. Get lost or I'll scream.'

'I'll find out where you live. I'll follow yer home. You won't know when, but I'll find you.'

'Oooh, I am SO scared.' Zena stepped on the smoking butt of her cigarette and turned on her heel, relieved that she hadn't been rumbled.

Zena headed back to the swingboats. She watched the burly man pocket her sixpence. No ticket. As they set off Zena pulled on the rope. The boat swung higher. And higher, as she pulled harder. The young lad standing at the other end of the boat saw this as a challenge. He started to tug harder still on his rope. The boat swung too high. Zena glared. He backed down, and the boat slowed. Even dressed as a teenage schoolgirl, Zena could still give a narrow-eyed teacher's stare that would stop grown men in their tracks.

As the boat swung, Zena worked out how the operator dealt with other customers. He pocketed the sixpence when a child was on their own. During her three-minute ride, Zena calculated that out of the six swingboats, all of which had two people in them, ten shillings should have been made. She saw him pocket three shillings. A nice little earner on the side. The gaff lads were casuals who would earn less than that for an hour of labouring at the docks.

Giddy from her ride on the swing-boats, Zena looped the perimeter of the fairground. She heard the dying putter of the motorcycles, as the bikers took a break from the Wall of Death. She walked around its smooth high wooden walls, her hand trailing. She wondered at its neat tight architecture. Not so much as a splinter. A hard, sharp yank on her pigtails snapped her into reality. She spun around thinking it was the coconut shy lad. Ready to give him a mouthful, Zena was instead confronted by the hard bulk of the man in the pork pie hat from the Wall of Death. He pushed Zena against the wooden frame, grabbed both her pigtails and twisted them hard. It took all Zena's nerve not to cry out from the pain.

'What you nosing round for? I saw you. Going on every ride watching everybody. Who sent you?' A mouthful of stained teeth snarled into her face.

A tight band of fear knotted in Zena's chest. It was almost more painful than the pull on her scalp. Looking up into the black eyes glaring at her, she said in her best haughty schoolgirl accent, 'I beg your pardon? How dare you accuse me of snooping.'

The man tightened his grip on her pigtails. Zena gasped.

'Too right you've been snooping. Who you working for?'

'I tell you sir, I am *not* snooping. I'm doing a school project on the life of a fairground. I have permission from the owner, Mr Collins. In fact, I should report you for making false accusations. Maybe I will.'

Hearing the name of the owner, he backed off, dropping Zena's pigtails. Afraid for his job, he mumbled an apology, touching his forelock. Zena suppressed a giggle.

'Look, it's OK,' she said, pretending to soften. 'I can see why you thought I might be snooping. My teacher told me I had to get as much information about the fairground as possible. I want to get top marks for my project. He gave me the school camera too. I should take some photos. Look, I'll take one of you against the sign for the Wall of Death.'

Zena pulled out her camera. Intrigued by the Polaroid Land camera, the man relented and allowed himself to be snapped leaning on the sign board. The camera gave instant photographs.

'Stay still. I'll take another one and you can keep it.'

Zena snapped another photo while the first was emerging from the haze of film.

'Here you go. The photo's nearly ready now. Don't tell Mr Collins I gave it to you though.'

'Oh no, miss, I won't. Thank you, thank you. Blimey! Is that me? I've never seen me own photo before. Me ma will be made up, she will. Thank you, miss.'

Zena walked off, relieved that she'd kept her wits and got away with it. She looked at the photo she'd taken and thought of her forthcoming report. It would be one in the eye for Charlie and Joe. If they ever did take photos, they were usually out of focus or of someone's foot.

Having been on most of the rides, observed all the operators, and taken photos of those she'd caught cheating, Zena had an idea how the swindles were happening, and how much was going missing. The owner might forgive some of the scams, but a massive profit was being pocketed. It was for Collins to follow up.

*

'How many of them were creaming off profits then, love?' Syd asked.

He stood up from his desk, and laughed at Zena,

pulling one of her pigtails. She'd forgotten that she was still dressed in her schoolgirl's garb. She'd been in such a hurry to tell her father that she'd solved the case, she'd not thought to change.

'A total of five operators. All gaff lads brought in for the autumn season. I think they might be in it together. They're on the rides where it's easy to pocket the cash.'

'Of course. Makes sense. How much do you reckon?'

'They must make a fortune each day. The rest of the rides are rented pitches where the families know each other. No wonder the owner hired us. A third of his profits must be going walkabout.' Zena didn't mention the bully from the Wall of Death. She was worried her father might not give her another case if he thought she was in real danger.

'Well done! You've done a grand job, my girl. Can't say I was too hopeful when you set off. Must have been the pigtails!' Her father laughed.

Zena ignored his sally with annoyance.

'Very funny. Now let me get on and type up my report. Mr Collins will be asking for it soon.'

Zena backed out of her father's cubbyhole and sat at the detectives' desk. Joe had his own desk, being the senior detective, but Zena still had to share with Charlie. She stared at the detritus piled on Charlie's side. Her elation at solving the case evaporated. She felt like sweeping the whole mess of papers, teacups, and overflowing ashtrays onto the floor. How did her father allow him to be so careless?

The clack and ring of the Remington soothed her rattled nerves. Zena finished the report with only a couple of errors. She could use the eraser. She hated typing. Even though she had been a clerk for the U.S. Army during the war, she'd never really got the hang of it.

'Woah, look at you! I love that St. Trinian's look!' As he came in, Joe's presence could not be ignored. His bulk ate up the space in the office. He thumped down in his seat and bent over the desk doubled up with laughter.

Ignoring him, Zena pulled out the final page of her report from the typewriter and went to staple it. She felt like stapling his tongue. She'd been waiting for this gag after what her father had told her. The St. Trinian's comic strip had been running for the past year. Even Zena had to admit she looked more like one of the unruly monsters of Ronald Searle's cartoons than a demure schoolgirl.

Being a woman in this profession brought her many such remarks. Some male clients had already refused to be interviewed by her. It was infuriating. She'd proven herself to be as good as the men if not better. They took the shortcuts that she wouldn't; illegal bugging, false reporting, bullying witnesses. Syd would always forgive them, but woe betide Zena if she even put a toe out of line. Not that she would.

Before she left that evening, she glanced at the headlines of *The Liverpool Echo.*

'Daddy have you heard this?' Zena took the paper into her father's cubby-hole.

'What? Another department store opening where you can go shopping?' Syd gave Zena a wry smile.

'Very funny. No, it's about the fairground. Listen to this: *Police are investigating the assault on five young men working as casual labourers at Collins' Fairground. The assault took place on the evening of 15th July 1948. Police are appealing for any witnesses to the assault to come forward.* It has to be Mr Collins Dad, don't you think? Should we go to the police and let them know what we found out?'

'No, no, we can't do that. We make our living from people like Mr Collins. If the police come calling, we'll not lie, but we don't volunteer information unless we're asked.'

Zena hesitated. She didn't agree with Syd, but was loathe to contradict him. Especially in front of Charlie. She resolved to speak to Win. If anyone knew what to do, she would. She was always so sensible.

*

The weeks passed by in a whirl of writs, injunctions, and tracking down missing husbands. A stack of files waited for Zena back in the office. The divorce hearing for the Edwards was set for the following month. They were anxious for their divorce to be completed as quickly as possible. They just wanted to get on with their lives in peace and friendship. They would need her affidavit swearing that Mrs Edward was found in a compromising circumstance. Zena set to work, banging at the keys of her old Remington. Her attempt to persuade Zena's father to buy the latest electric typewriter had failed. She was stuck with the Remington and all its quirks.

As she handed the affidavit to her father to check, he looked at her with a quizzical air.

'What is it, Dad? You look worried about something.'

'Seems the ladies of the night switching up and down Lime Street are extending their patch,' Syd said.

'That's nothing new. What's the problem?'

'They're reaching Victoria Street corner.'

'So?'

'Some of our clients, including the solicitors in the building, are being accosted on their way home.'

'Or some of them are taking advantage, more like.'

'Either way, we can't have it, Zena.'

'What can we do about it?'

'We need to get evidence so the coppers can warn them off.'

'What do you expect me to do about it? Dress as a prostitute?'

Syd put his head to one side and looked at Zena with a wry smirk.

'No. No. I draw the line at that. You can't ask me to do that. Absolutely not! Get Harry to pose as a client.'

Syd carried on looking at her. She knew that look, and there was no arguing.

The following day Zena brought in her outfit. Tight skirt, low-cut blouse, blonde wig, high heels, and her make-up bag. She had to wait until early evening. The girls weren't brazen enough to work in full daylight. Dusk crept into the office, the low evening light filtering through the smoke and dust motes.

Zena donned her disguise. The heavy make-up took an age to apply. She settled the wig firmly over her tied back hair. Evening had greyed out much of Cook Street by the time she stepped out of the office. She walked up and down the end of the road into Victoria Street, handbag swinging, stilettos clacking. Nothing.

Zena went further down the road and stood against

the wall at the corner of Temple Court. She was in luck. The girls were waiting for the solicitors to empty out of the pubs. She pretended to eye up the punters while hoping to catch one of the girls also plying her trade. A couple of punters approached Zena, eyed her up and down and walked on. She felt sick, worse than a piece of meat on a butcher's hook, but strangely miffed when they passed her by. A grey Humber pulled over and a chubby-faced, mild looking chap wound down his window.

'Want a ride, love?'

'Nah, I'm waiting for me fella,' Zena said.

'Go on, you could fit me in while you wait, eh?' He winked at Zena.

'Nah, get lost or I'll have me fella stick one on you.'

'Your loss,' he said, as he edged his car down the street, no doubt looking for someone more obliging. He didn't look the type to go with a prostitute. But then who did?

'How much?' a familiar voice whispered in her ear.

Oh, my goodness. Zena jumped at the voice. She knew it well. Was it really him? No, it couldn't be. Zena's heart thumped. How would she deal with this one? It had never occurred to her that someone she knew so well would ever go with a prostitute. It was dreadful. His poor wife.

'Clear off, Eddie, I'm working,' Zena hissed. Eddie was one of the solicitors from Kenner and Associates across the hall from Scott's. Zena knew him well; he would always greet her as she ran up the stairs. They would comment on the ever-broken lift, or the trouble they had parking.

'I know, that's why I'm asking you how much?' he replied.

'Eddie, it's me!'

'What do you mean, "It's me"? I've never met you before.'

God, could the stupid idiot really be this thick?

'It's me, Zena! I'm working. Undercover. Move away, or I'll be rumbled.'

'Zena? Are you sure?'

'Of course, I'm sure. I know who I am, for goodness' sake.'

'Oh, no, oh, no, oh bloody hell. Please Zena you won't say anything, will you? Promise? I can't have my wife finding out.'

'No, of course I won't, you booby. Now go away!' Zena glared at him. He scurried off, cheeks flaming.

It was lucky that it was still late summer, or she would have been frozen standing there for the best part of the night. She had never felt so exposed in all her life. She was sorry for the poor girls who had no choice but to make this their living. At last she got what she wanted.

'Get off me patch, you whore ye. What you doing here?' A woman approached her dressed in a tight green, lizard-patterned dress, with a plunging neckline and bra that pushed up her ample bosom under her chin. Most uncomfortable.

'OK, OK. Don't take on so. I'm going in a minute. I just need to tell you something.'

'Tell me what? Why? Are you with the bizzies? I knew you wasn't one of us. I'm not talking to no bizzie. Gerrof with you.'

'Listen. I'm not with the police I promise you. I'm trying to do you a favour.'

'Who are you then?'

'Listen to me. There are people trying to get you off this patch.'

'Who? Who you talking about?'

'They're bringing in the police to move you on.'

'Move us on where? Who are you?'

'Never mind who I am. By this time next week, you could be in prison.'

'Why are you telling me this? Why should I believe you?' The girl eyed Zena with suspicion.

'You need to believe me. Move your patch before you get arrested.'

The girl grumbled something back at Zena and went to talk to one of the other girls. They looked back at Zena, unsure what to make of her.

Zena left. Her job was done. The recordings she had made, along with her statement, would be enough for the police to move the girls on if any were left. She hoped they would take her advice and move somewhere else. Zena wouldn't identify the girl she spoke to. She'd enough on her plate. If it appeared that the police had moved them on, then that would be enough for the solicitors. Oh, the irony.

The next day Zena blasted her father.

'Don't ever, ever ask me to do anything like that again.'

'Why? You managed didn't you?' Syd winked at her.

'It was humiliating.'

'Oh give over love. It can't have been that bad.'

'It was. It was, Dad. It was horrible. One of the solicitors from this building propositioned me!'

'Propositioned you? What do you mean?'

'You know full well what I mean. He asked me…' Zena couldn't bring herself to say the words.

'You mean he actually asked you…'

'Don't say it Dad. Don't say it. I've never been so embarrassed in my life.'

'Who was it? Was it Eddie? Has to be Eddie.' Syd started laughing, a deep long belly laugh that rumbled the filing cabinet and sent the overflow of cups on his desk clinking.

'It's not funny! I could have been killed. Those girls didn't take kindly to another woman on their patch.'

'Eddie…oh my word…'

'Stop laughing,' Zena shouted. Her father had tears running down his cheeks. He couldn't stop himself. Zena almost weakened. His laugh was infectious, but she stayed firm.

'I'm not telling you who it was,' she said. 'But never again! I'm not the dogsbody you give the worst jobs to.' Zena turned on her heel and stormed back to her desk, hoping for an apology to follow. It didn't.

*

Zena had little time to think before another Christmas was upon them. The Scott family tradition of open house was a welcome distraction. The dining room was laden with Christmas cake that Marion had slaved over weeks before; mince pies baked by Madge, and canapés crafted by Zena. Dave inched out precise and measured glasses of Tio Pepe sherry. Nana's favourite. Mistletoe hung over the front door, and Zena and Madge greeted the neighbours and friends with a kiss as they came in. Marion dashed upstairs until the kissing was over, and she was safe from whiskery embraces. They all agreed it was the best year they'd had since the war.

The New Year of 1949 came with a blast of snow, quicky followed by a spring flurry of divorce cases. Scott's and Zena were busier than ever. It was with relief on a hot evening in June that Zena sat down in the cool and peace of the back room of Ripon Road, Campari in one hand and cigarette in the other. Until the telephone rang.

7

THE CASE OF THE BARCLAY AFFAIR

June 1949. The voice on the other end of the telephone was loud, demanding, and insistent that Zena track down her husband's latest mistress. One would have thought that one mistress would have been sufficient. Zena wondered why the woman didn't divorce him.

'Are you sure you wouldn't rather get a divorce Mrs Barclay? It would be a lot less costly,' Zena said after half an hour listening to her new client.

'No Mrs Archer. I can't help myself. I love him. He makes me laugh. Always has.'

'It's entirely up to you Mrs Barclay and if you're sure?'

'I'm sure. He's a bugger alright. He was off with the babysitter not long after we were married. He always comes back to me in the end. I just like to keep tabs.'

Zena couldn't imagine Dave being unfaithful. Ever. She understood Mrs Barclay even less. Why stay with a philanderer? Poor deluded Mrs Barclay. Maybe tracking down the latest mistress would open Mrs Barclay's eyes. But how to find her? Win would know.

'Win? Win I need some help,' Zena whispered down the telephone. Her father wouldn't approve. No way would he sanction paying Win as a detective. She would need to do this under the radar.

'Zena? What's happened? Are you ok?'

'I'm fine. Listen I was wondering something. You can say no. How about you do a bit of work with me?'

'Me? Work with you? As a detective? I'm just a housewife!' Win laughed.

'Exactly. That's why I need you. You know what Cyril's like. You know…not being…you know what I mean… Win you know don't you?'

'Sadly yes I do. Only too well. Dirty beggar. If it weren't for the kids…'

'I know. I'm so sorry Win. But that's why I need some help with observations to track someone down.'

'You mean you want me to keep you company. Like your mum does?'

'It's a bit more than that, but yes. I need someone else in the car and you know what Mum's like. She's just too difficult sometimes.'

'Why not. It might be fun. It'll get me out of the house and away from the kids. My mum can babysit. Just tell me when.'

*

It was Saturday and buttered sunlight warmed a strip of the patchwork quilt. A wedding gift. Zena drowsed, trying not to remember that it was July 1949 and the Barclay case remained unsolved. Even with Win's help, weeks had gone by. The case was no further along.

An imperious shout of, "Breakfast on the table,"

scotched any hope of a lie-in. Woe betide Zena if she missed her mother's weekly full English. Dave was lucky. He was off early to work. She pulled on her dressing gown with a shrug and headed down to the kitchen. Everyone else was dressed and halfway through their sausage and bacon.

'Will you go to Birkenhead Market with me this morning, Zena?' Madge's wheedle grated. Syd hid behind the *Liverpool Echo*. Zena hesitated, her eye caught by the weekend's headlines.

'Zena!' Madge's voice changed from wheedle to command. It was as sharp as her father's when she wanted something.

Zena tried to avoid the weekly trip to the market which had become a ritual rather than a pleasure.

'Can't you go with Marion this week?'

'Marion doesn't like shopping. You do,' Madge replied with a pained look.

Zena drove her mother through Wallasey Village towards Birkenhead in the old Austin A10. The day was bright, but muggy and damp, and condensation formed on the inside of the windscreen as Madge clattered on about the purchases she wanted to make. As they approached the market building, the white relief letters 'BIRKENHEAD MARKET, ESTABLISHED 1835' stood proud over the massive domed arch, the two coats of arms either side. There was one with a motto that always appealed to Zena: *By Faith and Foresight*.

They parked at the rear of the market, beside a new but filthy Ford pickup. The flatbed at the back was full of empty wooden crates. Rotting fruit and vegetables littered the floor. A lone potato rolled out and rested by the mud-covered wheel. As they walked into the echo of the iron-buttressed warehouse, they were deafened by the clang and chatter of stallholders shifting and selling their wares. Madge shouted something at Zena, who tried to ignore her. She wanted to stand and soak up the atmosphere. She loved the market. There was everything one could want here, and more.

'I said, let's go to the Nuts Corner. I want some fruit,' Madge shouted right into Zena's ear.

Zena gritted her teeth and smiled back.

'Fine. But then I want to go to the fabric stall. I've had my eye on some marigold linen there for ages. With any luck they might have it on sale.'

'OK you go. I want to talk to Mrs McKinney.'

'Maybe we could buy some material for Marion too. Run her up a summer dress. When does the poor girl ever get new clothes?'

Madge ignored Zena's comment and beetled round to her favourite stall. Most times Madge unpicked or remade old clothes into dresses for Marion. Zena felt it was time Marion had something new. She might be an annoying teenage sister, but she often got a raw deal.

Zena left her mother gossiping with the lady at the Nuts Corner and circled back round to the fabric stall. The drab utility woollens of the war had given way to a riot of colour. Bolts of pinks and bright blues jostled with spring greens and clashed with autumn rusts and cardinal red. Heaven. A dress length remained of the marigold linen Zena coveted, and she bought three yards of dark green poplin for Marion. More her colour.

Walking back to collect her mother, a brown paper bag of material heavy in her basket, Zena saw a familiar figure. It was Mr Barclay. Zena started running.

'Come on, Mum, we have to go,' Zena hissed.

'What an earth is going on? I hadn't finished talking!' Madge was furious at being interrupted, but Zena knew she had to hide before she was spotted.

'It's a mark. I've been following this chap for his wife,' Zena said. 'I don't want him to see me. I've already been to his house, and he opened the door to me. He knows my face.' Zena kept her head down, and shuffled along next to her mother, looking as if she was more her mother's age than an energetic 28-year-old. Her father had told her that changing one's walk was the best form of disguise. Zena hoped he was right.

'Let's get a move on and follow him. I need to find out where his mistress lives. You keep an eye out where he goes and guide me. I can't look up.'

Madge got into the spirit of it straight away, enjoying her role as detective's assistant. Their mark led them a merry dance around the perfume and jewellery stalls, no doubt purchasing something cheap and nasty for his mistress. After half an hour he headed south out of the market onto Claughton Road, and got into a black Vauxhall 10. Easy to spot. They raced to their car and saw him drive off past the Astor Cinema.

He drove slowly and they followed him without incident through the dark of the Kingsway Tunnel. He turned right before Old Haymarket and into Crosshall Street, parking outside a large Victorian redbrick mansion block.

Zena drove past and pulled up further down the road. Her mother said, 'She must have some money if she's living in there. My friend Eve was married to a barrister who lived in an apartment in Victoria House. Too cold, she said. Lucky he died, and she could move.'

Zena turned the car around and parked on the opposite side of the street, hoping to get a glimpse of Mr Barclay or his mistress through her binoculars. She always kept a pair in the glove compartment just in case. Nothing. Zena had to figure a way to find out which apartment the mistress lived in. At least now she knew the street name and building. Finally a break in the case, no matter how small. Mother and daughter waited for another hour, before Madge started moaning. Time to leave.

*

Zena tried to track down the number of the apartment in Victoria House where she thought Mr Barclay's mistress might live. She'd taken Win with her to carry out some observations. Win was an easier cover to work with than her mother who could only manage an hour or two. They sat together cheerfully gossiping about the latest fashions and drifted onto the topic of Win's husband Cyril. A cad if ever there was one.

'What I don't understand is why you stay with him Win.' Zena was exasperated that her friend refused to leave her husband despite his terrible behaviour.

'It's ok for you Zena,' Win said. 'You have Dave and no children. I don't have the money to leave even if I wanted to. I have no choice.'

'Everyone has a choice.'

'That's easy for you to say. You just don't understand,' Win's eyes brimmed.

'Oh no. Win, no don't cry. I'm sorry. I'm just angry on your behalf.'

'I know, and maybe one day I'll be able to go. Anyway, Cyril isn't bad all the time.'

They sat in silence for fifteen minutes before leaving. Yet again they'd seen nothing and to cap it all she'd upset Win. Zena needed more information about the mistress.

'Mrs Barclay? Zena Scott Archer.'

'Ah, Mrs Archer. How you have been getting on? I've been waiting for your call. Have you found that floozy yet?'

'I think I might have, but I can't be certain she's the one. Do you have anything else to go on? Does he have a type?'

'Ha! A type? Of course he has a type. They're all the same. Blonde, bosom. You get the picture.'

'Yes, Mrs Barclay, I do. Are they always like this?'

'Yes, most of the time. I never bother when he goes for one of them. I've only ever worried once. Mousy thing five years ago. I knew there was more to it. And there was.'

'What did you do?'

'I threatened him good and proper. He even had the cheek to ask for a divorce! He came back to me eventually. He always does. As I told you, I just want to know what he's up to. I have the kids to think of.'

'Does Victoria House mean anything to you?'

'Not at all. Should it?'

'Possibly. I'll let you know if I get any further.'

If she could get into the entrance hall of Victoria

House, she might find out from the post boxes who lived there, and track the mistress that way.

After several days of boredom sitting in her car, Zena struck lucky. She noticed a woman striding out of the grand arched entrance of the apartment block. Fur coat and high heels. Blonde. Bosom. Taking a chance, Zena leapt out of her car and ran after the woman, holding her wedding ring outstretched in her hand.

'Excuse me, excuse me,' Zena shouted.

The woman stopped and waited for Zena to catch up. She looked Zena up and down. Zena bit her tongue and played her role.

'I'm sorry, but I think you might have dropped this. I saw something on the ground and thought it must be yours.'

'My husband wouldn't buy me a cheap wedding ring like that.'

'Oh, I'm so sorry. I wonder who else it might belong to. Do you live in Victoria House?' Zena said through clenched jaws. That wedding ring was all Dave could afford at the time.

The woman nodded.

'I wonder if I might trouble you. Perhaps I could write to all the tenants. I would hate someone to think they had lost their wedding ring. Even if it is cheap, it will be precious to someone,' Zena said.

The woman sighed, 'Oh, come on then. There are eight apartments. If you hurry up and take down the names, you can do what you like from there. You don't need mine, Mrs Irene Barclay at No.5, and No. 4 is a widower, so it's not going to be his.'

Mrs Barclay? It was too much of a coincidence for it not to be her. But were they really married? She followed the second Mrs Barclay into a spacious entrance hall. Black and white tiles circled a gated lift. Eight wooden post boxes lined the wall on the left. Zena hurriedly wrote down all the other names on the boxes, although she already had the information she needed.

'Thank you for this. I'll write to everyone and see if they have lost their wedding ring,' Zena said. She rushed off, not daring to look back.

Zena could hardly believe her luck. That woman had to be the mistress. Or the wife? Shocked at the possibility of bigamy, Zena returned to the office.

'What do I do, Dad? Should I report him to the police if I find out he's committed bigamy?' Her moral compass was not often tested, and she was uncertain which way it would swing.

Syd, however, was unambiguous. 'Keep your sticky beak out of it, my love. That's what I say. It's up to the wife if she reports him to the police. You present the evidence in your report and the client makes the decision. That's how we've always done it.'

Still unsure, Zena sat at her desk, and started typing up her notes. Charlie, in characteristic fashion, piped up. 'Good luck to him I say. Men need more than one wife. Haven't you heard the saying, Zena? A man needs a wife for the bedroom, a wife as mother to his children, and a wife for the house. Me, I'd have another one just for fun.' Charlie giggled at what he thought was the best joke in the world.

'Shut up, Charlie! You shouldn't have been listening.

It's no wonder no woman in their right mind would ever have you.' Zena glared so hard that, immune as he was to most rebukes, Charlie stayed silent.

*

It took a visit to Chester before Zena found the record of a marriage certificate for Irene Barclay. Case closed, or so she thought. It was up to the first Mrs Barclay to decide what to do next. She was shocked several weeks later to hear Mrs Barclay's voice on the telephone.

'You need to follow him again, Mrs Archer. He's got another one.'

'But, Mrs Barclay, I have sent my report to you. It shows that your husband married Irene Shaw in Chester in June. I thought that was what you wanted me to uncover. I thought the case was closed. At least from our side. Of course, if you want to report his bigamy, that's your decision.'

'Yes, I know, I know. I told you, I never worries about any of those blonde types. This one's more serious.'

Zena wondered what was more serious than bigamy.

'What makes you think that Mrs Barclay? It could just be another fling,' Zena said.

'No, no I can feel it. It's different…He's different. I want to know what he's up to. Please, Mrs Archer.'

'All right Mrs Barclay. What is it you want me to do?' Zena said, resigned.

'He's meeting her tomorrow, but I don't know where. I overheard him talking on the telephone when he thought I was asleep. Just follow him Mrs Archer. See what he's up to.'

That night Zena moaned to Dave, as they sat in the cool

of the back room, windows open to the garden. No point saying anything to her father. He'd give her short shrift.

'It's bad enough putting up with Charlie in the office, but now I have to go chasing after a bigamist!'

'It *is* the profession you chose.'

'I know, you don't need to keep reminding me. But I don't have to like it all the time, do I? After all, you moan about people at work as much as I do.'

'Not as much,' Dave said.

'Do I moan such a lot?'

'Yes quite a lot.'

'I don't mean to. But I can't say anything to Daddy. Who else can I tell except you?'

'I don't mind. Not really. It's just that you take on too much. These cases, well-' Dave hesitated.

'Well, what?' Zena said, starting to get rattled.

'They get you down.'

'What do you mean get me down? I don't get down. When do I get *down*?'

'Listen, stop now, stop. I don't mean anything by it. I don't like seeing you tired and upset. That's all.'

'I don't like being accused of being *down* and I'd rather you didn't say that again. I'm doing my job and sometimes, just sometimes, I want to talk about how hard it can be,' Zena said, as she slammed out of the back room.

*

Zena followed Mr Barclay from his house past Old Haymarket towards Lime Street the next day. A trickle of perspiration itched in the long furrow of her back. "A lady

111

perspires, never sweats." Her mother's voice was tight in Zena's ear. She wished she'd worn her marigold linen dress. At least she'd swapped her new patent leather high heels for sandals.

She watched Mr Barclay's anxious scurry past St John's Gardens. His head whisked round every few minutes, allowing the breeze to lift his carefully styled comb-over. Zena gave a wry smile. His coiffured hair was not the only thing she had noticed this morning. The scent of Brylcreem trailed him. Her stomach lurched.

A voluminous summer gabardine helped Zena's disguise. He might be a heel, but he was not stupid. The old lady wig scratched her head and she cursed him, the oppression of the unusual late summer heat, her argument with Dave the night before, and life in general.

Zena hung back as she watched Barclay enter Lime Street Station. She backed up behind a pillar avoiding his gaze as he made another eye-sweep behind him. A minute later, confident she was still undetected, Zena disguised her walk with a limp, and hobbled head down onto the domed concourse of the station.

The sour scent of hundreds of bodies clutching leather suitcases made her gag. Mustard appeared to be in fashion this year. Not a colour she had ever favoured. The hum of excitement under the meshed arch of the station roof distracted her.

With one eye on her quarry, Zena stood for a moment, observing her surroundings. She watched a young couple holding hands. They stared, faces skyward at the clicking departure board waiting for their platform number. The boy, tall and dark, sported a thin pencil moustache over his fleshy lips. He must have been hotter than Hades in the knitted sports shirt he was wearing. The girl, cool in her polka dot cotton dress looked up at him. Far too dewy-eyed. She'd soon learn. Zena's cynicism got the better of her. The past year working on so many divorce cases had taught her that not everyone was as lucky as she.

Zena wished that it *was* she who was heading off for a romantic weekend, or an exotic holiday. Not to be. She shook herself out of her reverie and scanned the eager faces of those heading for the seaside, or climes further afield. She saw Mr Barclay's tall, fleshy frame; his stomach pregnant tight against his pressed blue shirt. He moved on towards the lavatories. Zena limped over to a spot nearby and bent down to tie her shoelaces repeatedly, until she saw him emerge. He didn't even glance at the old woman in a bag lady coat stand up, and hobble after him.

The effort of making sure he wouldn't tag her was taking its toll on Zena's concentration and patience. She nearly lost him as he veered off to buy a newspaper at the stand under the clock. Five minutes later she was back on track. Where was he was heading? She had no clue where this journey would take her.

Tripping over a snappy Jack Russell, Zena was distracted again as the owner tried to engage her in apologetic conversation.

'I'm sorry, he's normally so well behaved in crowds.'

Zena tried to be polite, but had to stop the woman in mid-sentence. 'I have to dash. My train.' She cursed the woman and her stupid dog. She liked dogs, but this encounter had cost her dearly. She had lost Barclay.

She speeded up and ran past the bookshop. Once again

round by the lavatories. She hesitated in case he'd gone in again. Her head whipped round as panic set in. Where was he? Zena set off again. Ten minutes of careering round every corner of the station, she was hot, breathless, and ready to give up.

Turning the corner from the news stand, onto the main concourse, Zena nearly bumped into his protruding stomach as he marched towards the ticket counter. How had she missed him? She should have known that flat-footed walk anywhere. She mumbled an apology, and hobbled off, hunched back into shape. She tied a cotton headscarf over her grey wig. Zena couldn't believe that he'd not clocked her, but he'd not even looked at her. His brusqueness and impatience played to her advantage. Just in case, she changed her walk to a stride. With her head up he would never recognise her as the old bag lady who had bumped into him.

Worried she might lose him again, she beetled over to the arched window where he had bought his ticket seconds before.

'My husband has marched on ahead without me,' Zena told the ticket seller. She pointed to Mr Barclay striding away towards Platform 5. 'Please can I have a ticket in the same class?'

The ticket seller, a stylish young woman in a crisp white blouse, sympathised. 'Mine does the same. I might as well not exist. You know what the worst thing is?' Zena ignored her question with a quick apology, took the ticket and headed straight for the train waiting on Platform 5. No time for chit chat.

Fifteen minutes later the train steamed out of the

station. Zena sank with relief into a second-class seat. Her mark was safely ensconced further down. He wouldn't spot her in the corner seat of the compartment away from the window. All he would see would be the large hat of the old lady next to her. Ignoring any attempts from her neighbour to engage in conversation, Zena dived into her bag of tricks: notebook, recorder, Minox Riga mini camera, glasses, and of course high heels and pearls. She had no idea where Mr Barclay's outing would take her, and she needed to be prepared, disguised or glamorous. With a couple of minor changes to hair and make-up, she could be either.

Pulling out a red Shetland wool jumper she had bought at Keswick Market, Zena realised how badly it smelt of oil. She was about to apologise for its rankness, but guessed that the chatterbox next to her would seize on the opportunity. She struggled with the fiddly task of embroidering Marion's initials on to the jumper. The art of Swiss darning looked easier in the library book. It wasn't perhaps the most practical of presents, but Zena was sure it would suit Marion. The lady in the hat peered at the embroidery, and tried again to engage Zena in conversation. Letting out a large yawn, Zena let her head and embroidery drop. She had no patience for tittle-tattle, but she wasn't faking. The seats might be worn but they were still comfortable, and the dash round the station in such dreadful heat had made her very tired.

A sudden jolt whipped Zena's head back from an uncomfortable doze. 'Have we already arrived?'

'Yes, dear, you've been asleep all this time,' confirmed the old lady.

As the train hissed into Euston Station, Zena leapt up,

stuffed the jumper back into her bag, flung on her coat, and bolted for the door, anxious not to lose Mr Barclay. She almost fell down the two steps from the train and felt rude not holding open the heavy door for her neighbour. She need not have rushed. Barclay was taking his time. He helped a young woman from the carriage, his eyes fixed on her tight-fitting blouse as he took her case in one hand and clasped her hand in the other. Incorrigible.

Battling through the crowds to keep up with Mr Barclay as they exited the station, Zena overtook him on the Euston Road. She walked ahead, tracing his movements in the mirror of her compact. It was one way she could be sure he wouldn't suspect he was being followed. After less than ten minutes, he turned into Drummond Street, towards a white neon sign. It was missing a letter and announced, 'WELCOME TO THE -USTON HOTEL'.

The carpet sucked at her sandals as Zena walked to the front desk to sign in. Tight as ever. He wasn't splashing out on this one. She checked Mr Barclay's name and room against the register. As suspected, he was not listed under his own name, but as Mr and Mrs Jones. He and his supposed wife were due to check out the next morning. Zena was thankful it was only one night.

'Where did you say you were from?' The lank-haired reception clerk looked at her with suspicion. A woman checking in on her own, with no luggage. Zena managed to convince him that she'd had a row with her husband.

'I absolutely had to get away from him,' she said, dabbing her eyes and looking up at his acne-ravaged face. His eyes slipped over her as he pressed the key into Zena's palm and held it there for a second too long. She shuddered, but thanked him, and asked to use the telephone.

'Over there.' The young man pointed to the box in the hallway.

'Euston?' Dave's voice echoed annoyance and disappointment after Zena had explained to him where she was. They had left each other that morning on strained terms. Zena had hoped she would have been able to make it up to him that evening, and had planned a surprise dinner at The Midland. Following Barclay to London had scuppered that one.

'I'm sorry, I wasn't expecting him to head off to London.'

'Where did you say you were staying?'

'A dreadful hotel on Drummond Street. You could fry eggs on the head of the lad at reception. Revolting. I promise I won't be here any longer than I need to. What about you? Are you staying in?'

'No. As you're not here, I'll go to meet Fred. He's on leave from Burma. Only has a few days.'

'Oh, no, that's not fair. I stay in this godforsaken place while you go out gallivanting. I hate this job.'

'You don't hate it, and why shouldn't I go out if you're not here?'

'I hope you enjoy yourself!' Zena snapped and put the phone down. She hated others having a good time when she wasn't.

Zena headed up the narrow stairs to her room. The carpet, threadbare and grey with dirt, oozed a rotting stench. Stained curtains hung from sooted windows. A faded pink candlewick bedspread, worn and frayed at the edges, covered the narrow single bed. At least the sheets were clean. To cap it all the room backed onto the Northern Line. The endless rumble, with an occasional shout of 'Mind the gap', slipped into Zena's fitful dreams.

*

A breakfast of congealed fried egg, flabby toast and weak tea made Zena gag, but she kept her eye on her quarry. He was ogling a rather plain, mousy young woman. Not blonde, and no bosom. Was she being groomed to be wife number three? What was the attraction?

Zena hummed to herself, 'Mine is not to reason why, mine is but to do or die,' as she prepared the tiny camera in her bag of tricks. She shimmied past the couple, head down towards the tea urn, turned back and snapped the pair holding hands over the marmalade. They remained oblivious.

Zena kept Mr Barclay in her sights as he left Mrs Jones to her own devices in the breakfast room and headed into Drummond Street. The smell of diesel from the trolleybuses trundling up Euston Road lingered in the summer morning air. The streets were packed.

The heat pressed down, sapping Zena's flagging energy. Pausing for an ice cream, she sat on the station concourse, savouring a vanilla wafer. She had the evidence for Mrs Barclay, and she was sure the husband was headed home.

The train heaved out of Euston, on time for once. Mr Barclay was well and truly nabbed, and with her disguises stowed, Zena felt more like herself. Her hair was pinned high into its chignon, the gabardine and wig rolled and stuffed into her bag. She swapped sandals for high heels and clipped a string of pearls around her neck. A sweep of lipstick completed the picture. Every bit a lady.

Heading for the dining car for lunch where white linen and monogrammed cutlery decorated the tables, Zena saw Mr Barclay. She had guessed correctly. An amusing idea floated around her head. She would test whether he had recognised her. Zena asked if she could sit at his table. He was more than eager. His shirt button popped as he leaned over, half standing, pretending to be a gentleman. Zena suppressed a giggle at the dimpled hairless flesh squeezing out of his gaping shirt.

Over an excellent grilled sole, Zena engaged him in conversation, extracting that he was a travelling salesman, that his hobbies included fishing, and that he liked to eat fish. Of course. She knew it all, but pretended otherwise. She had followed him for long enough to know where he spent his time, the colour of his socks and what he ate for lunch. Zena knew when he was lying. Syd had taught her well. Tricks of the trade. "Look at their eyes, how they use their hands, and their posture," he told her. "Liars give themselves away every time." Zena watched Mr Barclay look down to the right, and his hand travel to his nose, when she asked, 'Are you married?'

'Widowed,' he lied. 'My poor wife, she died two years ago... cancer.' He whispered *cancer* through the side of his mouth as though it was a dirty word.

'Oh, I am so sorry for your loss. Do you have children?' Zena asked, knowing that the first Mrs Barclay lived in New Brighton with their two boys.

'We weren't blessed in that regard.' Mr Barclay rubbed his nose and shifted in his seat. He was more uncomfortable lying about his children. Denying a wife, or wives, came more naturally.

Zena found his slack mouth and sour breath hard to stomach, but he was enamoured. After an hour of tête-à-tête, they were on first name terms. 'Please call me John, Philipa,' he said, putting his hand over hers. As usual Zena had used her middle name as a ruse. Zena shuddered slightly. Her joke was beginning to backfire. As the train pulled into Liverpool Lime Street, Barclay made a dash for Zena as she got up to leave. Zena recoiled, incensed as he pawed her arm. She said, 'John, please. That's enough.'

'Oh but Philipa,' he said, backing her into the corridor, 'No it's not enough. I want you to marry me. What do you say?'

Zena almost rolled her eyes at him but managed to stop herself. 'Oh but this is all so sudden!' she said as she looked at Barclay, pretending to be coy. Then with a quick flick of her wrist she promptly squirmed out of his grasp, opened the door and dashed down the steps.

'Goodbye John Barclay!' Zena shouted, leaving Barclay looking out of the carriage window, his fleshy lips open in an 'O' of bemusement.

*

The next day Zena finished the report for Mr Barclay's suspicious wife. Leaving out the bit where he asked her to marry him. Her notes detailed the hours she had spent walking in front or behind him or following his car through New Brighton and Liverpool 8.

Monday June 27th, 1949: Barclay case.

Mr Barclay at Albert Dock café as usual. Coffee, eggs, toast, bacon. Went to work. Nothing to report.

Tuesday June 28th, 1949: Barclay case.
After typical morning, followed Mr Barclay at lunchtime to the Abbey cinema. He wore a long, grey overcoat. Not his usual attire. I watched from across the road as he queued. Men alone. No wives. No advertised show on the board. When all the men had gone in, I asked the ticket seller what was showing. "You don't want to know love. It's not for the likes of ladies." Not hard to guess what he meant.

Wednesday July 6th, 1949: Barclay case.
Victoria House observation. Second Mrs Barclay observed at the door of the apartment block dressed in pink negligee and pink, fur-capped mules. She appeared unconcerned by neighbours. Barclay arrived soon afterwards. She stopped short of kissing him on the doorstep, but immediately pulled him into the hallway.

Zena could never understand why the first Mrs Barclay let her husband off with the second wife. She appeared much more concerned by the mousy girl in Euston. Zena knew better these days than to ask or to judge. Her report typed, she packed it with the photos into a large brown envelope ready for franking and posting.

'Bye Dad,' Zena called out as she pulled at the heavy glass door on her way out.

'You leaving early? You sure you've finished typing

everything up?' Syd rasped back at her. Charlie and Joe had left even earlier, but her father never shouted at them. She always had to be that much better than them. And even then she wasn't sure her father noticed.

She bit back the tart retort rising to her lips, and said, 'Yes all done. The Barclay report is packed and ready for franking and posting tomorrow. It's Dave's early today, so we're going out. Bye Dad.'

'Bye love,' Syd said.

Zena hurried down Cook Street to the station, eager to get home to Dave and her evening out. They were going dancing. The last of the summer season. In the carriage home, she mused over the Barclay case. It had rattled her faith in womanhood. She had seen women strong and proud of their contribution during the war. Then when their husbands came home they slipped back to a subservient role. What was it about Barclay that kept his wife beside him no matter what? She hoped her next case would bring her something different.

8

THE CASE OF YOUNG CONNOLLY

October 1949. 'Missing person.' Syd handed Zena a slender brown file. The name Connolly was stamped in black across the top. The Connollys' son was missing and they had called in Scott's to track him down.

The following day, Zena headed for the 1930's tenement block in Toxteth. The cheap brass knocker made a hollow noise on the thin door. Zena feared what she might find inside. She'd heard rumours about Irish families keeping their horses in these tenements. A tall man with a full head of salt and pepper hair opened the door. Zena took in his clean grey cardigan, pressed trousers and shined shoes.

'Good morning, Mr Connolly. My name is Zena Scott Archer. You called our office about your son, Paul.'

'Mrs Archer. Won't you come in now.' Mr Connolly's face broke into a wide smile as he showed Zena into a spotless living room. Zena was disarmed. A heavy wooden framed picture of Mary and Jesus hung above the mantlepiece. The hissing coal fire was banked up against the chill wind that whipped outside.

Mrs Connolly was as smart as her husband. She wore an immaculately pressed wool two piece. She busied herself making tea and fussing around Zena. After what seemed like an age, the couple, who Zena guessed were in their mid fifties, sat down on the edge of a creased brown leather sofa. Mrs Connolly twisted her hands and Mr Connolly's leg twitched up and down so furiously that Zena wanted to put out a hand to stop him. She didn't. She slipped into her sympathetic, professional manner.

'Please tell me what happened?' Zena asked.

'It's the boy. Our Paul,' Mr Connolly said, his large florid nose trembling. 'He's missing.'

'Have you called the police? It's a police matter if a boy has gone missing,' Zena said.

'You're right there, missus, but they've said they can't help.'

'That's unusual. I wonder why they wouldn't help. How old is Paul?'

'We say he's a boy,' Mrs Connolly interjected. 'It's more that he acts like a boy still. But he's really a man.'

'A man?'

'Yes he's 21,' Mrs Connolly whispered. 'I know that he's only just come of age, but boys younger than him fought and died in the war.'

'But we still need to find him, missus,' Mr Connolly said. 'He's simple in the head. Not right, if you know what I mean.'

'We married late. Maybe that was it,' Mrs Connolly looked downcast as though this was all her fault.

'Do you have any idea where he might have gone? Did he take anything with him?' Zena asked.

'Ah, the poor eejit, he doesn't know what he's about. He's taken my mother's wedding ring, and his post-office

124

savings book, his identity card and a few clothes. Nothing else.' A tear slid slowly down Mrs Connolly's soft cheek.

'OK I see. Do you have any idea why he might have wanted to leave home? Has there been any trouble at home?' Zena said.

'No, no, no trouble at all,' Mr Connolly interjected. He looked surprised and hurt at the suggestion.

'But…but the lads at our local where he's the pot boy, say he's always asking any girl he sees to marry him. As if…That's all we know,' Mrs Connolly's soft lilt trembled.

'Don't worry, Mrs Connolly, we'll find him. It might take some time, but I promise you we will,' Zena said, wondering how an earth she would manage it. Still a missing person's case was different from serving injunctions and the continual flood of divorce cases. She would work out a strategy to track him down.

*

Zena started her investigation at The White Lion. Young Paul had worked there as a pot boy, clearing glasses and mopping the floor. The landlord Mr Preston accompanied her into the public bar. Her father would never have approved of her going into a public house on her own. She wouldn't tell him.

'Kevin Richards is who you need to talk to,' Mr Preston said.

'Kevin Richards? And he is?'

'He's a regular. Nasty piece of work. You shouldn't mess with him,' Mr Preston said. 'But if anyone knows where the lad has got to it'll be him.'

'And why would that be, Mr Preston?'

'Paul idolised him. Never mind that Richards was forever bullying the poor sod.'

'Bullying him? How?'

'He'd make the lad cry, and then wheedle round him again for money. Young Paul followed him round like a puppy. God knows why.'

'I'd better meet this Mr Richards then, hadn't I?' Gone were the days when Zena would have baulked at confronting a nasty piece of work. She'd encountered too many of them during her few years as a private detective. Part of her relished some of the encounters. It gave her a sense of pride when they backed down.

Zena caused a stir when Mr Preston led her through the latched wooden door into the public bar, where women were not allowed. He pointed to where Kevin Richards was hunched over the *Racing Times* at a corner table, nursing a half-finished pint of Guinness. Walking over to him, Zena ignored the stares and mumbled comments of the group of navvies, drinking their after-work pints of bitter. She had to hide her immediate dislike of Richards. His long fingers were nicotine yellow. A black coat dripped from his scarecrow frame, rank with something Zena preferred not to imagine. A greasy black fedora lay on the beer-stained oak table.

'Mr Richards?' she said, trying to hold her breath at the same time.

'Who are you? Should you even be in here?' he growled, his Northern Irish accent cutting through the noise of skittles in the alley next door.

'I believe you are a friend of young Paul Connolly.'

'Aye. And what's it to you?'

'He's missing. His parents are worried sick about him. They've asked me to help try and find him.' Zena handed him her card.

'A woman? A detective? You've got to be kiddin' me.' He looked at the card and laughed into Zena's face.

'I can assure you that I am both a detective, and a woman. Can you please answer my question?'

'Now why should I do that?' Richards stared back at her, pushing his ravaged face further towards Zena.

'Because a defenceless young man is missing and his parents are frantic.'

'Do I care?'

'You might if the police get involved,' Zena bluffed. 'I'll ask you again. Do you know where Paul Connolly has gone?' She summoned up reserves of politeness to stop herself from slapping his face.

'How should I know where he's gone? Stupid bloody boy, hanging round me. Go talk to his other friends.'

'This young man, Mr Richards, is somebody's son, and we need to find him. His poor parents are going through hell.' Zena tried to appeal to the merest hint of Richards' better nature.

'Parents? More like jailors if you ask me. The boy hated his parents.'

'Why do you say that Mr Richards? They seemed very caring.'

'Caring shmaring. The lad said they mollycoddled him. Treated him like a baby. He wanted a proper life, like a man. Now bugger off and leave me to me pint.' Richards turned his hollow eyes back to his paper.

'You know where to reach me if you hear anything further,' Zena said. She turned on her heel and marched out of the bar without a backward glance. Much as it galled her to believe a man like Richards, she did wonder whether he might be right about the Connollys.

Zena trudged up to the office, annoyed that the lift was broken again. She sat at her desk with the new case file in front of her. What next? It seemed young Paul had no other friends other than Richards. Or none who she knew of at least. She needed advice. She looked at her Strad watch, the tiny emeralds flashing in the sun. A present from Dave. She'd been waiting nearly an hour for her father to finish talking to Joe. Staring at the case file brought no further inspiration. She peered round the filing cabinets.

Syd ignored her until at last he ground out a smoking butt, and emerged from his cubbyhole. He flicked the ash off the lapel of his double-breasted charcoal grey suit, and came over to kiss her cheek.

'I thought you were never going to finish. He does go on, doesn't he, Joe?'

'Ah, now you leave Joe alone. He's all right, is Joe. And shush, or he'll hear you. What is it you need from me?'

'It's this Connolly case, Dad. The missing boy. I don't know where to go to next. Maybe the parents drove him away. Should I even try and bring him back?'

'The parents are employing us, my girl.'

'But what if he doesn't want to come back? He's an adult.'

'It's your job to bring him back.'

'OK but how?'

'Go back to the beginning. Look again at who he spent time with. Keep trying. Time and patience will see you through. Now leave me be, I've a complicated fraud case on.'

Zena sat in the office fug, a frown line worrying her forehead. She flicked through her notes once again. Charlie winked at her from across the desk. Zena sighed.

*

'At last!' Zena shouted.

'What?' Joe's over-large ears pricked up. He took a great gulp of tea, stubbed out his cigarette and edged around the papers that were in danger of falling from his desk. He stood behind Zena, wheezing from his slight exertion, as she waved a letter at him.

'It's the Connolly case. It's from the manager of the pub. Listen.'

Dear Mrs Archer,

Please find enclosed a letter from young Paul. I hope it might help in finding him.

Regards,

Jim Preston.

'Here's the letter from Paul Connolly,' she continued.

Hello Mr Preston,

This is Paul. I'm sorry for not telling you where I was going, and for leaving my job. Kevin told me not to. He's taken me to Ireland. He says anyone can

*find a wife at the farmer's fair in Lisdoonvarna. I'm
there now, and I won't come home until I've found
a wife.*

Yours,
Paul Connolly.

The letter was on headed notepaper with an address
of a hotel in Lisdoonvarna. At last, a solid lead. Joe looked
at her in amusement.

'Well you know what you'll need to do now lass don't
you?' Joe said.

'What's that Joe?' Zena was close to speaking sarcastically
to Joe, but stopped when she saw the genuine interest in
his face.

'You'll need to follow him there.'

'Oh no really?'

'Yes really.'

'But...what about...' she was about to say, 'But what
about Dave?' but managed to stop herself. She didn't
want Joe to think that Dave disapproved of her work in
any way. He didn't. But she knew that going away, and to
Ireland of all places, might be one step too far.

'This is your job Zena, and despite myself, I have to
admit you're good at it.'

'Thanks Joe...but don't let Charlie hear you say that!'
She laughed. It felt good to share such a rare moment of
connection.

*

'Do you really have to go?' Dave said when Zena told him

about her imminent trip. Zena could tell how unhappy he was that she was travelling, and overseas at that.

'I have to do it for the Connollys, Dave.'

'How about staying for me?'

'I can't. It's my job.'

'I know. But you're spending more time on your job than with me.'

'Dave, please. This couple are frantic to have their son back. How can I not go?'

'It's because I miss you,' he said, neither willing nor able to put his foot down.

'Oh, I know, my love, and I miss you too. But it would mean a lot to me if you could try to understand.'

Dave got up silently and left the room. Zena knew he would give in eventually. She let him be.

The next morning, laden with her suitcase and knitting bag of tricks and with Dave's blessing, Zena set off to Holyhead in her father's Austin. It would be a long journey to Ireland.

*

It was true what they said about the Irish weather. And what they said about Irishmen. They never gave you a straight answer. Zena asked directions at the Roadway Tavern in Lisdoonvarna, where she'd stayed the night. At the bar, she encountered a right eejit: a great Irish word she had learned from Mrs Connolly.

'Well now, what would you want to be going there for?' he smirked at her over the top of his pint.

'I'm looking for a missing young man,' Zena replied,

trying to keep her cool. This was the third time she'd asked the same question and got similar answers each time. They couldn't, or wouldn't, say they didn't know.

'What's he done, this missing lad?' he said, more interested now.

'He's been abducted by a criminal. He sent a letter to say he was going to the farmer's festival,' Zena said.

'Aah, he's here to find himself a wife then?'

'How did you know that?' Zena asked, intrigued.

'Farmer's festival might be what some call it, but we all know what it means: farmer wants a wife, farmer wants a wife, eee-aye-ah-dee-oh, the farmer wants a wife.' He chuckled at his own humour, tears running down his cracked grizzled cheeks.

'That may be, but do you know where this address is?' Zena was getting frustrated. The old man might amuse himself, but not her.

'Ah now, that'd be telling,' he laughed, and tipped back his pint. Zena was about to turn on her heel and walk out, when he added, 'Follow me, lass. I'll take you.'

And there she was, soaked to the skin, following this caricature of an Irishman down the bleak main street, the only street in a town that brought farmers from all over the country to find a wife. They walked without speaking towards the stark grey church.

Zena had to put out a hand to stop herself bumping into him as he stopped opposite the church and pointed up at a sign that read MCLAUGHLIN'S HOTEL.

'There you go, missus,' he laughed.

'You knew all along!' Zena exploded.

'Of course! But then I wouldn't have had the chance

to escort a pretty young lass down the road, now would I?'

She couldn't help but laugh back, charmed by his last-minute honesty. She thanked him, and watched him walk back towards the Tavern. No doubt to drink another pint.

The lemon-yellow paint on the lower half of the hotel was peeling, but the curtains framing the window looked fresh and clean. Zena rang the bell. Within a few seconds the door was opened by a short, stout, middle-aged lady with cornflower blue eyes, and a frizz of dark hair.

'Aaah now, look at ye. You poor wet thing ye. Come in, come in.' She ushered Zena in without even asking who she was or what she wanted. The front room, which was the guests' sitting room, was bright and spacious. Zena gasped as she entered. China horses of every size and colour, along with mini-trotting carriages, covered every surface. Leather-backed horse brasses and horseshoes adorned the walls. A massive water-colour of wild horses galloping along the beach hung over the mantelshelf.

'You must love horses,' Zena said, not knowing what else to say. Her own collection of silk flowers was paltry in comparison.

'Aaah, they were my daughter's passion. She died,' the woman said, looking out of the window in the direction of the churchyard opposite.

'Oh, I'm so sorry for your loss. It must be devastating to lose a child,' Zena said, moved by the woman's distress.

'Ah, I'm grand now. Don't you be worrying about me. My Aoife is in a better place to be sure.'

'How did she die, if you don't mind me asking?'

'It was a riding accident. Obsessed is what she was. Obsessed since she was tiny. Would sneak off with those yokes over the hill.'

'Yokes?'

'The gypsies. Them and their horses. It was them as was after getting her hooked on the china and the brasses like.'

'Really. How was that then?'

'Their caravans were full of them. Can't stand them, but they're all I've left of her now.' Mrs McLaughlin stroked the back of a shire horse taking pride of place on the mantlepiece.

She was a sad-eyed, tough woman, and Zena's admiration for her grew as they exchanged stories of their lives over tea and hot buttered scones. Zena got around to the purpose of her enquiry. Paul Connolly.

'Sure now, he was here, bless the lad,' she said. 'With a nasty streel of a man who said he was his da. I didn't believe him. I was that suspicious of him.'

'You were right to be Mrs McLaughlin. You were right. He's more or less abducted young Paul.'

'That explains it. I could see the lad was scared.'

'Were they here for long?'

'Yes for a couple of weeks. The lad did whatever the man wanted. Except one evening, he gave me his post office book and identity card to look after. Told me to keep it away from his da.'

'Were you able to give it back to him?'

'Sure, just before they left. Young Paul was lucky it was me he gave it to. Some folks round here would have had it away as fast as Sheila's Cottage.'

Zena looked blank, and Mrs McLaughlin explained, 'This year's Grand National winner. Aoife never missed the National. Thought herself a right National Velvet after seeing Elizabeth Taylor in the film. She died the year after and I like to keep the connection.' She coughed back tears.

'I'm so sorry,' Zena said. She didn't want to press the poor woman, but she was getting impatient to know what happened to young Connolly.

'You're grand. Don't mind me. Now then, where was I? The lad was that upset he'd missed the matchmaking festival. Coming all this way too.'

'Matchmaking festival? I thought it was a farmers' festival?'

'Ha ha that's what the farmers would have you believe, but they're all here to find a wife. Single women come from all over to find themselves a husband.'

'Paul didn't find a wife then, I presume?' Zena asked, trying to push the conversation along.

'No, no, bless the poor lad. I tried to find out what was going on with him, but his daddy would shut him up when the lad tried to talk to me. Young Paul got a job in The Roadway Tavern, and still he asked every lassie he met to marry him.'

'Every girl?'

'Yes, yes it didn't matter their age, or what they looked like, he'd take out an auld wedding ring, and go down on one knee. Even asked me, can you imagine the like! Bless the poor boy,' she chuckled.

'When did they leave, Mrs McLaughlin?'

'It was less than a week ago. Paul asked me for his post

office book and identity card back. Not that there was much in it. His daddy had seen to that.'

'You mean he stole the boy's money?'

'Young Paul said his daddy had borrowed it, but nothing was ever put back in. He cried leaving me. I must say I was fond of him.'

Zena had got a lead from Mrs McLaughlin. On the rare occasions young Connolly was on his own, he had told Mrs McLaughlin that he had an aunt in Galway. Zena had her starting point.

It was a simple matter to telephone the Connollys back in Liverpool. Mrs Connolly's soft as butter voice sounded far away when the operator eventually put Zena through.

'Jaysus, Mrs Archer. What on earth is the young eejit up to now? After all these years? He's never even met his aunt. Michael crossed swords with his sister twenty years ago, and they've never spoken since.'

She gave Zena the last known address for her husband's sister Deirdre. Cold and tired, Zena went back to the Roadway Tavern to ask about Paul Connolly. While she waited for the landlord, the barman persuaded Zena to take a glass of Guinness and what they told her was a traditional Irish *tater pie*. The bacon was a little salty, but the potatoes and onions in the rich, buttery, open pie crust were delicious.

The landlord was a florid-faced man, with a shock of grey hair and a drinker's nose.

'Yes, Paul was here, missus. With his father. He earned a few shillings from me, working as a pot boy for a couple of weeks. Which his daddy spent at the bookies. They moved on sharpish like, when the local Garda took an interest in the dad,' he said.

'Garda?' Zena raised an eyebrow.

'Policeman, missus. He said that someone matching the description of the boy's daddy was wanted for burglary with menaces.'

'That sounds like Richards. He's not Paul's father. He abducted the boy, and has been using him as a cash cow ever since.'

'Doesn't surprise me, missus. He's a right scoundrel that one all right.'

'Do you have any idea where they might have gone?'

'Now then, I don't make a habit of listening to customers' conversations,' he said.

'I'm sure you don't, but his parents are desperate to have their son home. You know he's, he's a bit slow, don't you? Do you have sons, Mr.. Mr..?'

'Curtis, missus. James Curtis. Yes, yes, I do. John. Good lad.'

'Then you'll know that to lose a son would be devastating. If there's anything at all you can tell me, it might help.'

'Ah, I suppose there's no harm. All I heard was some talk about the Galway Races. The lad was excited. Maybe they've gone there. Can't promise you, missus, but worth a try.'

This fitted with Mrs McLaughlin's lead, and Zena contemplated her next move. Galway it would be. She might as well make the best of it, and see a bit of the countryside. Looking at the map, she saw that if she drove from Lisdoonvarna to Gort, and then on to Galway, it would take her through the famous Burren.

The Burren was as stark as she had been told.

Loneliness leached out of the sloping terraced hills. They rose ghost-like, chalk-grey, out of the wisps of early mist that hovered above the lunar landscape.

Within twenty minutes Zena was lost. Every road she took led nowhere, and all the signs were in Gaelic. She must have taken a wrong turn. She stopped the car to reorient herself, but even looking at the map gave her no clue.

The only option was to turn around, and try and retrace her steps. Even that was easier said than done. It started to rain and everywhere looked the same: that bleak, grey-crazed landscape, leading to nothingness. A church appeared through the mist. There would always be a church. Zena parked outside and taking the map, hurried in to escape the endless rain.

An oppressive hush hung in the air. The statue of the Virgin Mary loomed large behind the altar. Zena was close to crossing herself when a black-frocked priest startled her. He stepped out of nowhere, as she breathed in the incense-laden mustiness of the nave.

'Can I help you, my dear?' The priest's voice was deep and soothing, and his kind expression calmed Zena's frazzled nerves. Over a smoky cup of tea, brewed on a camping stove in the sacristy, he pointed out where she had gone wrong. Coming out to wave her off, he directed her again towards the road to Gort.

Gort, despite the name, was a pleasant town, and Zena parked in the elegant square. Nearly every corner had a pub. She headed for the one that looked the brightest and cleanest. The lunch menu was basic but adequate, and Zena chose the Irish stew. A classic, and something that she thought no one could get wrong. But wrong it was. The lamb was stringy, the potatoes undercooked, and shiny globules of fat winked on the surface. Zena forced down as much as she could without retching. She paid and hurried out before they saw the half-empty bowl and asked what was wrong. She would have found it hard not to be rude.

Arriving at the harbour in Galway, the rain stopped, and the sky pinked over the sea. The town was delightful. Iced candy coloured cottages edged the rain-shined horseshoe of the harbour. Bright red sails peeked over the walls. Galway Hookers: the traditional fishing boats of the region.

After booking into an hotel overlooking the harbour, Zena was glad to have a bite to eat and fall into bed and the deepest of sleeps. The following morning she dreaded facing the distinct possibility that Paul and Richards had already left.

The address Mrs Connolly had given Zena was not far from the Claddagh, the most historic part of old Galway, outside the old city walls. A few of the ancient thatched cottages remained, and she wished she could explore instead of following young Connolly on his daft goose chase. Leaving her car outside the hotel, Zena walked in the rain-freshed air, admiring the local scenery.

The street was narrow and curved, with a small park nestling in its belly. The cottages grew larger the further round the crescent one went. The house Zena was looking for was on the cheaper, smaller end. A two up two down, painted in familiar candy pink. A ruddy-cheeked woman with dark red hair, wearing a long skirt and shawl, opened the door when Zena knocked. She looked nothing like her brother Michael Connolly.

'Who are ye really, come on now?' she said, after Zena introduced herself. 'Why did he send ye?' She was suspicious, even when Zena presented her card. Still standing in the street, Zena explained again how she was looking for Paul Connolly, the woman's nephew. The woman's florid face softened, and she stood aside to let Zena in and sat her down in front of a roaring peat fire.

'Aah now, that young lad. He was here all right, with his dirty, skinny pal. But sure, I'd no room to keep them. Him a great hulk of a thing, and as mad as a box of frogs. The spit of his da,' she said.

'Do you know where they might have gone, Miss Connolly?'

'I gave them their tea and packed them off to me cousin across the river. She runs a lodging house. They'll be there,' she said, standing up to make it clear that it was time for Zena to leave. Tough old bird.

Zena started to wonder when this was ever going to end. She trudged on to the lodging house, feeling in her bones that they would have moved on. Mrs Devlin the landlady opened the door. She had the same complexion as her cousin but was as chalk and cheese in terms of temperament.

'Ah now, I was hoping someone would come for himself. Him and his pal are after running out of money, and I can't keep them for nothing,' she whispered. 'He gave me his money book, and I can see what a merry caper yer man's been on. I'm awful glad you've come for him.' She stood aside to welcome Zena in.

'His *friend* is with him then?' Zena didn't relish the thought of confronting Richards.

'Yes, he is, but he spends most of his time out, and up to no good, from what I gather.'

Zena hadn't thought about how she would persuade Paul to come home with her, and out from under the influence of Richards. In a eureka moment, an idea flashed in front of her, and she felt pleased at her own genius. She would move to Mrs Devlin's lodging house.

There were a couple of hours before dinner at the lodging house. Zena left her bag in her room, and set out to do some shopping in Galway. She would have to take something back with her to make up for the time away. Mrs Devlin recommended the old Galway Market, where Zena might still find some trinkets from the tinkers who plied their trade off their traps.

The main market was closing; the fruit and vegetable sellers had packed up, their remaining stock already loaded on to their wagons. There was a whole line of them along the wide street, ponies drooping their sad-eyed heads, weary of the wait. It was not at all as Zena had expected. She had imagined a smaller version of Birkenhead Market, but this was in the open. A few shops faced the square, but the market was held all along the main street. Crowds were thinning out, milling around the heavy wooden traps: dark-haired women in traditional long skirts and shawls; grey Irishmen in heavy overcoats and wide-brimmed hats. They looked as if they were from a bygone age.

Zena watched fascinated as an old man, clay pipe fixed to his lip, mended the handle of a large, blackened tin kettle. He sat on a three-legged stool, leaning against the wheel of his trap. His pony was content to wait as it lipped and crunched at vegetable scraps. The man saw Zena watching, tipped his hat and smiled, before bending over the kettle once more.

Zena looked around the remaining stalls and few shops on the square. Bit by bit she collected some traditional gifts. She was pleased with herself and her finds. A soft cream Aran scarf and gloves for her mother, a pretty little Claddagh ring for Marion, and one for herself. She saw a long clay pipe like those the old men in the market smoked, perfect for her father. Zena sighed. Syd didn't believe she would find Connolly and thought she was on a hiding to nothing. Zena was determined to prove him wrong. She picked up an embroidered Galway shawl for her grandmother and smiled at the woman who could have been the sister of Deirdre Connolly. Her skirt and shawl a Galway uniform. For Dave she hesitated between a tweed trilby or flat cap to add to his collection. She chose the trilby.

Zena was back with time to wash and change before dinner at the lodging house. It was a formal affair, with a tablecloth, napkins and porcelain plates. She was nervous waiting for young Connolly to make an appearance. A tow-haired, gangling young man appeared and sat down opposite her. Was this him? Zena barely recognised him from the photograph his parents had given her. He had lost a lot of weight, but he still had the same open innocent face. His sun-filled, sky-blue eyes shone when he saw Zena. He wore a tweed jacket and tie, and was smartly turned out for dinner. Zena hadn't expected him to be so together after all the time he had spent with

Richards. She half thought he would be as grimy as his malicious friend.

'Who are you? You're new. Where are you from? When did you arrive? How did you get here?' A torrent of questions was blurted out in between mouthfuls of potato. It gave Zena a chance to size him up, and work on her strategy to bring him home. She smiled at him, and was attentive as he showered her with questions. Instead of answering them, Zena asked him about himself, and how he liked Ireland.

This prompted an explosive description of places he'd been to, what he'd seen, who he'd met, and what he'd eaten. Zena listened, nodding and asked more questions to set him off again. All the while, she looked at him, staring straight into those startling blue eyes.

'I understand you have a friend with you?' Zena watched a cloud of doubt and fear wash over Paul's face. He looked down.

'Yes. Kevin is the one who decides where we go. But I can do what I want when we get there,' he said.

'I'm sure you can, Paul. Where is Kevin this evening?'

'He went to the races. He's always at the races.'

'Do you like the races, Paul?'

'Yes I love them! He said he'd take me, but he never does.' Zena was relieved that at least she wouldn't have to face Richards that evening.

By the end of the meal Zena was exhausted and excused herself. Paul's face dropped, and he looked about to burst into tears. Zena said she would see him in the morning, and he brightened. Tired and glad to end the day, Zena trod upstairs. The house had an inside bathroom, and Zena was grateful there was no need to go outside to use the privy. Her bed, small as it was, had never felt so appealing.

*

Breakfast was as formal as the dinner the night before, and Mrs Devlin served Zena first, without waiting for other guests to arrive. A travelling salesman joined Zena soon after, full of depressing tales about his travels across the country.

He told Zena he felt sick that he was selling insurance to poor people who barely had enough to eat. She reassured him. He had to make a living.

At the harsh, nasal whine of Richards' voice, shouting at the top of the stairs, the insurance man scuttled off. Zena wished she could do the same.

'You'd better get up now, fella me lad, we've work to do,' Richards bellowed.

Zena's heart hammered as a heavy tread thumped towards the dining room. She'd rehearsed what she would say to Richards if she saw him, but words flew from her mind when he entered the room. He was a cadaverous wreck of his former self. It was hard to imagine him getting any thinner. Zena almost felt sorry for him.

He didn't look at Zena when he sat down, hat still on. His manners had not improved. She felt the rapid thud of her heart and a lump caught in her throat. She swallowed, her mind whirling. She pinched her thigh to distract herself and focused hard on Mrs Devlin, who brought Richards his breakfast. The full Irish. With a grunt, he tackled the black and white puddings. Stabbing a sausage with his fork, he looked up to see Zena staring at him. He paused, sausage in mid-air.

'Hey, you,' he shouted, jabbing the sausage-laden fork towards her. 'What you gawping at?'

Zena lowered her eyes and said nothing.

'Oi, don't I know you?' Richards continued, slurping tea and cramming more sausage in his mouth. 'Where do I know ye from? I know you from somewhere. Now let me think.'

Zena tried to ignore him. Her mouth dried. The black pudding stuck in her throat. She'd hoped he wouldn't remember her. Her luck was out. She swallowed with difficulty.

'Aye, that's it. You're that nosy witch from Liverpool. What ye doing here? You following me?'

'I think you know why I'm here, Mr Richards. I've not been following *you*. I'm here for Paul. His parents want him home,' Zena said.

'Stay away from that lad. He's better off away from all that mollycoddling. I've made him into a man.'

'And a thief too, Mr Richards?'

'What? What you accusing me of?' Richards snarled.

'I'm not accusing you, Mr Richards. The police are.'

'Police? You been talking to the Gardai? I'll have you, so I will.' Richards smashed down his knife and fork. The remains of his breakfast scattered across the table. He stood up, and leaned over the table, his face inches from Zena's. 'You talk to the guards and it'll be the last thing you do.'

'I have not talked to the police, Mr Richards, but rest assured they are looking for you,' Zena's said, her voice wavering. She knew the only way to deal with bullies was to face them down. She stared hard at Richards. 'But if you threaten me again, I will inform the police in Galway that not only are you wanted for burglary in County Clare, but also for abduction in Liverpool.'

'What you mean, abduction?'

'I mean what I say Mr Richards. Abduction. You took the boy from his parents.'

'That's not true. You ask the boy. There was no abduction. He wanted to come.'

'Really? Is that true?' Zena held firm.

'There was no abduction I tell you! The police can't get me for that.' Richards' voice rose in semi-panic.

'I assure you they can. There are enough witnesses to suggest you coerced the boy. Manipulated him. That he didn't travel with you willingly. That you stole his money.'

'No. No. They can't pin that one on me.'

'Do you really want to find out?'

'I tell you, I'm not having it. You dare to call the Gardai on me and I swear, I swear, I'll have you.'

Zena dug her nails into her palm to stop her hands shaking. She couldn't let him see an ounce of fear in her face or body.

'You don't frighten me, Mr Richards,' she said. 'I suggest we work out an arrangement. Let me tell you what is going to happen.'

*

Half an hour later, a bleary-eyed Paul Connolly appeared. A cow-lick of hair was plastered down on his forehead, his shirt collar was scuffed and dirty, and his tie askew. He looked dreadful. He sat down opposite Zena, who had waited for him, another cup of coffee in front her.

'Where's Kevin? I heard him shouting. I didn't want to come down until it stopped.'

'Kevin's gone, Paul. Gone for good.'

'What do you mean, gone? Gone where?'

'I'm not sure, but he said to tell you that you're not to try and follow him.'

Paul sat for some time hunched over his breakfast. But with some gentle questioning, Zena was soon able to draw him out. By his second cup of tea and a double helping of rashers, he had returned to his voluble self. Zena continued to chat him up, flattering his ego. She felt mean at the ruse. But it was one that was working.

As Zena made to get up to leave, he put a hand on her arm.

'Please, please, don't go. I like you. I like you very much. Please wait! I need to tell you something.' His eyes flashed in panic in case Zena walked out.

'OK then, but you need to hurry and tell me what it is. I'm leaving soon for Dublin.'

'Oh no, please…please wait.'

'Hurry then, I can't stay long. My boat back to England is this afternoon,' Zena said.

'Stay. Stay here. Please. Don't move. Stay here,' he pleaded, itching to dash out of the room, but not sure if Zena would stay.

'All right, all right. I'll wait. But be quick,' Zena said.

He beamed at her, and clattered full pelt up the stairs to the room he'd shared with Richards. His boots made a loud bang on each step and Mrs Devlin came out from the kitchen to see what all the noise was about. Zena winked at her and whispered in her ear. Mrs Devlin nodded in understanding. Zena waited until Paul charged back downstairs again, breathless and delighted that she was still where he'd left her. A sweet, shy look came over his face, and his blue eyes swam a little. Zena felt dreadful, but she knew it was for the best.

He stood in front of Zena and fished around in his pocket. He pulled out a load of tissues, rubber bands, and scraps of paper. He was flustered, and searched again. He held out a thin gold wedding band.

'Will you...' he faltered, 'Will you marry me?' He dropped down on one knee, his wide-eyed open face trusting and loving. Zena hesitated. Could she do this to him? She shook herself and thought of his parents at home, desperate to have him back.

Zena looked shocked, and then delighted, and then confused.

'Oh my goodness. I don't know what to say. Are you sure? This is so unexpected,' she said, looking at his eager face.

'Oh please! You'd be doing me the most tremendous honour.' He must have rehearsed his speech many times.

'Are you really sure?' she said.

'Yes, yes! Does that mean yes? Are you saying yes?' The poor lad couldn't believe his luck. So many women had turned him down.

'I am saying yes. But there is one condition,' Zena said. 'Anything, anything,' he said.

'I have to go back to England today, I have no choice.

My travel identity card runs out tomorrow. You would have to come back with me, and we would get married in England.'

Zena waited for his reaction. He was so elated with the acceptance, that she could have suggested going to Timbuktu and he would have agreed.

'Of course. I understand. In fact, it's fantastic! Maybe my mother could come to the wedding.' A shadow crossed his face as he thought about his mother. Shaking it away, he beamed a headlight smile at Zena. Mrs Devlin clapped as he slipped the ring on Zena's finger. With luck Zena had remembered to take off her own wedding ring the day before.

Zena refused a celebratory sherry from Mrs Devlin and hustled poor Connolly to pack his bag, get his savings book and identity card from Mrs Devlin, and get on the road. They had to be at Dun Laoghaire by early afternoon to catch the Princess Maud ferry to Holyhead.

*

'Can we go up one of the lighthouses? Or the Martello Tower?' Paul said, his feet dancing in the front seat as Zena drove towards Dun Laoghaire. 'I read about those in the encyclopaedia before I came to Ireland with Kevin. He said he would show me one day. They were built in case Napoleon invaded. He never did.' It was hard for Paul to contain his excitement.

They had arrived at Dun Laoghaire harbour with an hour to spare before the crossing. Like a child, Paul squirmed in his seat looking this way and that as they drove into the harbour. The old east and west piers protected the harbour like a ballet dancer's *porte de bras*, and the Princess Maud was in dock. Her single funnel was sending out plumes of steam, and a trail of passengers lined up to board.

'Sorry Paul, we don't have the time. We only just made it. Look, people are boarding already.'

'I wouldn't take long I promise.' He was crestfallen and Zena almost succumbed.

'No you can't. The boat leaves in less than an hour. We must get our tickets, and they will want to check our identity cards before we load the car,' Zena replied. 'Come on. We can see the lighthouses from the boat.'

Getting the Austin onto the Princess Maud was a feat. Only a few cars could be carried in the holds fore and aft. Zena had to drive the car up a steep ramp to allow the dockside crane to lift her up and over. She made Paul get out and stand with the foot passengers. She revved the engine, clenched her buttocks and inched the car up the ramp. There was a cheer when she reached the top of the platform. They weren't used to seeing women drivers. Zena got out on to the deck, and watched as the hefty chains clamped the wheels and swung the car into place.

With relief, Zena took Paul to the far end of the ship to look at the lighthouses and the Martello Towers. A moment of calm before they set sail.

'Look, Zena, look, there's a cormorant. There, there on the lighthouse wall,' Paul said. He knew his birds. In fact, he knew a lot about many things. It was as if he had memorised the encyclopaedia. Maybe he had.

The crossing was awful. Only after several passengers were seasick Zena found out that the Princess Maud was notorious. She had no stabilisers and rolled constantly, even though the weather was calm. Good job Dave wasn't with them. He could get seasick merely looking at a boat. He hadn't come on any trips with her. He probably never would.

The boy – Zena couldn't help but think of him as a boy, even though he was twenty-one – was a trooper. No complaint, no sickness, just boundless and somewhat wearing enthusiasm. An hour into the journey, Zena feigned sickness and went for a nap in one of the reclining seats below, leaving Paul to his own devices.

They approached the Welsh coast in a blaze of autumn colour. A low evening sun washed the treetops gold. Zena felt a bony hand feel for hers as they stood on deck, watching the bustle of the crew in stewards' whites, preparing to dock at Holyhead. She had to stop herself leaping backwards at his touch. She still had a while to go before she released him back to his parents. After a minute or so, she prised her hand from his.

'Excuse me for a minute. I need to use the lavatory. Then I should check on the car. And I need to know what happens when we reach the port. I'll be back soon,' she said and walked towards the hold.

'Oi, hold up, pet, you can't go near there,' a gruff voice shouted as Zena looked over the rim of the hold to see the dark blue of her car, wedged between a gleaming green and white Morris Oxford, and an old Austin 7.

'I wanted to find out what I need to do when we dock. That's my car down there. The blue one. It's my first voyage,' Zena said, looking back at a middle-aged man in pristine overalls.

'Same as happened when you got on, love,' he said, laughing. 'They'll lift her out, and off you go. I can lift you in and out as well if you like?' he laughed even louder.

'No, I don't think so. Just the car will be fine, thank you,' she said, copying Nana's gimlet-eyed stare to put him in his place.

'Paul!' Zena shouted to him as he stood eyes skywards exactly where she had left him. 'Come on, come on. We need to get going. They're going to dock soon. We have to be ready to take the car away as soon as they have lifted her off the ship,' Zena said as she half dragged him to the queue already forming to get off the boat. He was gazing at the murmuration of starlings over the port. It was a sight that Zena also loved, but there was no time to stand and stare. Not that day.

Half an hour later the super-efficient crew had them offloaded and on their way. Nearly there. Another couple of hours or so and Paul would be back with his parents.

*

That night Zena couldn't help but break her golden rule not to tell Dave about her cases. She was full of the stories from Ireland and the denouement when she returned Paul to his parents.

'Oh, Dave, it was tragic. His face didn't know what to do. He was ecstatic one minute and then in tears the next. When I told him I couldn't marry him, you should have seen his face,' Zena said. 'I felt such a heel. I had to tell so many lies.'

'Oh, you poor lamb,' Dave said.

'He was the poor lamb. Lamb to the slaughter.'

'But it all ended well didn't it?'

'He's such an innocent. That snake Richards took advantage. The poor boy wanted someone to love, and to love him back. Like we all do,' Zena said, curling into Dave's arms.

'In the end I had to say that my mother was dying and I had to go to London to look after her. I said she couldn't bear to have strangers around.'

'Your mother often does say she's about to die. And she also hates having strangers round.'

'You're right! Oh, thank you, my love. It wasn't a complete lie after all,' Zena laughed.

'You didn't tell me how you got rid of Richards in the end.'

'He realised soon enough that the game was up. As soon as I told him he was wanted by the police for abduction as well as the burglary, he was more than happy to leave.'

'Was that true?'

'No, not at all, but he wasn't to know, was he? I sweetened the pill by giving him five pounds. I thought it might keep him away for a while. No doubt he'll look for some other sap to milk when he runs out.'

'But shouldn't you report him to the police?'

'No point. He'll be long gone. I'm just glad Paul is home with his parents. They might mollycoddle him, but at least they love him. They need to keep a better eye on him. Or maybe get him a dog. Something he can love.'

9

THE CASE OF THE JERSEY
ADULTERER

November 1949. The following week at work, Zena whipped the evening's *Liverpool Echo* from the paper boy's hand before he could deliver it to Syd. Plastered across the front page was the headline: WANTED FOR BIGAMY! LIVERPOOL MAN ESCAPES TO CANADA'

It had to be Mr Barclay. It was. Zena had been due in court to give evidence. At least that burden of recounting Barclay's endless infidelities would no longer be required. After receiving Zena's full report, Mrs Barclay decided to shop him after all. He had come clean to her and declared his undying love for the plain young woman from Euston. He was going to leave both Mrs Barclay and Irene. Mrs Barclay decided to have her revenge in court. Zena read on to the article below the headline.

'Dad, my goodness, listen to this. You remember that Barclay case I went on? Can you believe it, that dreadful bigamist has gone and done a moonlight flit to Canada!'

'Canada? Why Canada?'

'Yes, he jumped his bail. Can you imagine that?'

'Stupid fool. He'll be for it.'

'It gets worse! Mrs Barclay – the first one – followed him out there with the children.'

'Blow me,' Syd said. 'What on earth was she thinking? She's dafter than I thought.'

'I know,' Zena said. 'How he had the nerve to crook his little finger at her.'

'You said she was besotted. Seems she lost her mind over him.'

'She was going to court next week. I thought she would go through with it. Stupid woman running after him like that. What do you think, Dad, will he get away with it?'

'Mark my words, he'll be brought back soon enough.'

'It'll serve him right if he is.'

Zena had no sympathy for the sweaty Lothario. She had worked on a lot of adultery cases, but none had been as lascivious as him. Although it did make her laugh to remember his proposal on the train.

Later that night, Zena was glad she had bought tickets for her and Dave to see Mantovani play at the Liverpool Philharmonic Hall. The Barclay affair made her appreciate how lucky she was to have Dave. He was a rare find. The concert was sublime. Zena wore her long black silk dress with the sequinned bodice and feathered epaulettes. Dave looked dashing in his air force uniform. Mantovani played all the favourites to rapturous applause. Zena could feel Dave's hands moving next to hers. She looked down and smiled. Dave's hands conducted the orchestra in his lap. As Mantovani played their tune, *The Way You Look Tonight*, he took her hand and smiled into her eyes.

*

Winter sped into spring that peeked through frost. Bulbs greened the flower beds. Snowdrops, crocuses, and winter aconites had already pushed their way through hardened soil.

In the office, Joe had the biggest grin permanently on his face. He had found his one true love – Iris. His marriage to her the month before had done wonders to his appearance, and attitude. Zena had never seen such a change in a man, and was delighted. He had even stopped making those awful jokes about Zena's clothes.

The same could not be said of Charlie. She could swing for him. That smirk. Those splayed legs. She could swear he was leaving them out to trip her up. Every time she came into the office, Charlie would goad her. His latest trick was to ignore her requests.

'Charlie, please can you update me on the Fisher case. Dad has asked me to take a look.' Zena tried to remain polite.

Silence. Typical Charlie. He was in the wrong and refused to admit to it. The Fishers had asked for photos to be taken of the wife with Charlie in an hotel room. Joe was to take the photos, and Charlie would be the stooge. The couple had an unhappy marriage and were desperate for a divorce so they could marry the new loves of their lives. The trouble was that Mrs Fisher had rung to say that every time she tried to arrange an assignation with Charlie, he cried off.

'Charlie! I swear I'll have you fired if you don't answer me,' Zena hissed at him across the desk. There was no way she would let her father know she couldn't handle Charlie.

She had more responsibility these days as Syd's health got worse. She wanted to spare him the upset.

'In your dreams, sweetheart,' Charlie said, his usual smirk playing on his lips.

'Oh for goodness sake, just get the job done and done quick!' Zena left it at that, vowing to get her own back.

When she arrived at the office the next morning a roar came from Syd that reverberated across the corridor.

'After all I've done for you, you, whippersnapper you,' Syd shouted, slamming his fist down on the table. The filing cabinets rattled.

'Ah, now then, Syd, now then. You can't have expected me to stay here forever?'

'No, of course I didn't. But to set up down the road. In competition with me. That's down right out of order. You're a right-' Syd looked at Zena who cast her eyes down, '… a right… snake,' he said. The ashtrays rattled on the desks as he stomped about the room.

'Come on, Syd, there's enough work for everyone. You know that. You can't keep up with all the clients you've got as it is. Let someone else have a crack at it.'

'Get out. I can't bear to look at you. Get out!' Syd shouted. Charlie smirked back at him.

'You're a loser Syd. I'm the one that's kept you going. Joe, if you've any sense you'd come with me.'

Joe stared downwards; silent. Zena wondered how much he had known of this betrayal in advance. She knew Charlie was a snake as soon as her father hired and trained him. It wasn't until days after Charlie had left that they realised how underhand he was. He had taken half of Syd's clients with him.

'Dad, you should do something. Sue him for breach of contract or something. It can't be legal can it? He shouldn't get away with it.'

'That would be a fine thing, love,' he said. 'Trouble is, I never bother with contracts.'

'For goodness sake, Dad. No wonder they take advantage of you. Get John Kenner across the hall to draw something up for you. It'll pay in the end,' Zena said.

'Yes, good idea, love, maybe I will,' he replied, scratching his chin.

*

Charlie's departure piled on the responsibility and work for Zena. Now it was she who had to take the photos while Joe played the unlikely stooge for the Fishers. The scene was to be set at the Adelphi Hotel. Zena photographed Joe and Mrs Fisher holding hands in the elegant dining room on one day, entwined in the swimming pool two weeks later, and finally in a compromising position in a bedroom as the culmination of their supposed affair.

'No Joe, don't put your hand there. You look like you're stroking a dog.' Zena was exasperated at Joe's ineptitude. How Iris put up with him she couldn't fathom.

'Where should I put it then. Iris wouldn't like it if I was too intimate.' Joe's face screwed up in embarrassment.

'It's a job Joe. Remember that? A job. Iris doesn't need to know.'

'Listen Joe, pretend you're acting in a play. You're Errol Flynn having to sweep a lady off her feet. Zena's right, it's only a job and Iris wouldn't mind,' Mrs Fisher interjected.

'That's right! Come on Joe, it's make believe,' Zena said, looking at Joe half amused, half annoyed.

'Is this better?' Joe put his meaty arm around Mrs Fisher's waist and leaned over as if to kiss her.

'Much better,' Zena said, snapping photos as Joe and Mrs Fisher continued in their fake embrace.

There was a time when Zena would have been horrified at the thought of being party to such shenanigans. But Zena liked the Fishers. They had married too young and grew into different interests as they aged. They were friends who wanted to be friends, not husband and wife. But the law meant someone had to be a guilty party. If Mrs Fisher took the blame then they would get the divorce more quickly. Antiquated divorce laws always favoured the man.

Photos in the bag, report written, the Fishers had enough evidence for their divorce. There were plenty of couples like the Fishers and with her earlier sense of morality on marriage softened, Zena felt she was almost doing a public duty.

The Nuttall case was another where the law was an ass. It riled Zena that a wife who wanted a divorce from a philandering husband had to resort to a private investigator to prove his infidelities when he refused her a divorce. Yet no matter how hard she tried, Zena could not catch the slippery Mr Nuttall in the act. Maybe she would have to ask Joe for help. No. That would be the last resort. There had to be another way.

*

'I'm sorry, Mrs Nuttall, your husband is very clever. He's

avoided any liaison with this woman in public. I haven't got the evidence you need, Zena said with a touch of exasperation.

'I don't understand Mrs Archer. What does it mean?' Mrs Nuttall's voice rose in panic.

'It means I won't be able to serve the divorce papers in time for court. I'm sorry Mrs Nuttall, Zena explained.

'Please, Mrs Archer. I'm begging you. Try one more time, Mrs Nuttall said. 'He told me he's going to Jersey on business this weekend. I know it's not for business. He's meeting that woman, Mary. I know he is. Please say you'll go. I'm desperate.'

Zena could hear muffled sobs down the line. She gave in. She couldn't stand people crying. Anything to make it stop.

'Alright, alright Mrs Nuttall. I'll go. I'll see if I can get what you need, I promise.' The gratitude was nearly as nauseating as the crying.

That afternoon, Zena went to Lime Street. She booked an early train to Southampton. She would have to take the Southern Railway channel crossing on the Isle of Jersey ferry to St. Helier. She was fed up. If Mrs Nuttall hadn't cried she would have left it.

'Not again!' Dave said.

'Dave, you promised. Do we have to do this every time?'

'*You* promised not to go away unless absolutely necessary. Remember?'

'It *is* necessary. Everyone else is booked up, Charlie's left, and the divorce hearing is coming up. The poor woman is desperate.'

Despite his upset, Dave went with Zena to Lime Street

to see her off the next morning. It was with a lighter heart that she sank back to the soothing rhythm of the train as they sped southwards.

'Tickets please!'

Zena awoke through a fog of dreams and fumbled for her ticket as the door to the compartment slid back.

'Thank you, miss. Off to Euston I see. Anything special, miss?' the conductor said.

'No, not really.' Zena was not in the mood for chit chat. 'Is the restaurant car serving breakfast?'

'Yes, miss. Three carriages down. Enjoy your breakfast, miss.'

Zena took up her bag of tricks without a reply and headed for the restaurant car. It was altogether a modern affair. Zena sat down in a swivel seat upholstered in tan leather. It was deep and comfortable, and the glass-topped table was laid for breakfast. She ordered coffee, toast and poached eggs. Very sophisticated. Zena whiled away the rest of the hour eating, smoking, and reading the *Liverpool Echo*. Provided free of charge. After seeing an advert for the 1950 spring fashions at C&A Zena made a note to call in when she returned from her trip. She looked out of the window as the train slowed. The drip of willows over the river running alongside were sparked by a dart of blue. A kingfisher. It could be nothing else.

Euston was as busy as ever, and Zena hailed a hackney cab rather than venture with the hoi polloi on the underground to Waterloo. The driver was a chatterbox. An East End boy, hamming up his cockney accent as soon as he knew that Zena was from out of town.

'London belonged to the blooming gangsters between

the wars. Mind you, the bleedin' rozzers was as bad. Did nothing to stop them. I had to drive Jack Cromer one time. Biggest gangster in London in the '30s he was. He said, "Call me Spot. Everyone else does." He'd just got out of prison. He said he'd fought in the Battle of Cable Street in '36, but I heard different. Where were you in the war, love?'

Without giving Zena a chance to answer, he carried on, 'London bought it all right during the war. Frenchies bottled it and we copped the lot. Sorry, love, you was about to speak. Me missus tells me I don't half go on.'

His missus was spot on.

'I worked in Liverpool during the war,' Zena said. 'But we're from London originally. My father was in the Flying Squad before the war. He put away a few of those gangsters you're talking about. Not all rozzers are lazy and do nothing,' Zena said. That shut him up.

The following morning, the ferry chugged towards Jersey and headed around the bay into St. Helier. Zena admired the imposing pile that was Mount Orgueil Castle, shrouded in March mist. When the job was done, maybe she would get a chance to explore the old-fashioned Victorian town.

Mrs Nuttall had discovered where her husband was staying and had booked Zena into the same hotel. The Reveller. An old, converted coach house. The white brickwork formed a bright contrast to a hedge of dark green laurel and the grey of an aged wisteria. It was charming. Zena felt she might enjoy this job. If things been different between her and Dave, they might have come together. It could have been a perfect spring break.

Zena flicked through the guest register, as an ancient

hobbledehoy faffed over finding the key to her room. Mr Nuttall hadn't even bothered to use a pseudonym, confident he wouldn't be caught. His signature had a slapdash air. Zena already disliked him as she read *Mr and Mrs Nuttall, Room 12*. The real Mrs Nuttall was at the family home in Wallasey. Zena went to her room, everything decorated in pale rose chintz: bed cover, curtains, wallpaper. She was glad that she wasn't wearing her rose print suit.

It was dark when she awoke from an afternoon nap. She kicked herself for losing time and mulled over her strategy. It required patience and charm. Easy. Her first task was to befriend the staff. She headed down to the bar.

A curved, polished oak counter took centre stage. The rotund, florid barman passed trays of drinks to two white aproned waitresses who served customers with speed and professional courtesy. Zena was impressed. It was a cosy place, bathed in soft lamplight with deep plush armchairs and low tables. Zena could sit in here without being seen. She ordered a Campari. Chatting up the waitress was not hard. The girl was curious and protective of a woman sitting on her own. For once honesty was the best policy. No half-truths needed. Zena explained to her that she was a private detective. This sent the girl into a twitter.

'A lady detective? Ooh how novel. Are you like Miss Marple then, miss?'

'Sadly no, not at all. Mind you, I do love Miss Marple, and Modesty Blaise. The best though is Philip Marlowe.'

'Not heard of him. Who's he then?' the girl asked.

'My dad started me off reading them. He's a private detective. Have you heard of Raymond Chandler the author?'

'No never.'

'His books are well worth a read. The Big Sleep is my favourite. It was made into a great film a couple of years back after the war. Starred Humphrey Bogart.'

'Oh I love him. Casablanca's my favourite film ever. It was so romantic. Maybe I can get the book in the library tomorrow. Tell me miss, is it exciting being a detective?'

'It's interesting, always different, but nothing like the books. It's no murder mystery!' Zena didn't tell the girl what hard graft it was. Often very tedious. Better to let the girl think of her as a bit of a celebrity. It would help her case.

'What are you doing here then, miss, or do you have to kill me if you tell?' the girl giggled at her own joke.

'Ha ha that's funny,' Zena said. 'No, no, not at all. In fact, I need your help. Do you think you might be able to help me… er… can I ask your name?'

'Effie, miss. Oh yes, miss, I'll help you with anything.'

'I'm following a man with his mistress. The wife knows her husband is having an affair, but he won't give her a divorce. Dreadful man.'

To her surprise Effie, a slight, serious, bespectacled girl swamped by her black uniform, burst into tears. 'My dad, he's like that. Off with all sorts. I don't know how my ma puts up with it. No divorce for her. Not with six babbies at home.'

Zena handed Effie a handkerchief and waited for her to continue.

'I'm the eldest. I've got to bring in the money. Dad, he drinks it all and goes off whoring. The dirty bastard. Oh, pardon me, miss, for swearing.'

'Don't worry about that, Effie. I hear much worse

believe me. I'm sorry for you and your family, my dear.' Zena appeared much older and wiser than her twenty-nine years. 'I've had an idea Effie. We can't solve the problem for your mother. But how about you help me to stop the cheating rat in Room 12? What do you say? Not a word to anyone else mind you.'

'Yes, of course, miss. Like I said, anything. What can I do?' Her myopic eyes blinked in excitement. Zena whispered into her ear, and Effie nodded and giggled at the proposed plan.

Zena ordered another Campari and sat back in the winged armchair, smug in the knowledge that by tomorrow evening she'd be on her way home. She didn't even bother to look up at the high-pitched voice, 'Oh Jimmy, you are naughty.' She knew it was Mr Nuttall and his mistress Mary. It was enough just to hear it, and it could go in her report.

*

Zena rapped on the door to Room 12. 'Good morning, sir, my name is Marion. I have your breakfast as requested.'

It tickled her to act as a maid called Marion. Her sister would enjoy the joke too. Zena knocked harder and shouted, 'Good morning, breakfast!' The door was flung open, and Zena almost fell into the room. She saw a young woman sleeping. Her long, black hair splayed on the pillows, sheets awry. Mr Nuttall snapped his silk dressing gown together, and held the door aside to let Zena enter.

Zena wheeled the breakfast trolley into the alcove of the window. She turned, whipped her camera from her apron pocket and snapped a photo.

'I am Zena Scott Archer, private investigator. I have witnessed you, James Nuttall in compromising circumstances with Mary Tatchell. I am acting on behalf of Mrs Barbara Nuttall, who is taking out divorce proceedings against you.'

'Wake up, Mary, wake up!' James Nuttall shook the girl awake.

'What is it, Jimmy? What's going on? Why is the maid standing there like that?' The girl rubbed her eyes.

'She's not a maid, she's a bloody detective! It's my wife. She's sent this woman to spy on me. She's going to divorce me,' he said, looking at Zena with venom.

'What a rotten thing to do. Why did she do that? She knows you want a divorce. All she had to do was ask. She needn't do this, need she?' Mary hesitated. 'Jimmy? Jimmy?' The penny started to drop. 'You have told her you want a divorce, haven't you? Jimmy?'

Their shouting could be heard halfway down the hallway, as Zena slipped out unnoticed.

Pleased as punch, Zena returned the uniform to Effie and gave her a generous tip. Effie was delighted. She said that if ever her mother had the wherewithal to get a divorce, she would know where to come.

With a couple of hours to spare before she had to return to the ferry port, Zena followed Effie's suggestion to visit the Central Market. 'Been there two hundred years, miss!' It was a visual treat, and put Birkenhead Market to shame.

The January sun shot rainbows through the glass roof, matching the myriad colours of the stalls. Zena searched for gifts and found two sets of lace antimacassars for her mother and grandmother. Jersey cream fudge was enough for Dave and Marion. That would do. Syd always grumbled at whatever she bought him. This time he could do without.

On the long journey home Zena reflected on her marriage, her job and life in general. She knew how lucky she was. Dave was tolerant, up to a point. He had taken time to accept that he had to be kept in the dark about most of her exploits. It was her trips away that bugged him. It annoyed her when he made a fuss. It was part of her job. Would she be allowed to complain if he was a travelling salesman?

*

Back in the Cook Street office, Zena felt they had barely noticed her absence and her father showed little interest in her trip and the case. Work and life continued with Syd full of opinions about George Kelly who was executed on 28 March 1950 for the Cameo murder. It was all he could talk about. The manager of the Cameo cinema and his assistant had been shot dead the previous year by a masked gunman. It had taken months for the police to catch the criminals. At the time Zena had asked Syd if he might be drafted in to help. He wasn't, and had been miffed.

'What a shower,' Syd shouted through the cloud of smoke in his cubbyhole. 'Worst trial in history I'd say.'

Zena ignored him, and typed up the final invoice for Mrs Nuttall. She'd been granted her divorce in the court. Irrefutable proof of adultery the judge had said. Zena was pleased for her. She could start her life over.

'Zena! Joe!' A shout that meant a new case. What this time? Zena felt the familiar wave of excitement at the thought, but was puzzled as to why had Syd called both her *and* Joe.

10

THE BIGSBY CASE

April 1950. Syd stabbed his Craven A at Zena and Joe. 'I want both of you on this case. No arguing now.'

Zena murmured a 'But…' and thought better of saying more.

'I can see your face Zena my girl, and I'm not having it.'

'Dad…I-'

'Enough. There's a packet to be made from a rich client, and it needs to be done pronto. This is a job for the both of you. I want you working together. A team. Got it?'

Zena and Joe nodded as Syd continued.

'Shipping magnate. Right rich fella. Seems he heard of me through my mate George, down the docks. He wants us to investigate his daughter's fiancé.'

'What's wrong with the fiancé?' Zena asked, her curiosity now piqued.

'He's too good to be true it seems. The father wants to know if he's kosher.'

'What's made him suspicious?' Zena interrupted.

'That's for you to find out. Now just listen.'

Zena sat on her hands as her father continued. 'Joe, I

want you to investigate the boy's army background. His stint at Oxford was interrupted by the War. He was in the Coldstream Guards. So he says. You've still got some old army buddies, haven't you?'

Joe nodded.

'Zena, I want you to track down school records and what college he was supposed to have attended at Oxford. Got it?'

'How am I supposed to do that Dad without going to Oxford? I told Dave I wouldn't be travelling for a while.'

'You'll just have to untell him won't you? Telephone enquiries won't work in this case. And you're to go undercover to meet the client, the daughter and fiancé. Next weekend.' Syd stared back at Zena. She knew there was no point arguing.

She nodded, her heart sinking at the thought of telling Dave.

The argument with Dave was predictable and Zena was tired and frustrated.

'Dave, it's only for a couple of days. The client has asked me to his country house next weekend.'

'Why? Can't you interview them at the office? Why do you have to meet him over a weekend?'

'No, I can't. You know I can't. I'm undercover.'

'As what?'

'That's all I can tell you. You know I can't talk about my cases. Please stop this.'

'Stop what? I'm just asking. It's perfectly reasonable for me to ask when my wife says she's going away for a weekend but won't tell me what she's doing.'

'It's my job. You know this and it's boring that you keep

on like this. What will you say when I go to Oxford? This is getting too much. Come on now. You promised to support me.'

'There's supporting and there's being taken for a fool. That's what some of the boys say. How do I know you're going away for the weekend on a job?'

'Dave! Where an earth has this come from? Why are you being like this?'

'I saw you. I saw you! Don't deny it. Flirting with that Marston the photographer.'

'Oh, for goodness sake. He was making a joke. I wasn't flirting. I was having a laugh. Really? Oh, you do give me a pain.'

Dave got up, left the house and slammed the front door behind him.

*

It was the Friday before she was due to leave for Mr Bigsby's country mansion, Zena had a telephone call. A bellow exploded in Zena's ear. It was Mr Bigsby.

'About this weekend. As I told your father, I've invited my daughter's fiancé and some of their friends for a shooting weekend.'

'Shooting?' Zena didn't like the sound of that.

'Yes, it's getting towards the end of the stag hunting season.'

'Oh, I see,' Zena said wondering how she might get out of the weekend. She wasn't sentimental but hated that such beautiful animals would be slaughtered just for sport.

'I've told her we want to know him better,' Bigsby

continued. 'You'll be posing as a reporter for a bridal magazine. Society engagement and all that. They'll expect you to ask questions. Perfect cover, eh?'

'Good idea, Mr Bigsby,' Zena said. 'Have you told them the name of the magazine?' Zena resigned herself. No way would her father let her escape the weekend.

'No, no you make all of that up. Choose a name they can't check. My daughter is a suspicious little minx. She thinks I'm trying to scupper her chances with her chosen one.'

'I've the perfect name in mind Mr Bigsby.' Quick as ever, Zena had already thought of a story. Her days at the House of Joseph stood her in good stead.

'Wonderful. If he is who he says he is, I'll be delighted. But I swear to God, if he's not, I'll swing for the blighter.'

*

Zena felt very humble the next day as she drove her father's old car into the drive of the mansion. A Jaguar and a Rolls Royce were already parked, waiting for a driver to move them to the garage. It was an old Victorian manor house. A great pile with so many wings that one might get lost. It even had a tower.

A young maid showed Zena to her room, which faced the rose garden. Amid the rose beds, the lawn was scattered with primulas, their cream and yellow faces pushing through the grass. The soft rabbit-ears of the pussy willow below her window had broken into the chick-yellow fluff of catkins. If she reached out she felt she could almost touch them.

She turned back to the room which was clean and neat, although the mustard and black striped wallpaper and matching curtains made her queasy. With a quick slick of lipstick, she headed downstairs. Afternoon tea was being served in the drawing room.

Left to her own devices, Zena took photos of the couple and their friends as her fake magazine had requested. Their young friends were shy of talking to her, and she bided her time. The fiancé was handsome, if a bit of a dandy. He was several years older than the nineteen-year-old daughter. Tall, with thick dark hair cut short at the back and Brylcreemed into a wave at the front. His well-fitting tweed jacket and high-waisted wide cord trousers, suited his frame. Zena could see why the girl had fallen for him. The daughter was petite, honey-blonde, richly elegant, with delicate freshwater pearl earrings and a matching necklace. She hung on his every word; her eyes tilted upwards to his face.

After tea, the group of young friends went off to play billiards, or walk the grounds. Zena sat in the drawing room, looking at the bridal magazines the daughter had shown her friends. The silks and trains on display were very different from Zena's own wedding outfit – a black utility suit topped with a small white veil that her mother had made for her. She had carried a tiny posy, and Dave sported a carnation in his buttonhole. They snatched the day when Dave was home from India during the war. Liverpool was in the middle of the Blitz, and they had wondered if they would find the church still standing. It was.

Mrs Bigsby stood by the fire. She was a taller version

of her daughter. The same honey-blonde hair piled high in a chignon, dressed in a stylish black tea dress studded with polka dots of white, jade, and grey. Zena admired it, remembering her days modelling similar dresses at the House of Joseph. A double string of pearls complemented the sweetheart neckline.

Mrs Bigsby gave a nervous laugh. She knew the secret of Zena's identity.

'It's all very extravagant, isn't it?' she said. 'We're from humble beginnings.'

'Oh, I didn't know,' Zena replied.

'Yes, Bert, I mean Albert, made money from shipping during the war. He started off as a dock worker, you know.'

'Wasn't that a reserved occupation?'

'Yes, it were,' she said, her accent slipping. 'My family was angry about that. Thought he should have been off fighting.'

'We needed men in the docks too. It was important work.'

'Try telling me mam that. Me, I don't like all this fuss. Bert bought the house two years ago. It was run down after the war. They used it as a hospital. Do you think it looks good?'

'I think it's beautiful,' Zena lied. It explained the mustard and black.

*

Zena dressed for dinner in her long black silk, and at seven o'clock a loud gong sounded. Bigsby had clearly watched too many movies. Zena walked down the wide curving staircase, the deep richness of the polished oak sliding under her white-gloved hands. The curlicue of the volute at the end of the banister formed an ornate double clef. It led Zena's hand to a satisfying conclusion. She almost started up the stairs again, so she could experience the pleasure of the return.

The five-course dinner was an attempt at sophistication, and at Zena's request she was placed next to one of the fiancé's Oxford friends. She pressed him into conversation, over the somewhat underdone salmon *en croute*.

Zena could always detect when someone was lying. The young man licked his thin lips as she quizzed him about the fiancé and their time as friends at university.

'The magazine wants me to get the background on Oliver and his bride-to-be. I hope you don't mind me asking, but you're Oliver's best friend, aren't you?'

'Yes we've been friends since school. Then we went up to Oxford together.'

'Gosh that's a long friendship. Do tell me more about your time in Oxford. Which college did you both go to?'

'New College,' he mumbled. His wide blue eyes looked down to the right. Another sure sign he was lying.

'And what did you study there?'

'History and Latin.'

'Both of you?'

'No, no not both of us. We studied different subjects. Ollie history and politics. Mainly the Commonwealth. I did history and Latin,' he said, pulling on his ears. He was displaying every tell-tale sign of a liar. The problem was deciding whether he was lying about himself, or his soon-to-be married friend. Or both.

'And what about when the war started?'

'We both signed up and joined the Coldstream Guards.'

'Coldstream Guards? That must have been something.'

'It was. We'd done our first year up at Oxford by then.'

'Did that make you officer class?' Zena knew something of how the armed services operated from Dave, and working for the U.S. Embassy during the war.

'Of course. We started together as lieutenants, but Ollie was made captain very soon after. Born leader, our Ollie,' he shifted in his seat.

Zena knew that something was very wrong with the stories of these two young men. She had to prove it. Her father always told her to trust her instinct. If young Oliver Stafford was a liar, he was more skilled than his friend. Zena had a chance to speak to him after dinner. The Bigsby household was very modern, as the ladies did not withdraw. The guests had coffee and liqueurs together in the drawing room.

'Yes, we went up to Oxford together, James and I,' he said, looking Zena directly in the eye. 'We even shared a scout.'

'A scout?'

'Yes. A scout. Someone who cleaned our rooms for us, brought us tea sometimes. Turned a blind eye even more.' He winked.

Such a life of privilege. Zena doubted her instinct for a split second. This young man appeared so confident and in tune with the lifestyle and the terminology. Maybe he was telling the truth.

*

A summer haze hung over Cook Street; newly laid tarmac lifted, and black bubbles oozed. Everyone in the office was scratchy with heat. Except Zena. She loved it. She could wear the linen dresses she'd chosen with Win and her favourite Bangkok straw hat. If she was not meeting a client, she even went without stockings. Joe sat at his desk dripping with sweat. Even his tie was damp. It was an advantage to be a woman and Zena gloated over her coolness.

Zena was angry at Joe's laxity on the Bigsby case. She looked across at him. He was laughing and smoking with Harry, the new detective Syd had hired to replace Charlie. Harry appeared to be as lax as Charlie. She had already noticed how he had been keen at first, but quickly slipped into Joe's bad habits. Zena wished her father had let *her* interview the next detective. She would have employed another woman. Maybe Win would have liked the job. On the observations she'd secretly done for Zena she was excellent. Paid attention. Kept awake – a major plus. Even typed up the report herself. If Win had money of her own, maybe she could get away from Cyril. Zena was brought back to earth by Harry's bray of a laugh.

'How far have you got with the Bigsby case, Joe? Have you been in touch with those army mates of yours yet?' Zena said.

'I'm still following up some leads. My buddy knows a colonel in the Lilywhites – that's the nickname of the Coldstream Guards, in case you didn't know Zena,' Joe said with a smirk. He'd stopped trying so hard to impress Iris and the weight he'd lost when courting, lay heavy on his belly.

'It's not enough, Joe. I'm making all the running in this case. You need to get a move on – it's been two months now.'

'I'm working on it. I'm working on it.' Joe turned back to the Racing Times and ignored Zena's harrumph of anger.

She could have slapped him.

'Dad, I'm not working on a case with Joe again,' she told Syd that evening on their way home. 'He might be more cheerful now he's married, but he's a slacker. He's done nothing to help me on the Bigsby case. The lazy-so and-so has not come up with a single lead on the boy's army record. He's hopeless!'

'Leave him be, love. He's a good sort is Joe. He gets there in the end. He might be slow to you, but he's stood by me. Throughout everything. Not like that young fella me lad Charlie. Let's hope Harry has got it in him to be better.'

'I think you might have replaced Charlie with his younger brother, from what I can tell,' Zena said.

'Ah now, come on, love, give him a chance. He's still young, yet.'

'Age is no excuse, Dad. I'm young and I work hard.'

'I know you do, my girl, I know you do. Give the lad a chance is all I'm saying. OK?'

'OK.' Zena wasn't convinced, but would do anything to please her father.

*

Oxford was rich and honeyed in the late summer light. Zena walked the half-mile from the station to her hotel to clear her head. It was easy enough. Her little turquoise overnight bag was light to carry. Drifting past a raft of ancient buildings along the High Street, she peered in the mirrored interior of the Grand Café to see what delicacies were on offer. A plethora of scones. She paused at Shepherd and Woodward, the gentlemen's outfitter's, wondering if there might be something suitable for Dave. Maybe a tie? She would come back.

Zena was booked into the Randolph Hotel, a ten-minute walk from New College, the supposed college of the fiancé. Bigsby could afford to pay for a decent hotel if she had to be away from home. The Victorian Gothic architecture was somewhat overblown for Zena's taste, but her room on the third floor was well appointed, with a view across to the Ashmolean Museum. After a freshen-up she went downstairs and looked out from the hotel lobby, undecided about where to dine. Zena had assumed Oxford would be safe, but there was a gaggle of rowdy young students, careering around on bicycles. Never having cycled herself, it would be unwise to venture either on bicycle or foot. Better to stay close. She dined at the hotel and retired early to bed.

Breakfast the next morning was a formal affair in the dining room, with linen napkins and silver-plated cutlery. Very impressive. After a second cup of coffee and her full English breakfast she felt ready to face the porter at New College.

College porters knew everything that went on. Maybe she could even talk to the scout. If anyone knew whether the boy had been a student there, the scout would. She walked down Holywell Street, a pretty road of pale painted cottages, bowed with age. Halfway down, Zena headed through the unimposing arched entrance to New College. Not as grand as other colleges she'd seen. She carried on walking around the archaic flint walls, through another tiny archway. Then from dark into light, everything opened onto a charming quadrangle, the ancient buildings fringing the central green lawn. This was more like it.

'Excuse me, madam, can I help you?' a voice called out. A portly gentleman in a black three-piece suit, bowler hat and silver watch chain, appeared as if from nowhere. He stopped Zena in her tracks as she was about to proceed across the grass to yet another archway.

'You're not allowed to walk on the grass,' he said, glowering.

Zena knew he was going to be tricky. 'Oh, I do beg your pardon,' she said in her politest and poshest of accents. 'I wonder if you might help me. I appear to be a little lost.' His face softened. 'I've travelled down from Liverpool, you see.'

'Liverpool? That's a long way to come, miss, if you don't mind me saying.'

'Yes it is rather, isn't it?'

'My Uncle Ted hailed from Liverpool way. New Brighton in fact.'

'New Brighton? I live ten minutes from there in Wallasey.'

'Well I never. Small world. My best summer holidays were there, before the Great War. Loved that beach I did.'

He walked with Zena back towards the porter's lodge.

'Would you like a cup of tea, miss? Then I can't set you on the right road. You can tell me what you're doing in Oxford.'

Over tea and biscuits, they reminisced over New Brighton and the delights of whizzing down the Rocket. They were soon firm friends.

'And then he pulled my pigtails!' Zena said. The porter laughed as she embellished the story of the fairground swindle, as though she genuinely had been a fifteen-year-old with pigtails.

'Can I let you into a secret?' Zena whispered, looking round to check there was no one in the vicinity. The porter had already been interrupted several times by strangers asking for directions, or someone asking him to sign for a letter or receive a telegram.

'Of course. Anyone who has been on the Rocket has my ear!'

'I'm trying to find out if my niece is marrying the right chap. He seems too good to be true, and my niece can't see it.'

'Stop. Stop right there miss.'

'What? Why? I've promised my sister I'll try and find out if what he's telling us is true.'

'What? Are you fishing for information from me?' his round face flushed, matching the colour of his tie.

'No, no, well, yes, maybe. It's just that he told us he was up at Oxford. At this very college.'

'We don't snitch on our students you know. What happens in college, stays in college.' He frowned. He reverted to his earlier haughty self, and stood upright. His watch chain was at Zena's eye level. She contemplated the shiny buttons on his waistcoat, and her charm offensive kicked in again.

'Please believe me, Sam. May I call you Sam? I feel

we're friends already,' Zena said. 'I can assure you, there is nothing, nothing, I need to know about the goings-on in the college.'

Sam softened slightly. Enough for Zena to continue. 'Has the boy ever been here? That's all I need to know. I promise. If we find out that he did attend the college, then you won't hear another peep from me. I swear. Is that a deal? Sam?' Zena said. She saw the hesitation in his eyes.

'OK, deal. But nothing else mind you?'

'Of course Sam, I promise,' Zena sighed with relief.

'Tell me then. Who was this boy?'

'His name is Oliver Stafford, came up in 1941-42, and read history and politics. He joined up and went to France in 1942. That's what he told my sister. If you can find out anything about whether he was here, she and I would be very grateful Sam.' Zena looked directly into Sam's eyes.

Sam flushed again, this time with pleasure.

'Give me half an hour, miss, and I'll check with all the scouts if they remember anyone by that name. My lists here are for the students currently studying in college.'

'Do you mind if I stay here, Sam? It's so cosy.'

'All right, but no snooping like a bleeding private eye, mind you,' he laughed.

'Very funny, Sam. Me, a private eye? Maybe I should think about it?'

'Oh no. Definitely not. It's not a suitable job for a woman.'

Zena chuckled to herself as she waited for Sam. After half an hour, he came panting back to the lodge, wiping his ruddy face with a handkerchief.

'Nope. Noone was here under that name. He was not at New College. I'm sure,' Sam said.

'Could he have studied here, but not lived in college?'

'No, all students have to live in if they study in Oxford.'

'Is there a central register of all students who attend the different colleges in Oxford? Perhaps he went somewhere else.'

'No. Each college is independent. They all have their own records. There's talk of one day having a central registry, but I doubt it'll ever happen.'

After trying unsuccessfully to press a half-crown into Sam's hand, Zena thanked him and returned to the Randolph.

'Mr Bigsby? Mr Bigsby? Can you hear me?' Zena shouted down the telephone. The line was crackling, and the voice was distant at the other end.

'Mr Bigsby. I need to know for sure if New College was the college that Oliver Stafford claims to have attended. Mr Bigsy? Did you hear me? I need confirmation of New College. I will telephone again in the afternoon.'

Unless she received confirmation Zena would have to go through the same process for every college in Oxford. If when confronted, the boy stated that he went to New College, then he was lying.

Zena telephoned Bigbsy later in the afternoon.

'My daughter is adamant he went to New College, and was there for a year, studying history and politics. Is it true, Mrs Archer?'

'Oh dear, Mr Bigsby. Your answer means I have bad news. The boy is lying. If he told your daughter that he had been to New College, then there is no doubt. I shall put it all in my report.'

'Thank you, Mrs Archer. Please can you bring the

report directly to the house? I don't want any risk of it getting into the wrong hands.'

*

Oliver Stafford, Bigsby's future son-in-law, was an accomplished liar. He had lied about Harrow, and then Oxford. Zena also discovered that he lied about the Coldstream Guards. No thanks to Joe, who had found nothing. Zena gave up waiting for Joe's report and searched the war records for Stafford's name. He *had* been in the army, but as a private, not an officer, and not in the prestigious Coldstream Guards. Neither had he seen active duty. He had served as a trainer for the Home Guard.

The icing on the cake for Zena was when on a whim she searched through the Liverpool county court records for his name. She found an injunction against him to stay away from a Miss Ellen Grey, a factory owner's daughter. Zena contacted Mr Grey, and discovered that Stafford had played the same trick. Like Bigsby, Mr Grey got suspicious, uncovered his lies and took out an injunction. Stafford was a charming, clever young confidence trickster.

After typing up her report, Zena took a trip out to the family's mansion to hand it to Bigsby in person. The sun blinked through the tall birch trees lining the long driveway. Zena shook her head and pinched her cheek to avoid the mesmeric effect. Waiting in the vast entrance hall, Zena was still dizzy when Mr Bigsby appeared.

'My daughter is devastated Mrs Archer. How she'll recover from this, God knows!' Bigsby said, as Zena handed him the report heavy in its brown envelope.

'It must have been very traumatic for you all.'

'I'll say. But I am incredibly grateful for everything you've done, Mrs Archer. What a charlatan and an utter cad. I've told him that if he ever shows his face in here again, he won't make it out in one piece. He got the message.'

'We were glad to help, Mr Bigsby. I really hope he doesn't move on to some other poor girl.'

'I've taken out an advert in all the local and national newspapers, warning people off him. The swine. The police aren't bothered. He's small fry to them. He had better stay away from other young women, or I'll 'ave him.' Bigsby's accent slipped in his fury. Shaking his head, he held out his hand and Zena shook it, proud to be regarded as an equal.

*

The first crisp chill of autumn arrived. Nana's lumbago was playing up. To say that she was crotchety was an understatement.

'Zena! Bring me my knitting bag.' An imperious voice shouted down the stairs.

'I'm late Nana. I'm just about to go to the office. Can't Marion help you?' Zena pulled on her kid driving gloves.

'I'm asking you! You've become far too hoity toity, young lady, since joining your father. Why you ever wanted to work when you've a perfectly good husband earning money, I'll never know. Now hurry up and bring me my knitting.'

Zena bit her tongue. Nana was harder to argue with

than her father. She would never win. She went up with the knitting bag which was received with a grunt. Annoyed, she set off for the office hoping her father wouldn't blast her for being late.

She soon found out to the contrary. He was giving her a dream job. If only it weren't for the travelling.

'Paris?' Zena looked at her father across the table in his cubbyhole. He smiled at her.

'I thought you'd be pleased. Excited even. A chance to see all those sights.'

'I've seen them, remember. Dave and I went.'

'It won't hurt you to go again. Anyone would think I was sending you to Hades not Paris! Wait until you see the case. It's a cracker. You won't be able to resist my girl.' Syd slid over the brown case file, watching Zena's reaction when she flicked through the notes. She grinned. The case her father had given her was a divorce with a twist. He was right – it was a cracker. Zena couldn't wait to find out more and telephoned the client – a Mrs Valois – immediately.

11

THE PARIS CASE

October 1950. 'You see, Mrs Archer, I am desperate for a divorce,' Mrs Valois explained on the telephone. 'Me and my new beau Ernest want to get married. To be honest, Henri and I were never that suited, if truth be told.'

'Henri?'

'Henri, Henri Valois. He's my husband. A horse trainer.'

'What kind of horse trainer? For the races?' Zena imagined going to Longchamp. Those outfits.

'No no. Not at all. Did you not read what I sent your father?' Mrs Valois sounded puzzled. Zena didn't want to admit she'd been too excited to read everything. She just wanted to get on with it.

'I did briefly, but just to be clear what kind of horse trainer?'

'A circus trainer.'

'Oh I see.' She didn't, but decided not to let on. 'Remind me again why you want the divorce.'

'You see Ernest worked at the hospital where my mum died. He was lovely to me. There through thick and thin, he was.'

'And what about Henri?'

'Oh no. He was nowhere to be seen. Off with his trapeze artist. Good luck to her I say.'

'Trapeze artist? Sorry Mrs Valois you've lost me.'

'That's who he's off with. The trapeze artist. Claimed to be my best friend at one point.'

'But you say you don't mind?'

'No. Not anymore. I want to be together with Ernest. Proper like. As a couple. Henri can keep his new girl with my blessing. But you know, Mrs Archer, how hard it is to get a divorce for someone like me.'

Zena knew the familiar story very well. Many women during the war found love and wanted to divorce their husbands but couldn't.

Mrs Valois had been an acrobat with the circus when she married Henri. But now she wanted to be free to marry Ernest. She needed to prove Henri's adultery with the trapeze artist to get the divorce and start her new life.

'But won't he provide the proof himself if he's having an affair?' Zena asked, puzzled as to why Mrs Valois would pay for the evidence.

'Oh no, Mrs Archer, no that's not possible at all. Henri he's a Catholic, you see. He's French. Divorce is against his religion. I must be the one to do it. Please get me the proof I need, Mrs Archer. We'll both be happier if you do.'

Zena was to follow Henri Valois to Paris, where the circus would open at its regular haunt in Montmartre. Mrs Valois had booked a flight and reserved a room for Zena in an hotel for two days hence.

*

Speke Airport's art deco roof hooded the concourse as Zena walked to the Air France check-in desk. She was delighted when the chic French stewardess upgraded her. Practising her French and exchanging pleasantries about their scarves paid off.

On board, she sank into the wide leather seat in the first-class cabin, where she revelled in smoking, drinking champagne and writing up her journal. The only disturbance was the steward offering her more food or wine. Heaven.

A gruff Parisian taxi driver met Zena from Orly airport, and he slung her case into the boot with a grunt of annoyance. Zena tried to engage him in French. Waste of time. The Peugeot 203 made quick work of cruising out of the airport and the driver sped in grim silence through the hazy dampness of the Parisian streets. As they reached the brow of the hill on Boulevard Saint Jacques, Zena looked to the right down the long road. It was the famous starting point for the pilgrimage leading to Santiago de Compostela. She could almost make out the turrets of Notre Dame in the distance. Zena had been to Paris once before with Dave. For their anniversary. They had been struck by the wonder of the gothic cathedral, illuminated in the half-light of evening, the flying buttresses gargoyled and blackened from centuries of soot.

Zena had expected to be taken to a modest *pension* somewhere in Montmartre. She was intrigued, as she soon realised it was not Montmartre. Pulling up outside the Hotel Lutetia on the wide Boulevard Raspail, Zena was awestruck by the massive Hausmann-style hotel.

Liveried doormen whisked away her luggage, and led her into the opulent lobby to check in. The clerk was polite in the classic French way, but Zena defrosted his grimace by speaking in her halting French. He was gracious enough to say that her accent was charming.

Zena's heart leapt into her throat when later that evening, there was a sharp rap on the door and a voice shouted, '*Télégramme pour Madame Archer.*' Zena immediately thought of her father. Was he OK? With trepidation she opened the telegram and read: *To Mrs Zena Scott Archer COMMA Hotel Lutetia Paris France STOP Circus delayed due to storm STOP Stay until they arrive STOP Regards COMMA Mrs Valois STOP*

Zena could imagine that the circus manager would refuse to sail in choppy seas with animals on board. She was annoyed but could hardly complain. She was being paid to stay in luxury and enjoy Paris until the horse trainer arrived.

*

A chill shivered down her back as Zena looked across to the pinpricks of scattered light in the black hedge on Quai Branley. Where to next? Zena had had her fill of tourist attractions: the extravagance of the Grand Palais, the gaudiness of the gold cherubs on Pont Alexandre III, and the overblown statuary of Opera. She didn't know why she had taken against such a beautiful city. She'd loved it when she was with Dave. Perhaps it was the memory of the war: London and her beloved Liverpool blitzed, while Paris remained in perfect museum mummery. Even the opulent

Hotel Lutetia was once a billet for the German intelligence service, the infamous *Abwehr*.

An explosion of light behind her made Zena jump, as thousands of lights framed the lattice of the Eiffel Tower. It was one tourist attraction of which she would never tire. She stood for a while watching in awe, before striding across the bridge to the metro station of Alma Marceau. The sharp, hot smell of urine rose from the stairs below, and she took out her lavender-scented lace handkerchief.

A resounding rattle echoed across the tiled subway, as the carriage ground into view. The sweat-shined seats of the banquettes smelt sour. She thanked Dave for his idea to douse her handkerchief with perfume. A godsend.

Emerging from the metro after two hellish line changes, Zena faced the water-spewing horses of the Saint Michel fountain, greened with verdigris. Dismissing the cafés on the river, Zena tried her luck at the oldest café in Paris – Le Procope. She'd read in her Baedeker that early regulars included Voltaire, Rousseau, Victor Hugo and more recently Oscar Wilde. She would catch a little bit of history. Walking down Boulevard Saint Germain to the cobbled ginnel that backed onto Le Procope, Zena ducked her head into the waxlight of one of the many rooms that formed the café's interior. She was surprised by how little must have changed from the time of the patinaed photographs bedecking the bowed walls. Although the booth into which she sank was a modern feature, the smoked ceilings looked as though they hadn't been painted for at least a century.

Like Oscar Wilde before her, Zena became impatient with the delay in service, but shied short of banging the table, Oscar style. The black-aproned waiters ignored her for half an hour too long. Enough was enough. Zena marched up to the bar. 'Am I ever going to get a drink in here?'

*

The next morning, breakfasting in the hushed opulence of the hotel dining room, the young man from the reception came in with another telegram: *To Mrs Zena Scott Archer COMMA Hotel Lutetia Paris France STOP Cirque Medrano arrived Montmartre STOP Husband and trapeze artist together STOP Photos STOP Regards COMMA Mrs Valois Adelphi Hotel Liverpool STOP*

Zena read it and wrote her reply: *To Mrs Valois COMMA Adelphi Hotel, Liverpool, England STOP Message received STOP Am on the case STOP Regards COMMA Zena STOP*

Mrs Valois must have some money behind her if she was staying in the Adelphi and paying for Zena to stay in the Lutetia. Where from? A life as an acrobat could not be well paid.

The Basilica of Sacré-Cœur shone a luminescent white, proud on the hill overlooking the rest of the city. It was ethereal in the crisp, blue-bright autumn afternoon. Zena walked from Saint Georges metro towards Boulevard de Rochechouart, where the Cirque Medrano was housed in an enormous, sixteen-sided rotunda. A big top in stone. It was magnificent. She paid in advance for a three-day pass. That had to be time enough.

The matinee started at two thirty and lasted two and a

half hours. With half an hour to spare, Zena watched the world go by in a little pavement café on Rue des Martyrs; fascinated as a bustle of people slid by on the narrow strip of pavement. The coffee was strong and good. She walked back to the Cirque Medrano, heady with caffeine.

The rows of seats were banked high to the ceiling. Zena sat midway. The inside was decorated with flower garlands painted on the periphery of the cupola. Pink marbled columns held up the roof, rising high above the central ring. Zena was surprised to find how much she was enjoying herself just looking at the décor.

A rumble of drums announced the start of the performance, and Zena sat back to watch a star-spangled extravaganza. Margaret Jordensen a Danish dancer and contortionist made Zena's legs ache in sympathy. At last, Zena saw what she had come for. The horse trainer, Valois. He looked very dashing. His tight sequinned waistcoat shimmered in the spotlights. The long featherlight whip was an unnecessary adjunct to his hand. The horses galloped. Jumped. Flew. They twirled as acrobats tumbled on their backs and through their legs. Zena's heart raced with the excitement of it, waiting for someone to fall.

Gradually all the horses bar one trotted out of the ring. A lone black horse remained. Valois made it stop. With the slightest of gestures, the horse stood on its hind legs. It kicked up towards the roof, the long black mane dripping down its withers. With a heart-stopping clatter, a rope unfolded from the ceiling. The audience gasped.

The horse whinnied, and trotted in a circle underneath the rope. A young woman, wearing an outfit of spangled pink, twisted and turned upside down on the rope. She edged towards the trotting horse, one delicate ankle after the other. With one mighty swing, followed by a double back flip, she landed upright on the back of the horse. They set off at a gallop around the ring, to thunderous applause.

Zena watched Valois lock eyes with the girl. As horse and girl passed Valois, Zena could see the girl's lips part in a smile. Their act was for them alone, as she twisted down and around the horse's neck. It was obvious to Zena that they were in love, but she would need better proof than just a look.

In the small bar where they served refreshments during the intermission, the artists and spectators mingled together. Zena saw Valois and the trapeze artist, and squeezed her way through the crowd towards them.

'*Excusez-moi, monsieur,*' she said, as she approached Valois.

'It's OK, I speak English,' he said, flushed from the success of the act.

'I wanted to say how marvellous you both were. You have such command and poise. Do you think I might get a picture of you together? I'm a journalist for the *Liverpool Echo* in England,' Zena said. They nodded, and Zena took out her camera. They stood close, looking into each other's eyes, and smiled back at Zena with the casual intimacy of lovers.

'Oh, that's perfect,' Zena said. 'I would love to interview you about life in the circus. Behind the scenes, as it were. My boss wanted me to interview Buster Keaton, but he got the dates wrong. He'll kill me if I come back with nothing.'

Zena paused. 'Can I come tomorrow and interview you both for the newspaper?'

They agreed to meet her in the morning. The journalist story was a good ruse.

Zena skipped the clowns billed for the second half. All that falling about had never appealed, even as a child. She had achieved her purpose, and with luck she would get a chance to talk to some of the artists, and get more proof for Mrs Valois.

*

The stables that housed the circus's sixteen horses were behind the massive façade of Cirque Medrano. The following morning Zena skirted round the back of the Medrano and found Mr Valois with the horses. The rich, earthy scent of straw and manure was heavy, but not unpleasant. Valois looked marginally less dashing in his shirt sleeves and jodhpurs. He had a curry comb in one hand, and was brushing the long mane of the black stallion. There was a clear bond between horse and trainer.

'Good morning, sir. Thank you for agreeing to be interviewed this morning,' Zena said, as he turned at her approach. 'Our readers will be delighted. Where is the young woman I met yesterday? I would love a feature on you both if that's possible?'

'*Non, ce n'est pas possible, Madame*. She is in her room,' he said.

'Oh dear, maybe next time then?' Zena was annoyed. It would mean she would have to come back again.

The interview went well. He was lively, and keen to tell her about his background. His father had been a stable manager, and he had grown up around horses. He had an affinity with them. Zena had witnessed it the previous day. His dark eyes sparkled as he talked about his horses. They dulled as soon as Zena mentioned his family.

'*Non*, my wife, she is not here,' he said. 'She is English like you, and is in London. Her mother, she died. She will come later.'

After the interview, Zena wandered around taking photos, telling stable hands and other members of the troupe that she was a journalist. She was waiting for a chance to catch the girl. No luck. She still had the three-day pass, and watched the matinee performance again. It was as spectacular as the day before. This time she stayed to watch the clowns. They were of the French tradition, a combination of the tragic Pierrot and the comedy of the Fratellini brothers. To her surprise Zena found them funny. Valois and his girlfriend were still as patently in love, but Zena did not have her proof.

Back at the Hotel Lutetia, Zena asked the manager for a diverting place to spend an evening suitable for a woman on her own. Good food, and maybe some entertainment.

'For a woman alone, Madame, as sophisticated as you, in Paris? It must be La Coupole. It is on Boulevard de Montparnasse. I will order for you a taxi. All the famous artists in the world have dined there, Picasso, Man Ray, Matisse. And Edith Piaf sings there. So many famous people! Maybe, Madame, you might meet someone there also.'

He winked at Zena. He must have thought she was

a woman alone, coming to find a husband. Zena was amused. She'd never heard of the artists he mentioned, but Edith Piaf, now that would be something.

Zena hoped she was dressed appropriately for her evening at La Coupole. She wore the Dior MJ had given her, with white lace gloves, diamante necklace and earrings. La Brasserie la Coupole was everything the manager had led her to believe: elegant, sophisticated, with a stunning art deco interior. Unlike Le Procope, where she had to force a waiter to look at her, here they were used to providing excellent service. Zena was immediately seated at a table. Looking around her, she couldn't take her eyes off the marbled pillars painted with figures and colourful scenes.

The restaurant buzzed with elegant diners, the young women wearing the latest Chanel or Dior designs. She was glad she'd worn the Dior.

Zena started with the oysters. It was the done thing, so they said. They were fresh and salty, and she loved them. The waiter suggested she try the famous lamb curry. Too risky. She chose the peppered steak. Tender and pink, the way she liked it, washed down with a large glass of Beaujolais. Superb. Dessert was harder to choose. There were endless dishes on the trolley. Profiteroles dripping in chocolate, millefeuille, crème brûlée. In the end she chose Crepes Suzette, flambéed in Grand Marnier.

A small wiry gentleman with round glasses in a pin stripe suit kept staring at her. Zena nodded back and carried on eating, a little more delicately, conscious that someone was watching her.

'Can I interest you in a glass of champagne, Mademoiselle?' Zena jumped at the voice in her ear, and turned around to see two huge eyes behind bottle-bottom glasses staring at her. The man was standing behind her, breathing hot whisky breath into her face.

'No, thank you,' Zena said, incensed. Trying hard to keep her voice calm and polite, but firm, she said, 'I am a married woman here on business. Now if you don't mind, please leave, or I shall be forced to call the manager and have you removed.'

Nonplussed, the man swayed back to his seat, and carried on smiling. He was harmless enough, but such behaviour was unwelcome. She was enjoying herself too much on her own.

The waiter suggested she might like a *digestif* downstairs, where there was music and dancing. Zena was tempted but declined. After the debacle with the myopic drunkard, she'd had enough.

*

It was day three and Zena had been wandering around the outbuildings of Cirque Medrano, with no luck. She had not got the proof she needed. Just hints and lovers' looks. The journalist story was wearing thin, but she wheedled some gossip from the stable lads, confirming that Mr Valois and the trapeze artist were lovers. It could go in her report.

'It sounds a perfect love story doesn't it?' Zena pressed a young lad curry combing one of the magnificent white horses in the horse-riding troupe. Valois always groomed his own black horse.

'Oui, Madame. C'est formidable. Ils ne sont jamais

séparés. J'espère qu'un jour je trouverai l'amour comme ça.'

'I'm sure you will find love too, one day,' Zena replied in her halting French.

The boy told her that Valois and the trapeze artist often spent lunchtimes before the matinee show in his caravan.

Taking him at his word, that lunchtime, Zena sidled around the caravans hoping to catch the couple in an embrace or more. She needed irrefutable proof of their affair for Mrs Valois to get her divorce. A high-pitched laugh startled her, and she jumped behind a dark red caravan. Dropping down beside the ladder leading up to the front door, Zena peered round to see where the laugh came from. There they were. Valois pulled the girl into his wide, strong arms, oblivious. He held her hand and they went up the ladder into the adjacent caravan. Zena crept around the side, heart pounding. She knew she had only moments to spare before she was caught. No one in sight. She couldn't quite reach up to see into the any of the windows. She searched frantically for something to stand on. Nothing. Taking a gamble Zena reached up as high as she could, pointed the camera and snapped, and snapped again several times. Good job she was tall.

'Oi you – what you doin' there?' Zena was surprised to hear a strong London accent behind her. A baggy trousered man with deep brown eyes stared at Zena waiting for her reply.

'Oh gosh you're English. I thought everyone here was French,' Zena said.

'Course I'm English,' he replied. This man would be hard to win round.

'It sounds like you're from London. Am I right?' Zena

smiled directly into his eyes, trying to soften him up.

'On the nose love. Olympia. Bertram Mills Circus.'

'Oh, so you're with the tour. Monsieur Valois and his horse troupe who are over from England?'

'The very same. Personal invitation from Jerome Medrano himself. Anyway, what were you up to back there? I saw you outside Henri's caravan.'

'I've been doing a piece for the *Liverpool Echo*.'

'You the journalist then. I heard you'd been sneaking around.'

'I just wanted another photo of Henri and his young trapeze artist together and I saw them go into the caravan, but I couldn't reach and didn't want to disturb them.' Zena wasn't sure her story held up and was surprised at his response.

'Come here,' he said, cupping out his hands.

'What? What do you mean?'

'Come on, come here. I'll give you a bunk up.' He held his hands out again so she could put a foot in and get up to the window ledge.

'Shhh,' she hissed worried that Valois would hear him.

Zena looked in the window and wished she hadn't. The photos she snapped would be more than enough to prove adultery and she quickly jumped down red faced.

'They deserve to have a naughty photo printed in the paper. Can't say I like what he gets up to,' the man said.

'Really? Why's that?' Zena asked.

'I was mates with his missus. Ditched her for a younger model he did but even then won't divorce her. Poor Mabel. She was a cracking acrobat. I miss her.'

'Oh no. I didn't know that,' Zena lied. 'I thought the

pair here were an established couple and planned to do a feature on love in the circus.'

'Well now you know. Do your worst. I would.'

The man turned on his heel and marched off. At least now she had her proof. What a set up. With relief, Zena rushed back to the hotel and asked the receptionist to book the first available flight.

Dave's voice was full and tender when she rang home. 'I'll come in a taxi and pick you up. No argument.'

'But you hate being in a car, love. I can get a taxi on my own, please don't worry.' Zena held the telephone receiver tight to her chest. She'd missed Dave more than she'd expected. He would meet her, no matter what she said. At that moment she felt the luckiest woman in the world.

Zena was overjoyed to be home. It seemed more like a year than the two weeks she'd been away. Comfort and belonging washed over her as she walked through the door of Ripon Road – until she was greeted by her mother's ire.

'You could have got an earlier flight, so we didn't have to wait up all hours for you to get home,' Madge grumbled. Zena knew, however, that her mother was secretly pleased to see her. Ignoring Madge's sour face, Zena fished out a little painting of Sacré-Cœur she had picked up in Montmartre. Her mother loved it.

The weekend rushed by and Zena wished she had had one more day before returning to the office and the smirks of Joe and Harry. At least Mrs Valois was delighted to hear from her.

'Maybe we can both be happy now,' Mrs Valois said. The line crackled.

'Sorry Mrs Valois. It's a bad line. Can you speak up?'

'I was saying that we married too young.'

'Ah I see.'

'Yes Henri, he's a charmer all right, but such a boy. He loved his horses more than he did me.'

'I can see that,' Zena replied.

'And that young girl too by the sound of it.'

'I saw that too.'

'I just want us both to be happy. I do. But he won't go against his faith.'

'That's why you need the divorce?'

'It is. He wouldn't budge. I had to do it. I had to. No other way.'

'I understand Mrs Valois. I'm not here to judge.'

'Thank you. It means I can get on with my life with Ernest. I hope you understand.'

'Of course I do. You, like us all, deserve happiness. My report and the photos will give you all that you need,' Zena said. 'But Mrs Valois, you may not wish to look at all of the photos,' she warned.

'Don't you worry about that. I'll be waiting for them. Thank you Mrs Archer.'

*

The Valois case came to court before Christmas, and Zena was called to give evidence. Judge Clarke granted the divorce, nodding to Zena in recognition as she gave her statement. After the hearing Mrs Valois grabbed hold of Zena.

'Oh Mrs Archer, thank you, thank you.'

'No need. No need Mrs Valois.'

'Call me Mabel.'

'OK Mabel. Really I was glad to help.'

'But you don't know what a difference you've made to my life Mrs Archer. I'm a free woman. I can marry my Ernest,' Mrs Valois said, clutching at Zena's hand.

'As I said I was glad to help.'

'Help you did, Mrs Archer. You will never know how much.'

'You paid us handsomely for it,' Zena replied, extracting her hand.

'I used money from my inheritance. I tell you it was worth every penny.'

'I'm glad to hear that.'

'Henri took it bad. But he's the one who chose religion over love,' Mrs Valois said.

Zena wished all her clients were as happy to hand over their money. Zena left the court and Mrs Valois with mixed emotions. She was delighted that the case was successfully closed, and her client had got what she wanted. Yet a doubt niggled. Who was in the right? Henri or Mabel?

12

WINTER AT HOME

December 1950. The Scott household settled into quiet. The tensions of the days sighed into the nights' dreams. Life was winding down for Christmas and Zena wanted to make up to Dave for all the times she had been away.

'Dave, I've got us tickets to see *Whisky Galore!*'

Zena tugged at Dave's sleeve to drag him out of the back room. Coats and hats on, they linked arm in arm, walking tight together down the street. *Whisky Galore!* according to the poster outside the cinema, was a Highland romp. Joan Greenwood played the fiery redhead featured in the poster.

'Did you know the name of the real ship was S.S. Politician? It left Liverpool in 1941 carrying 250,000 bottles of whisky,' Dave said, as they sat in the worn seats of the Ritz. 'It sank two days later in the Outer Hebrides because of severe weather.'

'Shhh!' someone behind them hissed, but Dave continued, oblivious. 'The locals gathered up as many bottles as they could find before the custom men arrived.'

After the film finished, Dave suggested a nightcap at The Grange.

It was gone nine o'clock, but Charing Cross, the massive crossroads in Birkenhead, was as bustling in the evening as it was during the day. The Grange was a big barn of a place, and they went into the lounge bar. Dave had a whisky and Zena a Campari. They could hear the piano and singing in the public bar.

'Why can't we go in there? No one would mind. I'd love to hear the music,' Zena said. She was cross that just because she was a woman, she was restricted to the lounge.

'No, love, please don't make a fuss. Why don't we go into the snug instead?' Dave looked at Zena. Although she was annoyed by the rules of the public bar, Zena didn't mind a cuddle in the snug. A perfect way to round off the evening.

The oak table and settles in the panelled snug were gnarled and worn with decades of couples hoping for the same as Zena and Dave: some peace and quiet to themselves. They clinked glasses, and Zena leant on Dave's shoulder, content with the world. With a start, she leapt up as the door burst open and a stocky, bandy-legged drunkard lurched into their space. Staring at them bleakly, he thought better of whatever he was planning, and heaved himself out of the door. Laughing, Zena settled back with Dave and sipped her Campari.

The next day was Stir-up Sunday. Madge always made a big thing of it. They all had to be there, or it would be unlucky. The family stood around as the ingredients were carefully mixed. The Scott family followed the old tradition of stirring the pudding mixture from East to West in honour of the three wise men who visited the baby Jesus.

'Go on Zena, hurry up, go on, give it your stir. You're the last!' Madge was impatient to get the pudding into the basin.

'Hang on a minute, I always forget which way is East.' With a quick pretence at hesitation, Zena added an extra sixpence to the Christmas pudding.

They all clapped and Madge spooned the heavy mixture into the muslin lined bowl ready for steaming.

*

When Zena went into the office the next morning, Joe and Harry were huddled around the old Valor paraffin heater in the corner, smoking and cracking jokes. The noxious fumes made Zena queasy. Her old patchwork blanket gave her warmth enough.

Joe glanced over at Zena, and whispered something to Harry. They both laughed.

'What?' Zena asked.

'Nothing,' Joe replied, smirking.

'There's something, Joe. What are you laughing about? Are you still miffed?'

'Now why on earth should I be miffed?'

'You know why.'

'Go on tell me.'

'For goodness sake, Joe, this is ridiculous.'

'You're the one that's ridiculous.'

'Ah, now we're seeing your true colours. It's lucky for you Dad isn't here.'

'Yeah, you'd run off to Daddy, wouldn't you? Like you did about the Bigsby case. Got my pay docked for that one, thanks to you.'

'Joe, come on. You have to admit you did nothing on that case.'

'That's not true and you know it. What about the army records?'

'You spent more time at the bookies than you did checking old army records. Dad asked me, and I told him.'

'Told him lies just to get back at me.'

'That's not fair Joe. I told Dad the truth. I found those records. If you don't do the work, you can't expect to get paid.'

Zena turned away from them and ignored their continued whispers and snide remarks. She carried on typing up the final invoice for Mrs Valois.

An hour later Syd barrelled into the office slightly tipsy from a lunch with Mr Leonard, the owner of Leonard's department store.

'Zena, get this! Mr Leonard asked for you in particular,' Syd slurred.

'What do you mean Dad?'

'Stockings and lingerie are going missing from the stockroom. Why do you think he asked for you then?' her father said.

Zena bit her lip to stop herself retorting: 'Because I get the job done?' Scott's and now Zena, had a reputation in Liverpool for succeeding where others failed.

'They want you in there as a salesgirl.'

'A salesgirl? What would I have to sell?'

'Lingerie. Should suit you down to the ground!'

'Very funny.'

Zena was surprised that Mr Leonard had the wherewithal to call Scott's. The last time she had walked past the windows in Leonard's they were greasy and the display had remained unchanged for weeks. Leonard's was the biggest local department store to survive the Liverpool blitz. Zena had loved it in its heyday. Endless rationing had sent it downhill. Old, dated stock and utility wear reminded customers of the war. Zena, like many, craved something new and glamorous. Leonard's could not provide it. They should be moving with the times.

'You're to go in tomorrow. They reckon undercover is the only way to catch the thief,' Syd said. 'Mr Leonard was most insistent it was you. Where did he hear about you?'

'Maybe Hart's recommended me.'

Regardless, Zena was delighted that she was well known enough to have caught Mr Leonard's attention. Acting as a salesgirl might be a bit of a challenge, but she rather enjoyed the thrill of being someone else. Living another life.

*

The following day Zena walked through the white Portland stone frontage of Leonard's, still pocked with shrapnel dents. She was to report to the manager in the lingerie department. It was reminiscent of her job in L.J. Hart's. Hopefully without the startling discovery of someone naked stealing the clothes.

A similar refrain echoed in the lift: 'Going up all floors, lingerie, haberdashery and menswear.' She stopped at the lingerie floor, where three of the young shop girls were grouped around a bank of glass-fronted cabinets, fiddling with the half-bodied mannequins inside. Their heads turned one by one to stare at Zena like startled rabbits. She walked towards them and pretended to be nervous.

'Excuse me, good morning. I'm the new girl, Phillipa. I was told to come here to report to the manager in the lingerie department. Am I in the right place?' she said, eyes down.

With one voice they replied, 'Yes!' then they all laughed as if it was the best joke in the world. Zena laughed with them. She felt immediately at home.

After meeting the manager, a flat-footed beef of a man, Zena was soon established on the shop floor and introduced to the salesgirls, Joyce, Jean and Mary. After lunch, Jean said, 'Do you want to have a go?'

Zena nodded.

'All right then, Phlipa,' Jean said.

Zena opened her mouth to correct her, but the mispronunciation tickled her. She let it go. Phlipa she was.

'Next customer's yours,' Jean said.

A hefty woman trailing three snot-nosed children browsed the more functional undergarments. She appeared taken with the Playtex girdle, brand new from America. The clips for stockings were integrated. No need for a corset and separate suspenders. Zena had had her eye on it herself.

'Can I help you at all, madam?' she asked. 'Are you looking for something in particular?'

The woman swung round, knocking off the little girl hanging on her skirts.

'Geroff me, Jenny,' the mother shouted. She started to raise her hand, but the look on Zena's face stopped her in her tracks. 'Ta, love, but I'm just looking. It'd be too much for me anyroad,' she sighed.

'You never know,' Zena said, keen for her first sale. 'There is a special offer on these new items. For example, this corselette, which is designed for, you know, the fuller figure.' Zena didn't mean to be rude, but the woman could do with the full corset, not the girdle.

'Why not try it on, madam? We can entertain the children here while you do.' Zena felt sorry for the poor woman, who probably never had time to shop for herself.

The woman agreed. After several squawks as she squeezed into the corselette, lo and behold, Zena had made her first sale. 'Me fella would kill me, but who cares. I never buy anything for myself and I work as hard as him,' she said handing over a ten shilling note. She bought a pair of stockings to go with it. Zena was cock-a-hoop as she gave the woman her change.

'Blimey, Phlipa, you've got the gift of the gab! There's no way I would have ever sold that woman anything,' Jean said.

'People sometimes don't know what they need, and I suppose we're here to help them find it,' Zena said.

*

Flushed with success, the next day Zena approached a woman in a dark green utility suit. Zena could see that the woman had transformed a man's uniform into a smart two piece. She also knew that the army material could be scratchy. She needed a slip.

'Good morning madam, is there anything I can do to help you?'

'No thank you. I'm just looking.' Startled green eyes stared back at her, and looked down.

'May I say, your outfit is smashing. Did you make it yourself?'

'Yes. It took a long time. But it's the only thing I have left of him.' The green eyes brimmed.

'Oh no. I'm so very sorry. That must be terrible for you. My husband was in the air force. India. He's fine. Never talks about it though. I can't imagine what it must be like to lose someone.'

'It's been tough alright. You must know. Bringing up the little ones. Hard to make ends meet. I come in here for some peace while they're at school.'

'We haven't been blessed with children, but I see why you come here. It's a bit of a haven isn't it?' The young woman nodded her reply.

'Why don't you treat yourself? Just this once. I'm sure your husband would want you to have something nice. This slip would be perfect under your suit.' Zena picked out a full silk slip in cream and held it against the woman's back for size.

Another sale but still no closer to catching the stocking thief. By the end of the week Zena had notched up quite a record. Mary laughed at her. 'You'll be winning the salesgirl of the week soon,' she said, 'and you've only been here a few days.'

They were a great bunch of girls, and Zena could see no sign of fiddling. The stock in the storeroom was counted each day, and they knew how much had been sold through the till receipts. The receipts were rolled up, placed in small metal cylinders, and sent up through the pneumatic tube to the manager's office. The pneumatic system fascinated Zena, and when she told Dave about it he said he would investigate getting one for Celia Manley's chemist, where he was now the manager.

Zena was as flummoxed as the store detective. Who on earth could be stealing the stock if it wasn't the salesgirls? Zena tried another tack. She did morning and evening observations, and worked during the day at the store. It meant long days, but the extra work paid off. After a week, she was sure the girls were clean.

'You'll need to give me a list of all the staff who have access to the stockroom,' Zena told the manager. 'I've been watching them all, and I would know if it was one of the girls,' she said.

'I can't think who else it could be, you've had all the names,' he said. 'There's the old night watchman Jack, but it can't be him. He's been here thirty years.'

'Have his circumstances changed at all?' Zena asked, knowing full well that even the most loyal of employees could be tempted if their life took a turn.

'His mother is old and sick,' the manager said.

'Does he look after his mother?' Zena asked.

'Yes he does. He's never married. His mother is his life.'

'What about when he's working?'

'Er…I think he has to pay for help to come in and watch her. I'm not sure. He says that sometimes she goes walkabout.'

Zena already had her suspicions but said nothing. The next evening, she sat in the car in the back alley facing the goods entrance of Leonard's. She wound a ball of dark blue wool, unravelled from one of Dave's old Air Force jumpers. She would knit him a smart new vest.

There he was! Jack, the night watchman. Zena

snatched for her binoculars. He was coming out of the goods entrance. It was him alright. He was staggering under the weight of several large packages. She picked up her camera. He looked around and then across at Zena's car. Zena ducked down, and peeked over the window edge to see what he was doing. She heard a crack. She sat up. Jack was jumping on the boxes. They were empty. He folded them, tied them with string and put them in the galvanised bins outside the entrance. He looked around once more, pulled out a pack of cigarettes, and lit up.

Zena watched him the next night as he followed the same routine. Take out the empty boxes, crush them, put them in the bin. Have a smoke. Return inside. She could see his torch sweep each floor as he moved up. He was thorough alright. It didn't look as if he was the thief. But who else could it be?

The following night, Zena was almost nodding off waiting for Jack to come out when a sharp rap on the window startled her. Her heart pounded. Was it Jack? Had he spotted her? She'd moved her car. She was sure she was well hidden.

'Excuse me miss,' a man's voice boomed. All Zena could see in her eyeline were shiny buttons. Jack wore brown dungarees.

Zena wound down the window, and looked out and up. A policeman. Thank the Lord.

'Yes sergeant? What can I do for you?' Zena learnt from her father to always go up a rank. Flattery worked where confrontation would not.

'Constable, miss.'

'Sorry, constable. What can I do to help?'

'I was wondering what I might be able to do for you miss. You've been parked here rather a long time.'

Zena handed over her card. *Zena Scott-Archer, Scott's Detective Agency, Member of British Detectives Association, 3 Cook Street, Liverpool.*

'A lady P.I. eh? That's novel.'

'Yes constable. I'm on a job.' Zena tried not to sound exasperated. How many times had she heard that expression before?

'May I ask what job miss?' the constable replied.

'It's routine shop theft. I'm keeping watch. Now if you don't mind officer, the longer you stand here, the harder my job becomes.'

'I think you should move along now miss. It's getting late. You shouldn't be out on your own at this time.'

Zena wanted to scream at him that she was on her own late at night doing observations all the time. And she was fine. His attitude was the reason she brought her mother or Win along to most observations. A woman on her own was a target. They couldn't resist telling her it was dangerous to be out alone. What did they think women got up to during the War? If only they knew.

'OK officer, if you say so. I shall say goodnight then.' No point in arguing and if Jack came out to start his routine, she'd have blown the case. No way was she going to admit to failure because she was a woman on her own.

The next night, Zena drove round to be sure no coppers on the beat were in the area. She pulled into a side street opposite the back of Leonard's and waited.

She noticed that tonight something was different. A battered looking dark green Bedford van was parked next to the bins. Zena watched. Camera ready. The streetlamps were bright enough to see a figure leaning out of the window on the third floor at the back of Leonard's. It was Jack. He whistled, low and loud. The driver of the green van leapt out. Looked around. Satisfied all was quiet, he ran to stand under the window. Jack lowered down a large box tied to a rope that he eased over the windowsill. It looked heavy. No doubt full of stockings.

Zena pressed the shutter on her camera. The photograph popped out in less than a minute. Fuzzy around the edges but with enough detail to back up her report. The stockroom was on the third floor. Zena felt no satisfaction at having caught the thief. She doubted it would end well.

'Jack? No, it can't be! I can't believe it,' the manager said. 'He's been with the family since Leonard's opened.'

'I know, it's sad when the most loyal staff betray you. I'm afraid as soon as you said Jack's circumstances had changed, I suspected something.'

'Why didn't you say something then?'

'I don't like to accuse until I have proof. I'm sure you can understand that?'

The manager nodded.

'What will happen to him?' Zena asked.

'Mr Leonard had already decided to retire him. Your findings won't change that. He won't pursue charges I'm sure. Jack's been with us for too long.'

'Oh I am so glad to hear that. He just needed extra cash for his mother, poor man.'

'Yes. This way he'll get a pension. It'll be enough for him and his mother. He'll never know we caught him out.'

Zena was relieved. It was the end of the case, and the end of her third week. The next day, she left to the sound of clapping from the girls, and the floor manager. Plus a bonus of a guinea as salesgirl of the week. If she ever got tired of detective work – it could pall, all that travelling – maybe she could try a new career in sales. Dave might be happier to have her working regular hours in a regular job. But would she? She loved the fact that each day was different. That she never knew if she'd be working undercover, or following a mark. Whatever it might be, she could safely say her life was never dull.

13

THE CASE OF THE MISSING ARTWORK

March 1951. 'You'll need to wear a uniform,' Syd said. It was three months after her last undercover role at Leonard's, and Zena's heart sank at the thought of thick stockings and flat shoes. Even with a belt to nip in the waist, there was no denying that a nurse's uniform was neither flattering nor comfortable. All that starch. And no make-up. Zena didn't relish her role as a locum nurse to the client, a Mrs. Wilson. Valuable art works were missing and Zena was tasked with uncovering the thief.

With any luck it wouldn't be for long. Undercover work was tough, even though she knew she was good at it. All that lying. It took its toll.

The following day, her footsteps echoed through the old manor house as the housekeeper showed Zena to her room. It was quaint, with heavy velvet curtains at the tall window overlooking the extensive grounds. Zena looked out across the spring landscape. A vast oak tree centred a wide bordered lawn edged yellow with early daffodils. Dark green Italian cypresses lined the back wall, tall and proud.

A wing-backed chair stood in the corner of the room, next to a Victorian marble-topped washstand. The blue willow-patterned bowl and jug reminded Zena of the one Nana used to have. Zena suspected little had changed in the house since Victorian times. A coal fire warmed the room as she unpacked her case.

Zena met her client, Mrs Wilson, the next morning. The housekeeper, Mrs Davidson, called Zena into a vast bedroom cum sitting room, where the rich widow spent much of her time. Heavy wood panelling and large framed paintings decorated every wall and darkened the room. Not that there was much light coming in from between the half-closed curtains. Zena's client dismissed Mrs Davidson.

'Come here, young woman. Let me look at you.' A claw-like hand grabbed at Zena's as she stood next to the huge oak-framed bed. 'You don't look much like a nurse, but I suppose you'll do.'

'How can I help, Mrs Wilson? My father told me you've had some valuable items stolen.'

'My husband and I were art collectors. He died two years ago,' Mrs Wilson said, then collapsed into a paroxysm of coughing. Her quavering hand grabbed for the oxygen mask that hung by her bed. Zena was transported back to the days of wearing her gas mask during the war. The memory of claustrophobia almost had her coughing as much as her client.

Mrs Wilson's tiny, lined faced was covered by the heavy mask, attached to the giant oxygen cylinder standing on wheels by her bed. She waved Zena's help away and fell back exhausted on her bank of pillows.

'Since my husband died,' Mrs Wilson gasped for breath as she took away the mask to speak. 'My favourite art works have been disappearing,' she coughed. 'It must; it must be one of the staff. No sign of burglary,' she collapsed onto her pillows and pulled the oxygen mask back over her face. 'Find out who it is…' she croaked as she waved Zena away.

The only other person connected to the household who knew Zena was a detective was the regular doctor. Zena was to assist him. Zena had not an inkling of medical issues. She would no doubt have swaddled Mrs Wilson up like a mummy had she been asked to change a bandage.

Everything was easy for the first few days. Zena's tasks were not onerous, and Mrs Wilson proved to be an entertaining if eccentric client especially on her good days.

'You see that photograph over there, Zena?' Mrs Wilson pointed to a photograph of a beautiful young girl, her eyes closed and black hair slick, holding a cigarette in an arched, gloved hand.

'Man Ray. He signed it for me. We met in Paris. He tried to seduce me. Said I looked like her,' Mrs Wilson said, giggling like a schoolgirl.

'Who's Man Ray?' Zena didn't dare ask if this person had succeeded in his seduction.

'What? You don't know who Man Ray is? Ignorant girl! I see I'm going to have to educate you.' Mrs Wilson reached for her mask, the exchange too much for her. The heavy rasp and click of the oxygen echoed in the heaviness of the room. Zena was glad to leave.

'The doctor's coming tomorrow to give Mrs Wilson her weekly injection and you'll have to draw it up for him,' Mrs Davidson told Zena that evening.

'No problem,' Zena replied, unconcerned. As the doctor knew she was undercover, she assumed he would draw up the injection himself.

Zena took up Mrs Wilson's sleeping pills and warm milk. She entered her client's room, which glowed in the soft gaslight. The old lady didn't trust electricity. "The devil's work," she called it. Mrs Wilson lay reclined on her pillows, for once not agitated about something that had gone missing, presumed stolen. Zena had already found several supposedly stolen items, which had been put in a safe place and then forgotten.

'Sit down, my dear.' Mrs Wilson patted the heavy cream quilt on her bed. 'We need to continue your education. Fetch that book on the table over there.' Half an hour of art education later, Zena was as exhausted as her client, trying to remember the names and the paintings Mrs Wilson had shown her.

The next morning, Zena prepared Mrs Wilson's room as instructed. She placed the heavy silver tray on the mahogany chest of drawers in the bay window. A clean muslin cloth covered the tray, and a large metal-topped syringe and hypodermic needle lay on top of it. Finally, she put some boiled water in a silver bowl, next to a small square of muslin. All was ready for Doctor Green. A sharp rap on the door announced his arrival, and Mrs Davidson came fussing behind him as he strode into the room.

'Good morning, Mrs Wilson, good morning, nurse. I am Doctor Tiplady. Doctor Green was called to an emergency.'

Zena gasped, close to uttering an expletive. A tall, severe, grey-haired gentleman with a clipped moustache stood in front of her. Her heart thumped. Would her disguise be revealed? It would be mortifying to be shown up in front of the supercilious housekeeper.

Zena mumbled something back. She tried to make a quick exit, bobbing down, and sidling towards the door. The imperious voice of Doctor Tiplady stopped her in her tracks.

'Nurse. Please draw up the usual injection for Mrs Wilson,' he said, signalling towards the tray on the chest of drawers. Zena stared back at him, horrified. She must have looked as if she was going to faint.

'For goodness sake, let me do it. Standing there gawping like a fishwife,' Mrs Davidson snapped. 'I've done it countless times for Doctor Green. This nurse is new, Doctor Tiplady, and we can't wait to have Nurse Timms back.'

Mrs Wilson's rasp came from the bed. 'Leave her be, Davey. She's getting used to how things work.'

Mrs Davidson glared at Zena, who didn't care, so grateful was she that someone else would draw up the injection. Zena watched as Mrs Davidson fixed the needle into the syringe and drew up boiled water before passing it to Zena with a sigh. Zena handed the syringeful of water to Doctor Tiplady, who winked at her before injecting it into Mrs Wilson's left buttock.

'But...' Zena was about to speak, but Doctor Tiplady interjected, silencing her with a sharp look.

'Now, nurse, please bathe the area I have injected.'

'Yes, doctor.'

'Then please see me downstairs. I have some more instructions for you.'

'Yes, doctor.'

A few minutes later, when Mrs Wilson was the calmest Zena had ever seen her, she joined Doctor Tiplady in the drawing room. Could it only have been boiled water he injected?

'Mrs Wilson is a hypochondriac, nurse. I assume you had already guessed.'

'Ah, I...'

'She doesn't need any medication, but a weekly injection of water seems to help.'

'But how does it help to calm her so much if it's just water?' Zena was curious. Maybe she could try it on her grandmother.

'It's all in the mind, you see, nurse. A placebo is as effective,' he said tapping the side of his head. Perhaps he was not as severe as Zena had first imagined.

'Fascinating.'

'Not a word to Mrs Wilson, you hear. We mustn't have her believing Doctor Green and I are a pair of quacks now, must we?' Doctor Tiplady winked at Zena, his grey-green eyes searching hers for a hint of hesitation.

'No, doctor.'

*

Some days later Zena walked around the house to admire some of the works of art. She started to appreciate the few artists she had heard of. Maybe the education was paying off. The Toulouse-Lautrec in the drawing room caught her eye. She had seen so many reproductions in Paris. The door opened a crack and Bert the handyman crept in. He was the one person on the staff who Zena thought might be wily enough to salt a few valuable items away when no one was looking. He worked in the garden and did odd jobs around the house. He lived in a tiny cottage in the grounds, little more than a shed. It suited him.

Zena slipped behind the long curtain as Bert looked around to check no one was looking. Bold as brass, he lifted a Modigliani painting off the far wall. Mrs Wilson had given Zena an article to read about Modigliani's almond-eyed beauties as part of her art education.

'Oh, that's a lovely painting. Where are you taking it?' Zena asked. Bert jumped, bemused as to where she had come from.

'Missus has asked me to put it away,' he replied.

'Oh, and where would that be?'

'Can't say. Missus says not to tell no one. Somewhere safe.'

'Look, it's big and heavy, and you wouldn't want to drop it and damage it, would you? The missus would be terribly upset, wouldn't she?'

'S'pose,' he said.

'Come on. Let me help you. I won't tell anyone, I promise,' Zena smiled at him.

His face crunched in uncertainty, tears filming his eyes.

'Look, we'll have it stored in no time, and no one will know. Don't worry, it'll be fine,' Zena said and took his arm.

'All right, but quick now. Missus told me to tell her when it's done, and I've been too long already,' he said, his eyes flicking back and forth in panic.

'You lead the way,' Zena said.

Bert picked up one side of the painting and Zena lifted the other. It was heavier than she'd expected. He must have the muscles of a weightlifter to lift it down from the wall. He stepped back into the large entrance hall of the manor house and headed through a side door, down a narrow set of stairs that led to the kitchens. Zena had been down this way many times before, and nothing had made her suspicious.

Bert stopped with a jerk, and the sudden jolt nearly made Zena push him down the stairs. He stood on a little landing and rested the painting on his large hobnailed boot. He motioned for Zena to put her end down. She did so with relief. With a quick sleight of hand, Bert pushed at one of the oak panels, which opened inwards. With a nod he picked up the painting once again, expecting Zena to do the same. It was pitch black and Zena hesitated, fearful she might fall into the darkness. A sudden light flooded the staircase. A large lantern hung on the wall, its battery-operated beam tracking the stairs.

'Here,' he said.

They carried the heavy painting down the steps into a vaulted basement. The vast room was cool and dry. As Bert turned on more lanterns, Zena could see that this was where the missing pieces of art had been stowed. There were hundreds of paintings stacked in dozens of upright wooden racks. They placed the Modigliani upright, in one of the few empty racks. Glass cabinets lined the far wall. They were full of bronzes, marble busts and colourful ceramics. Zena stood admiring the room. She had never seen anything like it. There must be a fortune down here. This was evidently the work of a professional, not a handyman. Bert was either a master of disguise, or he was in cahoots with a very sophisticated art thief.

'Come on,' Bert said, anxious to get back upstairs. Zena crept behind him up the steep steps. How had he managed to get so many of the stolen items down there alone? There had to be an accomplice. Perhaps someone on the outside, or even the inside. Mrs Davidson the housekeeper was too old, but what about her son, Philip? He was always loafing around. Zena had not taken to him. He reminded her of Charlie. That sly self-assurance. It riled her.

Resolving to keep an eye on Philip and question him next time she came across him, Zena took Mrs Wilson her nightly medicine.

'Mrs Wilson. Could it be Bert? Bert the handyman?' Zena asked as she placed the tray on the mahogany side table.

'Could what be Bert?'

'Could he be the one who has been stealing the artworks?'

'No, surely not. It can't be Bert.'

That night Zena tossed and turned. It didn't make sense. Bert appeared so genuine. But then she was pretending to be a nurse, and everyone believed *her*. Mrs Wilson did not believe it was Bert, but had no other explanation. Perhaps Philip was blackmailing him for some reason. Too many thoughts whirled, and Zena woke with a jolt from a dream that had Philip standing over her with a bronze statue, ready to strike.

A cool bath woke Zena into a semblance of calm and she took Mrs Wilson her breakfast. She would quiz her about Philip. The more Zena thought about it, the more she believed Philip had to be involved. There could be no other explanation. Bert could not have done this on his own. It had to be someone who appreciated art, who knew how to store it, and where to sell it. None of that sounded like Bert. He was not canny enough and had no reason to steal. But then she remembered Jack at Leonard's department store. No one could imagine him stealing either. It was often the most unlikely suspects who were the culprits.

'Zena! Come in, come in, my dear. Put that tray down and come and sit here. I've remembered. I knew it couldn't be Bert.'

'That's marvellous, Mrs Wilson. Is it Philip? I've had my suspicions about him. I knew Bert couldn't have done this on his own. He's been behaving very strangely around me for days now.'

'Zena, please, stop.'

'But surely you must see that it's got to be Philip. Who else could manipulate Bert in that way?'

'If you'd let me finish. That's what I want to tell you.'

'Please, do tell me.' Zena wasn't convinced that Mrs Wilson would have a better suspect.

'It's me!'

'What do you mean, it's you?' Zena said. Was Mrs Wilson delusional as well as a hypochondriac? Unless it was an insurance scam. Perhaps the hypochondria was a front. All kinds of thoughts raced across her brain.

'I told Bert to take those paintings.'

'I don't understand. Why?'

'He brings up another from the archive. I…I…' Mrs

Wilson paused to take in more oxygen from her mask. 'I have a chance to look at a different beautiful painting. It's a…it's a revolving art gallery. Don't you see?' Mrs Wilson gasped.

'You asked him to take that Modigliani to the basement?'

'Yes, I did. I completely forgot.'

'Forgot?'

'Yes. I forgot. My memory isn't what it was.'

'I must admit, I had noticed you often forget where you put things,' Zena agreed.

'I've been forgetting more and more these days. Today I asked Bert to bring up a Matisse.'

'A Matisse?'

'Yes the red one, the still life with a vase of magnolias.'

'Oh yes I think I saw that in the drawing room.'

'Yes that's it. Davey wheels me round to look at them.' Mrs Wilson paused to cough and take another deep breath of oxygen.

'Do you think any paintings might have been stolen? Bert has the opportunity.'

'No. No. My mind is clearer now. It can't be Bert.'

'Are you sure?'

'Of course I'm sure. Bert would never steal. He helped my husband and I build the archive in the basement.'

'The archive? That's what is in the basement?'

'Yes we started collecting twenty years ago. Bert is a craftsman. A different type of artist.'

'If the basement is his handiwork, then I agree with you. Why did you build such a big room?'

'Our rooms were full to the brim. Art needs space. The archive room was the perfect solution.'

'Ah. Now I see.'

'Are you starting to appreciate art a little more now, Zena?' Mrs Wilson chuckled. 'You weren't so keen on my lectures when you first arrived.'

'Mrs Wilson, that's not fair!' Zena laughed back. 'But seriously, perhaps I could come back and photograph your archive. In case anything goes missing in the future.'

'No, no, that won't be necessary.'

'I really do think it's a good idea Mrs Wilson,' Zena interjected.

'No absolutely not. George can do it.'

'George?' Zena had not heard mention of George before.

'My nephew. Now I know how bad my memory can get, he can deal with that side of things.'

'I see. Maybe you're right,' Zena said, not totally convinced. As she had not met George, she couldn't tell whether he was trustworthy.

'It's the best thing to do. After all, everything will go to him in the end.'

'I suppose if that's the case…Bert has been managing alone for a long time.'

'Poor Bert. He deserves a rest. I'll tell George the next time I see him.'

Zena left the house that evening not fully satisfied. The job was done. But would Mrs Wilson remember to tell George? How hard it must be to lose one's memory. Zena couldn't imagine it ever happening to her. A mind as sharp as hers would never dull.

14

SYD'S SCARE AND ZENA'S SURPRISE

September 1951. The year had skipped by. Zena could hardly recall the number of cases she'd been on, injunctions served and court appearances made. One of the judges would even comment on her style and the hats she wore. Life was a whirl. Thank goodness she had the calm of the back room, her needlework and knitting to take her mind away from the trials of work.

Zena was knitting quietly when Marion came in from work in tears. She was working as a junior clerk at Liverpool University's finance department and hated it. Most nights she came in tight-lipped and silent. As soon as the family had eaten supper, she would go straight to bed. A bad sign. Zena didn't want Marion being bullied as she herself had been by Croft. Better to leave. And leave soon. Marion finally confessed to Zena that she might have found a way out.

'Joan told me about it. There is a job going for the both of us. Working for a mill owner as girl Fridays. Doing odd jobs, but it pays well.'

'It sounds great. What's the catch?'

'What will Mummy say? She won't like it.'

'She may not like it, Marion, but it's your life. If you have a chance of a new job you should try. Maybe we can persuade her. Tell me some more.'

'He's a millionaire. We'd have our own rooms. He has a mansion. He grows orchids.' Marion loved orchids.

'That might help. Where is it?'

'Wilmslow.'

'Oh dear. Listen I'll back you up with Mummy. You go for it.'

The following night, Marion came home, excited instead of upset. She had news. She'd been offered the job.

'But Mummy, Wilmslow is not that far. It's a couple of hours on the train. I can come home at weekends,' Marion pleaded.

'That's too far, Marion. You've never lived away from home before. You're 17, for goodness' sake. You're not of age. How do you know what this man is like, anyway?'

'He lives in a mansion with his wife. He's very wealthy. He owns a paper mill.'

'Where would you live?'

'We'd have live-in accommodation. Our own rooms. It's not as if I am going on my own. Joan is going to work there too.'

'How often would you come home?'

'I don't know until I start. Look, I'm going. You can't stop me.'

'I can, young lady. You're not of age. And, and…who's going to look after that dog of yours while you're gadding about with your millionaire?'

'I'll be working, not gadding about! Kim doesn't need much looking after. She'll be fine.'

'Mum, let her go. You know how unhappy she's been,' Zena said in solidarity.

'Stay out of this, Zena, it's nothing to do with you,' Madge shouted back at Zena. Her face was puce.

'What do you mean, nothing to do with me? She's my sister. She's crying every night she comes home. It's not right.'

As the row escalated, Syd intervened. A rare occurrence.

'Enough! Leave her be, Madge. Let the girl go. That university is destroying the poor girl. She deserves a chance at some happiness,' he said, looking at Madge with his no-nonsense stare. Madge stopped, and Nana, who had been snoozing in her wing-backed chair, piped up, 'What, what? Go? Go where? Who's going?' They all looked at Nana and burst out laughing. Even Madge.

*

It was Harry who found Syd slumped over his desk. With the autumn damp eating into their bones, Zena's father had caught a chill. The coughing had gone on for weeks and despite their pleadings, he would not go to the doctor. He refused to rest.

Rushing in from a case, Zena was distraught to find two ambulancemen carrying her father out of the Cook Street office on a stretcher. She went with him to the hospital, where she telephoned her mother. It was a chest infection that had led to pneumonia. He was on oxygen, and they stood around his bed watching him struggle to breathe, hoping that the antibiotics would work a miracle.

Christmas arrived and was a miserable affair. Syd was still in hospital. They trooped up to see him every day. Zena appreciated how the hospital had done their best to make it a bit more festive. She was glad that Syd enjoyed the attention. He was rarely fussed over. There was a tree, and the main meal was turkey with all the trimmings, which was more than was to be had at home. Madge wasn't in a Christmas mood, and Nana took to her bed. It didn't stop her insisting on 'a liddle bit of sherry' on Christmas morning. Her baby voice appeared whenever she wanted something. Zena felt she was always the one who had to get whatever it was that Nana demanded.

Zena went heavy hearted into the office. Taking over the business had been tough while her father was sick. The books were in a terrible state. Invoices hadn't been sent and there were bills not paid. Zena passed over the lion's share of the investigation work to Harry and Joe and started on the mountain of paperwork her father had been too ill to attend to.

*

Syd's recovery was slow, and his return to the office in the damp chill of February added to the deep rattle in his chest. An explosion of coughing brought everyone in the office to attention. Syd turned up the wireless.

'Listen,' he shouted.

The calm voice of John Reith filled the room.

'... we make the following announcement. His Majesty the King passed peacefully away at a few

minutes before 12.00. He whom we have loved as King has passed from our midst. We voice the grief of all the peoples of his Empire.'

He was fifty-six. Lung cancer. Zena thought of her father, but said nothing. They all stood around in shock. What was there to say?

Joe coughed back tears. 'He stayed put during the Blitz, you know. He was a good and decent man, broken by that bloody brother of his. It's unfair, is what it is. Unfair. Poor geezer. Now that slip of a girl has to take his place.'

In mourning like most of the country, they closed the office for the day as a mark of respect. Zena and Syd returned home, where Nana was in tears. This set Madge off, and Marion was trying to comfort everyone with copious quantities of sweet tea. They sat glued to the wireless. The BBC had shut down all radio broadcasts except for news announcements. Later that afternoon, Winston Churchill's deep boom echoed around the front room: *'We cannot at this moment do more than record the spontaneous expression of grief.'*

They listened to the reports of crowds gathering in the cold and rain outside Buckingham Palace. Diplomats from around the world arrived to sign a book of condolence. The nation was in shock.

Flags on St. George's Hall and the Liver Building stayed at half-mast. Life went on, but in sombre grey. Faces dulled. In the office, the usual ribald jokes and guffaws of laughter were silenced. Even Harry stayed respectful and quiet. Zena tidied up loose ends and wrote reports. They agreed to take no new cases until after the funeral on February

15th. Nothing else was appropriate. Zena buckled down to tedious jobs at the office. Joe was in mourning clothes and refused to tell a single joke.

The Astor showed the Pathé Newsreel of the King's funeral, and the cinema was packed. Along with the rest of the nation, Zena and her family were in tears at the sight of the coffin pulled on the gun carriage by dozens of sailors. The body of the King was flanked by ten thousand men-at-arms carrying their guns reversed. It was a solemn and sad journey to Paddington where the coffin left by train to St. George's Chapel at Windsor to be buried.

*

As the shock of the nation and Syd's health improved, Zena was surprised to hear a shout from her father's cubbyhole, which for once was not about a case.

'You've been taking on more and more cases, love, and you're getting pretty nifty at the old undercover work I must say. Those pigtails...' Syd chuckled at the memory. 'What do ye say, love? Fancy coming in with me as my partner? We'll do it all official, like.'

'What? Partner? Are you serious, Daddy? You've never mentioned this before.' Zena was too shocked to be delighted at the suggestion.

'I'm not getting any younger, or healthier. Maybe I'll want to retire at some point. It would be a shame to lose Scott's if I did.'

'But what about Harry, or Joe? Wouldn't they want to buy in as a partner?'

'That wide-boy Harry? He'll run the business into the

ground with his shenanigans. And Joe's nearly as old as me. No, I need young blood I can trust, and you're it, my girl.'

'Gosh! I'm flattered, Dad, I am. Honestly. But I'll need to talk to Dave first before I say yes,' Zena said, thrilled that her father trusted her enough to suggest it.

All that afternoon, Zena rehearsed what she might say to Dave. What would he think? Being a partner at Scott's would be a permanent commitment. And more responsibilities.

That night in the quiet of their back room, Zena delivered her carefully prepared speech.

'...and it'll give me more freedom. To decide my own cases. That would be good wouldn't it?' Zena finished with a rush, looking up at Dave as he stood by the fireplace.

'It'll be much more work, Zena. You're hardly here as it is,' Dave said, not looking at her. Zena couldn't judge his mood.

'I know, love, but it's a wonderful opportunity. And for Dad to offer it to me. How can I turn him down?'

'I know it's hard to refuse your father, but have you thought about what it means? For you? For us?'

'I have, love, I have. Please. I can't take it without your blessing.' Zena cupped Dave's face in her hands and looked into his eyes, smiling her most charming smile.

'Of course you have my blessing. When have I ever been able to refuse you anything?' Dave laughed, holding her hands out wide. He drew her towards him and clasped her hands behind his back.

The next morning, Zena rapped on the breakfast table. Startled eyes looked back at her.

'You might already know Dad has asked me to become a partner at Scott's. Dave and I talked about it, last night. Dad, I would like to accept.' Zena looked at her father. 'So long as there are no more inappropriate undercover roles.'

'Of course, love, I promise,' Syd said, scratching his chin.

Everyone clapped and cheered, even Madge.

'Tonight we'll have a celebration!' Zena said. 'Dad, you'll have to tell Joe and Harry. You can invite Joe and Iris, but not Harry. Mum, you can invite Stan and the other neighbours. Marion, you can help me with the canapés. Dave, you can get the drinks.' Zena was flushed with excitement, happy giving everyone their orders. It would be a celebration to remember.

*

Zena settled into her role as partner with ease. Harry and Joe were not as keen now that Zena officially instructed them on cases. Her teacher's stare got harder. They backed down.

Syd had recovered slowly from his bout of pneumonia, but Madge was not happy that he was going to the British Detectives Association annual meeting.

'You're still not well,' Madge insisted. Zena looked at her father, who she had to admit looked a little grey.

'I'll be fine. Don't fret. Anyway, Zena will be with me.' He looked across at Zena with pride in his eyes.

'I'll take care of him Mum, don't worry.'

Madge grumbled, knowing by now that nothing would persuade her husband otherwise.

'Do you think your mother would notice if I stayed on for the cricket?' Syd asked a few days later when they were planning their trip.

'You know the answer to that Dad,' Zena laughed back at him.

India was playing England at Lords less than a week after the annual British Detectives Association meeting in London.

It was the first time Zena's father had asked her to go with him to the annual meeting. She'd be there officially as his partner. She rolled that word around her brain for size. They set off from the house on a cloudless June morning, fresh with the scent of cut-and-come-again sweet peas. Syd was on good form as they boarded the train to Euston. He told jokes all the way down and had Zena either in stitches or wincing with embarrassment. Syd's laugh ricocheted off the walls of the dining car.

'Ssshh, Dad, everyone's looking,' Zena whispered. Syd carried on laughing, ignoring the stares and clicking tongues.

At Euston, given Syd's chest they got a taxi. A rare luxury in Syd's book. Driving through Russell Square on the way to their hotel, Zena wished Dave could see the hanging baskets resplendent outside the Russell Hotel. He would have loved the red trailing geraniums mixed with the purple and red fuchsias. His favourite flower.

They arrived outside the Waldorf as the theatregoers lined up to get into the Strand Theatre next door. It was *Kiss Me Kate*.

'Come on, Dad, it'll be fun! You like musicals.'

'Your mother wouldn't like it.'

'Oh, don't bother about Mum. She'd be upset if you had a whisky without her. Whatever you do will be wrong.'

'Maybe, but still, I don't like the idea of it. It doesn't seem fair.'

'Oh, you're no fun, Dad.'

'You'll have plenty of fun tomorrow night, my girl. There'll be dancing. You love dancing. No. Best to rest up tonight. Save your energies. You're going to need them.'

Despite her height, Zena felt small in the executive boardroom of the Waldorf next morning. An overpowering sense of maleness filled the meeting room. Forty plus men in suits, and not a scruffy mac among them. Zena always laughed at the screen image of a private detective, so different from reality. Scrubbed up ex-police or army, not one of them would have looked out of place in an office.

A plump figure came around the enormous oval polished mahogany table, and bore down on Zena with a glint in her eyes. Her cheerful cut-glass voice belied her fierce expression.

'Welcome, welcome, m'dear! You must be Syd Scott's gel? Super that there's another woman here. Gets a bit lonely in the old powder room, what? I'm Charlotte, by the way. Charlotte Stephens. Pleased to meet you.' A dimpled hand reached out to grasp Zena's own.

'Mrs Stephens? My goodness. It's such a pleasure to meet you. I had no idea you'd be here. I thought you'd retired.' Zena was overawed to meet the renowned Charlotte Stephens, founder of the London Detective Agency. The first woman in London to own a detective agency.

'Haw haw,' Charlotte Stephens brayed. 'Try keeping

me down, young lady. I can still show these young men a thing or two.'

'Of course, I didn't mean…'

'Don't worry, m'dear, I'm only joshing. I have another girl working with me. Means I can come to these meetings. Splendid.'

'Another woman detective working with you? That's wonderful. I'm the only female private detective in Liverpool. I wish there were more of us.'

'These young fellow-me-lads think they're the bee's knees, don't they? I tell you; we two women solve more cases in London than the men, you know. You keep at it, my girl. I hear your father made you a partner recently?'

'Yes, I'm still learning the ropes. My father's a good teacher, but he needs more help with the business side of things,' Zena said. 'He begged me to join him after the war.'

'Yes, yes, there were so many cases after the war. Blackmail was big here in London.'

'Not so much in Liverpool', Zena interjected.

'Mostly divorce?' Mrs Stephens asked. Zena nodded.

'All those women wanting divorces when the husbands came back. Women got a taste for freedom during the war,' Mrs Stephens continued.

'Exactly. Women did the men's work and more. But now…'

'Don't get me started on that. Women pushed back in their boxes to be good little housewives. Makes my blood boil,' Mrs Stephens said.

'Mine too. But tell me Mrs Stephens. How did you get started? There are so few women in our business. Yet don't you think we make great investigators?'

'Too right we do, my dear. Trixie, the girl who is my partner as I told you, is taking over now. My eyes, you know. Blind as a bat, I am. Trixie's absolutely super,' Mrs Stephens laughed.

'It's not easy being a woman in this game. Did you find that?'

'Not easy at all. You know, I didn't need to work. But I was an independent sort of a girl. Went off to Switzerland as a singer and got roped into counterespionage. Of course, I had to tell my dear papa that I was only going for singing lessons. And the rest, as they say, is history.' Her loud bray of a laugh turned heads in the rest of the room. Mrs Stephens couldn't give a hoot, and her eyes sparkled as brightly as her diamond earrings. She had done well for herself, as well as for women in the profession.

A bell rang, and the meeting was called to order. Forty-three men and two women sat around the massive mahogany table. Syd looked serious. Mrs Stephens and Zena sat together, already thick as thieves. The meeting, with motions on this and that, was enlivened by Mrs Stephens' rapid-fire asides and caustic wit.

The meeting over, and it was time for the banquet. Dressed in her sequinned ball gown, Zena made her way into the lofty elegance of the Palm Court. Arched floor-to-ceiling windows reflected the fragile flames from high-branched candelabra edging the tables. Wives and families also attended the banquet, and the room sparkled with sequins and gold. Dave rarely liked these kinds of occasions, and Zena was glad to be on the arm of her father. Dapper in dinner jacket and bow tie, Syd accompanied his daughter to their table, his face beaming with pride. Such seriousness, and such manners. It was a novel experience.

Raymond C. Schindler was the first American to be elected president of the British Detectives Association. He swaggered onto the stage to accept the honour from the outgoing president. He might have been well regarded by Scotland Yard and a legend for decades in New York, but Zena found him rather overblown in both size and manner. Puffed up with a sense of his own importance. He stood tall, legs astride behind the podium as he made what Zena had to admit was a very eloquent and funny acceptance speech.

He finished with a hint that he knew the identity of the real killer of Sir Harry Oakes; a multimillionaire and the richest man in the Bahamas. Zena remembered the case in the news in 1943 when he'd been bludgeoned to death. The controversy raged for years because of the involvement of the Duke of Windsor.

A buzz of alarm circled the room. Was it possible? Schindler had worked on the case, but could he really know the killer? Before there could be further speculation, six dinner-jacketed men marched onto the stage. Schindler had no chance to put down the glass of scotch in his hand before he was held aloft and bumped in time-honoured fashion. Six times he was thrown up into the air, before being set back down. He held up his glass of scotch still intact to a loud cheer.

Zena had learned the foxtrot with Dave for the occasion. He hadn't complained at the weeks of tea dances they had attended, and practice sessions in the back room at Ripon Road. Raymond Schindler singled her out. He signalled to the band. In an explosion of trumpets, Zena was swung around first to the left, then to the right. He pulled her towards him, and then pushed her away. Where to put her feet? This was no foxtrot. Then Ray, as he insisted she call him, grabbed Zena's waist and swung her around off her feet. The whole room had stopped dancing, and they all clapped and cheered as the final drum roll signalled the end of the dance.

'Now *that* was the lindy hop!' he said, as Zena collapsed, breathless, back at the dining table. Syd sat there laughing and coughing.

'Did you put him up to that, Dad?' Zena said.

It was marvellous. She loved the fun of it, and the dance had galvanised the rest of the guests to try something more than a sedate waltz. It was past two in the morning before Zena fell into bed, exhausted, but elated. That night she dreamed of Ray's moon-face looming into hers. He was wearing bottle-bottom glasses, like the dreadful man she had met in Paris last year. She woke with a start, heart pounding, and for a second forgot that she was in an hotel in London. She'd travelled so much recently. She dozed lightly after her dream. Where might the next job take her?

15

A CASE OF KIDNAP?

October 1952. The excitement of the British Detective's Association ball carried Zena forward through weeks of boredom, filing reports and serving papers. Summer had drifted into the snap of autumn. Zena loved this time of russets and gold. She loved less Harry's continual moaning about the lack of heating in the office. At least Joe for all his faults just got on with it and wore an extra scarf. Thankfully she had her cashmere shawl to keep her warm as she answered the door to a woman knocking on the glass door. It took a cup of tea and copious quantities of tissues before Zena discovered what the problem was.

'He took me lad away, Mrs Archer. Bold as brass, while the boy was playing outside. How dare he,' Mrs Atherton wept. Her careworn face looked older than her years.

'And how can I help, Mrs Atherton?' Zena replied, impatient to get to the point of the job and home before the light failed.

'I need you to get me lad back and serve papers on me fella. He's living with his ma.'

'You're divorced or separated?'

'Divorced. He's taken my boy but I'm the one with custody of my boys, not him.'

'The papers. Are they for a custody hearing?'

'No, no. They're to enforce the custody. I've got custody. I told you.'

'So you did, so you did. I apologise.'

'It's OK Mrs Archer. It's just he's no right to take him. I just want my boy back. Bring me lad back to me. Please.' She started crying again, and Zena handed her more tissues and suggested she wash her face before leaving. The poor woman looked dreadful. Her face was smeared with lipstick, and mascara dripped clown-like down her lined cheeks.

'Don't worry, Mrs Atherton. We'll get your boy back very soon, I promise. I'll keep you updated,' Zena said, as she ushered the woman out of the office.

Zena went to Broudie's solicitors to collect the papers for the Atherton case. She didn't think much of Broudie. Greasy hair and thin lips. No doubt he was cheap. The enforcement papers appeared in order, and that evening Zena walked round to the address in St Andrew's Gardens that Mrs Atherton had given her. It was one of the tenement apartments built in the 1930s to replace the slums. Well-built and large. A little like the square-jawed woman who opened the door to Zena. She peered through the crack of the door, the chain still on.

'I'm here to see Mr Atherton,' Zena said. The woman hesitated and was about to shut the door.

'Look, if I don't see him, he'll be in serious trouble,' Zena continued.

'Who sent you?'

'Look, if I don't talk to him, the police will come round.'

'Are you from the welfare?' The woman narrowed her eyes and wiped her hands on her creased apron.

'No. I'm not, I promise. I'm a private investigator.'

'I suppose you'd better come in then.' The woman took off the chain and held open the door, showing Zena into the crowded front room.

'That's him,' she said pointing at a large dark-haired man with a square jaw, watching the wooden television set which blared out in the far corner.

Zena had never seen so many people crowded around one tiny screen. There must have been about fourteen of them, adults and children, watching Billy Bunter snoring at the back of the class. They were all roaring with laughter, and Zena had to shout to make herself heard.

'Mr Atherton, you have been served,' she said, handing him the papers. 'You do understand, don't you, that you have to appear in court on Monday?'

'I didn't kidnap him, missus. Honest!' he said. 'Turn that racket down,' he shouted. He had gone as white as a sheet. Sweat leaked from his face forming rivulets in the folds of his neck. No one took the slightest notice, and they continued pointing and screaming with laughter at Billy Bunter's antics.

'I happened to see him, and he came with me.'

'That's not what it says in the summons, Mr Atherton,' Zena said.

'It's true, missus. I swear on my Jimmy's life. He ran to me. I didn't go after him. I was going to bring him back to his ma, but he loved it here, so I told him he could stay.'

'You know your wife is frantic with worry?'

'Yeah, but she don't know what it's like not to see my boy, and she'll only let me see him when it suits her.'

Zena could see Atherton was getting agitated about his ex-wife, and his lack of access to his children. She had an idea.

'Look, Mr Atherton, I can see how difficult it is for you,' she said. 'If you like, I can take Jimmy back to your wife now, and there'll be no need for you to go to court.' He looked doubtful.

'It will save you a lot of trouble,' she added.

Without taking his eyes off the television screen, a small, tousle-headed boy of about six called out, 'I want to go home to me mam.'

Mr Atherton looked relieved. 'This nice lady'll take you back to your mam. Will you go with the nice lady?'

The boy nodded, his eyes still glued to Billy Bunter. He held out his little arms, so they could put his coat on. His grandmother stuffed his pyjamas and toothbrush in a paper bag.

'He's a good lad,' she said, with tears in her eyes.

'Tarra, son,' said the father.

'Tarra, Dad,' said the boy, putting his hand in Zena's as they walked out of the noisy, crowded apartment.

When they arrived back at his mother's house, Jimmy barely acknowledged his mother's embrace. He ran straight into the front room and sat down in front of the television next to his brother, who was watching of all things, Billy Bunter.

*

'Slow down!' Zena said the next day to the group of apple-cheeked lads charging down Cook Street. They laughed and kicked their heels in the air, daring her to stop them. It was hard for her to be cross with them for long; their excitement was too infectious. For once the lift was working and she emerged with a clang into the hallway of the third floor. A large brown envelope was pushed halfway through a letter box outside Kenner's door. She stared at it. The envelope was addressed to John Kenner, but Zena was surprised to recognise the handwriting as her father's. Shaking her head in wonderment, she stuffed the letter into the box, and opened the glass panelled door into Scott's and bedlam.

Harry was shouting at Joe, and Syd was shouting at Harry. Amidst the mayhem a tall, thin-lipped, well-dressed woman, sat head high, waiting for Zena. Apologising for the noise, Zena glared at all three men, who fell silent, one by one. Harry and Joe went back to their desks, and Syd retreated to his cubby-hole. The strike of a match the sole sound.

'How can I help you, Mrs...?' Zena asked, pleased at her sudden authority.

'Fletcher. Mrs Audrey Fletcher. I need a witness to my husband's threats so that I can get a divorce on the grounds of cruelty.'

'I'm sorry to hear that Mrs Fletcher. How do you suggest we witness these threats?'

'I can have a microphone put in. You can be in another room, listening to everything that is said.'

'That is not how we do things, Mrs Fletcher.'

'Can't you make an exception? He's left me nothing! One mattress, one chair, one plate. Can you imagine?'

'No I can't Mrs Fletcher. It must be awfully hard for you.' Zena felt genuinely sorry for the woman. Dave was the kindest and gentlest of men. She couldn't imagine the ignominy and humiliation of being bullied.

'And he beats me. Threatens me. Every Sunday. He comes round the house and if I don't give in...Well, you know what I mean?' Her voice wobbled, and a lone tear brimmed at the corner of her eye.

Zena softened. 'Perhaps just this once.'

On the following Sunday Zena arrived at the house long before the husband was expected. It was an old barn of a place, bare of furniture. It was true that the husband had left his wife with nothing. Mrs Fletcher showed Zena the ground floor room where the microphone was located inside the shade of a tall standard lamp, next to the lone armchair facing the fire.

'I had my neighbour wire it up,' she explained. 'It's very clever. Bill's so angry when he comes, he'll never notice anything. He'll think the wire is from the lamp. Come on upstairs, and I'll show you where you can listen.' She led Zena into another bare room. Headphones of the type used for an old crystal radio lay on the floor. The wire came up through the corner ceiling of the room below, but the neighbour had been more than economical with his wiring. To put on the headphones, Zena had to lie down on the floor. It was bitter, and no heating.

'Oh, my goodness, it's so cold in here. I may not last long,' Zena's teeth chattered as she spoke.

'I've an idea!' Mrs Fletcher said.

'Are you sure this is the best way to catch him? I'll come up with a better idea I'm sure,' Zena said.

'No, you're here now. Come with me.' Mrs Fletcher beckoned.

For days afterwards Zena chided herself for not refusing what came next. They dragged the mattress from Mrs Fletcher's bedroom into the room for Zena to lie on, and Mrs Fletcher found a spare blanket. Zena lay down, pulled the blanket around her, put on the headphones, and waited.

She heard Mrs Fletcher in the room below. Every so often she thought she heard a bang of a door slamming. Her heart would stop, and she would listen harder. Nothing. For hours. She lay there, shivering, uncomfortable and furious. She cursed the job, the woman and the husband.

*

The next week, Mrs Fletcher came back asking for more help. Zena nearly threw her out of the office.

'I found out he's bought a bungalow,' Mrs Fletcher said. 'He must have a woman in there. I need evidence of adultery. Please Mrs Archer. You have to help me.'

Zena's heart sank. It was the worst possible time. She couldn't lift her mood, and this daft case with Mrs Fletcher riled her. Harry could do it.

'Harry, I need you to do a job for me,' Zena called across to Harry, sitting at the desk across from her. Let that layabout do a bit of work.

'What does Syd say?'

'Never mind Syd. What he says is neither here nor there. I'm a partner in the business, and you'll follow my instruction, or you can look elsewhere for a job that pays you to sit around all day.' That shut him up.

Later that week, Harry came back with news that the husband visited the bungalow with a woman a few nights a week, and stayed for a few hours. There was still not enough evidence to prove the husband was committing adultery. They needed to be seen together in the act.

Now they had the measure of the couple's routine, the next time the husband and his girlfriend visited the bungalow, Zena called the wife. They both sat outside one evening, watching the house. It was as tedious as lying on the floor with headphones. But not as cold.

A light went on in a window at the left-hand side of the house. Then it went off again.

'They've got to be in bed together,' Mrs Fletcher said. 'We need to catch them at it.'

'I can't break into the place. I could be arrested,' Zena said. 'But of course, I can't stop *you* from breaking and entering.'

'I'll do anything. I want that divorce, and if I can catch him for adultery that'll do,' she said.

They crept up to the window, both holding torches. Mrs Fletcher shattered the glass with her torch and directed a sharp beam of light into the room. The couple were in bed together.

'That's my husband,' said Mrs Fletcher.

Now it was Zena's turn.

Through the broken window she said, 'I am acting for your wife, Mrs Audrey Fletcher, who is going to take divorce proceedings against you on the grounds of your alleged adultery.'

The wretched couple weren't listening. The girl sat bolt upright up in bed and screamed, 'Burglars!'

'Go away, or we'll call the police,' the husband shouted, as he scrambled out of bed.

They were both stark naked.

'Phillip!' Mrs Fletcher shouted. 'You've been caught in the act and I'm getting my bloody divorce now, and there's nothing you can do about it. You dirty old beggar.'

The husband blanched. At last he grasped what was going on. He leapt back into the bed, covering himself and the girlfriend.

'Go on then, you miserable old trout. I'll be glad to be rid of you. But don't think you're getting anything out of it. I'll take the lot, you'll see. I'll see you homeless,' he shouted, peering over the sheets, pushing his girlfriend down.

'You try! I'll take you for every penny. You won't get away with it,' Audrey Fletcher screamed back at him through the window.

The slanging match was set to continue, until Zena whispered in Audrey's ear, 'The court won't take kindly to you threatening him. You need to stay calm. Use the evidence to protect you. We'll get him, and see you right, don't worry.'

Some weeks later Zena appeared in court to give evidence against Phillip Fletcher.

'Mrs Archer. Looking as glamourous as ever I see.' Judge Ormerod smiled down at Zena. Zena always made the effort for court.

'Thank you m'lud,' Zena said before she swore the oath and gave the evidence that Audrey Fletcher needed to get her divorce.

*

Before Christmas sped into sight, Zena and Dave escaped to the Lake District to stay at the Crown and Mitre. It had become a home from home and Mrs Erwin the landlady greeted them like family. It was with a heavy heart that Zena went home to the ire of her mother and demands of her grandmother. Even her father was in a foul mood.

'What's wrong Dad? You're like a bear with a sore head these days.'

'It's these blasted no-goods.'

'What no-goods?'

'They're coming into our profession Zena and I don't like it. I don't like it one bit.'

'I still don't understand Dad. How are they getting clients if they're so bad?'

'They sell information given by one client to the very party they have been employed to shadow or bring to justice. In other words, they take a double rake off.'

'But surely that's illegal?' Zena was shocked.

'As it's all confidential, they just get away with it. That's their protection.'

'You mean no one will come forward to the police because they're worried their secrets will be aired. I see. We should do something about it.'

'I've got an idea, but I need the backing of the Association. I'm writing to them today and at the next meeting we'll confirm it.'

'Tell me. What's the idea?' Zena was intrigued.

'Hundreds of people since the war have been victims. If we invite them to send us details of how they've been defrauded we can treat every case with complete secrecy.'

'But how can we persuade people? They won't want to pay up again.'

'This will be the tricky bit to get past the Association. We should do it for free. For the good of the profession.'

'Good luck persuading them Dad. It won't be easy.'

'Maybe not. But I'll give it a go. These con artists can't be allowed to get away with it.'

*

Winter crept up dark and cold leaving the light behind. Zena hated this time of year. Even the increased responsibility as a partner palled. For once she wasn't looking forward to the meeting of the British Detectives Association in London. Syd's poor health stopped him from attending the winter meeting and Zena was tasked with defending her father's proposal to offer a free service for victims of fraudulent P.I.s.

'All aboard.' The slam of doors and a heavy chug signalled the train was about to move. The guard's whistle screamed in Zena's ear as she ran pell mell along the platform. Early mornings. She hated them.

'Get a move on, love, you can make it,' the guard said. He opened a door and Zena hauled herself into the corridor with gratitude.

'Thank you, thank you.' She waved back at the guard before clouds of steam enveloped him and he disappeared. Composing herself, she walked down the corridor to find a seat. The train was full, but at last she squeezed into a compartment, next to a brawny man with fat thighs.

She emerged off the train into Euston station. It was

heaving as usual, but there was something in the air that caught at Zena's throat. Gas or smoke? Could the station be on fire? Everyone appeared calm. Unlikely to be a fire then. As she headed for the exit, the thick, heavy smell got worse. Outside on Euston Road, the dense air had turned the sky black. Yet it was only mid-morning. Zena could scarcely see two feet in front of her. She jumped as a voice shouted in her ear.

'*Evening Standard*. Londoners dying. Worse peasouper in history. *Evening Standard*. Londoners dying. *Evening Standard*. Read all about it.' The boy's voice echoed as he disappeared into the smog behind her. She had barely walked a few yards.

Zena stared as people stumbled, arms linked for safety. A police officer wearing a white mask, carried a flare as a small crowd of people trailed in a line behind him, each clutching at the person in front. He edged down the Euston Road towards King's Cross.

'Excuse me, officer, I've just arrived from Liverpool. What's going on?' Zena said.

'It's been like this since Friday, miss. It's the smog. They say it's already killed hundreds of people. Where are you going to, miss, if I may ask?'

'I've got to get to Earl's Court. I was hoping to get a bus. I'm not a fan of the underground.'

'No buses running since Friday, miss. It's the underground or nothing. You can't walk far in this. My advice, miss, would be to go back to Liverpool.'

Within seconds the policeman and the line of stragglers had vanished.

Turning on her heel, Zena inched her way back into

the station, and headed for the underground. She couldn't let her father down. She had to attend the meeting. With one change at Edgware Road, the journey underground was far easier than the few minutes she had spent outside Euston. With luck it would be clearer at Earl's Court. The meeting was somewhere on Bolton Gardens, a ten minute walk from the tube station.

If anything, the smog was worse than at Euston. As Zena emerged from the Warwick Road exit, she was spooked by the smothered silence. She couldn't see a single soul. The street lamps had been turned on earlier but made no impression on the dark half-light. Zena was lost even before she started. It was hopeless. With no friendly policeman to light her way, it would be impossible to find her way to Bolton Gardens. Zena inched her way back along the wall to the tube station.

At least she could breathe again. At Euston throngs of people swirled onto the platforms out of London. The train from Euston to Liverpool Lime Street was packed as Zena struggled to find a seat. Everyone talked about the smog and what chaos it had wrought. It was a good thing her father wasn't with her. It would have played havoc with his chest.

'It was awful, Dad. I tried. I even went to Earl's Court. It was hopeless. Just to get out of the station was a nightmare. Let alone make it to Bolton Gardens,' Zena said, safe home in Ripon Road.

'I did wonder my love. It was even on the BBC lunchtime news.'

'It was all over the papers in London. Trying to find the meeting hall was nigh on impossible,' Zena said.

'It's the worst it's ever been. I'm just glad you got back safe and sound. Could have been much worse.'

'Yes it could. The Evening Standard said that hundreds have already died and they're expecting more. Think if you'd have come with me Dad. You know how bad your chest is these days.'

'It's not that bad. I'm fine. Never mind the meeting. It'll be all over by now. If anyone turned up.'

'Will they still vote on your proposal even if you weren't there?'

'Of course. The letter I sent to the members laid it all out very clearly and Ray Schindler is on our side. We'll just have to wait for the minutes.'

'Oh I hope it works Dad. All that work you've done.'

Her father had struggled for years on this. Zena was so proud of him. He commanded respect but never had the arrogance of some of the younger detectives like Charlie. Or Harry. She shuddered at their antics. Surely Syd should be recognised for what he had done. But how?

16

PRESIDENT SYDNEY J. SCOTT

December 1952. Marion came home for Christmas, full of news of her job with the eccentric orchid grower.

'It has a swimming pool?' Zena said, incredulous at such luxury. Even Madge was impressed.

'Yes, and tennis courts. And Mummy, you should see the greenhouses – they're heated and it has a vinery. Joan and I were allowed to play bowls on the bowling green on our day off.' Marion was breathless with excitement; unused as she was to being the centre of attention.

'And inside is as grand. There's a purpose-built ballroom with a sprung floor. Can you imagine Zena – it has a bandstand encircled with life size Wild West characters depicting Custer's last stand.'

'Sounds a bit over the top to me,' Zena said.

'Oh no, it's incredible, Zena. Beautiful. The ballroom is surrounded by a conservatory where he lets canaries fly free. There are enormous creepers climbing up the posts. And-' Marion stopped short, reddening in embarrassment. Zena nodded to encourage her.

'He has a bar upstairs with every imaginable kind of drink, and a mirrored floor.'

'A mirrored floor?' Madge said, horrified.

'Yes. Mirrored. He told Joan and I that we should walk on the floor only in trousers. If we wore a skirt, everything would be reflected.'

Zena laughed along with the rest of the family at the story, and Marion blushed.

Christmas was blighted by Syd's cough. It was painful for Zena to listen to him gasping for breath at night. He refused to call out the doctor, fearful of being dragged again to hospital over Christmas. Dave got him through with copious quantities of linctus, and Madge plied him with hot toddies. They had to wake him up to listen to the Queen's first Christmas message on the radio.

'Each Christmas at this time, my beloved father broadcast a message to his people in all parts of the world. To-day I am doing this to you, who are now my people. As he used to do, I am speaking to you from my own home, where I am spending Christmas with my family; and let me say at once how I hope that your children are enjoying themselves as much as mine are on a day which is especially the children's festival, kept in honour of the Child born at Bethlehem nearly two thousand years ago.'

They listened with quiet attention, until the end of the speech and her blessings to the nation, *'May God bless and guide you all through the coming year.'*

'Poor girl, taking on such a task after the death of her father,' Syd said, speaking for them all.

*

Zena couldn't have been prouder. Syd had been elected the first president of the Association of British Detectives. It was March 1953 and the British Detectives Association and the Federation of British Detectives had merged to become a new Association. Syd's proposal to rid the profession of fraudsters had been met with unanimous approval. This was his reward.

Zena felt hopeful of good times ahead. Her father's cough had abated, and he had high ideals for what he wanted to achieve during his year as President.

'What do you think to this one, Zena, love?' As the train steamed towards Euston, Syd read out the aims of the new Association. Zena had already helped him re-word some of them. They had to be presented to the Executive Council for endorsement.

'To maintain a high standard of detective methods, to guard the public against imposition and fraud, and by our example, make it an honourable profession; to assist and to act in conformity with the law.' Her father looked at Zena for confirmation.

'It's great, Dad, but don't you think we should add something about maintaining moral standards?'

Zena looked at the rest of the wording and jotted down a few notes.

'How about this? "To maintain a high standard of detective methods, to guard the public against imposition and fraud and by our example, make it an honourable profession; to assist and to act in conformity with the law and to preserve a strict code of professional morality." Would that work?'

'Perfect,' he said copying it down into his own notebook. He still used the flip-over black notebooks from his Flying Squad days.

They arrived in London to a drear grey pall. The Waldorf, however, was as glorious as ever. The chandeliers in the grand entrance hall brightened the gloom.

Zena had been looking forward to meeting Charlotte Stephens again. Her anecdotes the previous year were so enjoyable. But it was not to be. Zena was shocked to hear that the London agency had gone bankrupt. None of the members at the meeting knew what had happened. Mrs Stephens had come across as so successful. That was a lesson: never be complacent.

Syd was sworn in as president. It was a very formal occasion. Raymond Schindler asked Syd to stand. As he placed the president's medal around Syd's neck, he read: 'As the retiring president of the British Detectives Association, it gives me the greatest of pleasure to invest you with the emblem of your office as the first president of the Association of British Detectives. Your colleagues will be a constant reminder of the trust placed in you by them, to preserve the standards of the Association and to elevate our profession so that it may serve the best interests of the public in their particular difficulties and problems. Your position will require qualities of integrity, firmness and humility, but armed with the principles set out in our Memorandum and Articles, our Bye-Laws, our Code of Ethics and the support and encouragement of your fellow members. I trust you will have no cause to feel lonely in your high office and that you will be able to pass on this emblem to your successor with added lustre and significance.'

Everyone stood up and clapped. Syd's eyes misted, as did Zena's. His speech telling the crowd how he first became a private detective was entertaining, the crowd laughing at his jokes. She couldn't have been prouder.

'Being in the Met was all very well, but it was hard graft, and I'd already been injured several times.' Syd scratched the jemmy scar on his chin. 'I retired out of the Flying Squad for an easier life in insurance. Boy, was it dull.' A ripple of amusement went around the room. Syd continued, 'Anyway, one day I was on this train, and blow me, didn't the idiot who was sharing my compartment leave his briefcase. What to do? Being a nosy blighter, I checked inside the briefcase. It was full of important papers.'

Syd paused for effect. He continued.

'When I looked further, it turned out it belonged to a solicitor in Cook Street. As I was on my way to Manchester, I took a quick detour to Liverpool. The solicitor – I still remember his name to this day – Mr Slater. He said to me, "You've a knack for this. You'd make a good private detective, you know. Have you ever thought about it? I could put a bit of work your way." And the rest, as they say, is history. I took his advice, and here I am today. Proud to be called the first president of the Association of British Detectives.'

Syd sat down to thunderous applause and stamping of feet. There was no time to bask in glory, as immediately after the swearing in it was straight on to business. The rest of the meeting discussed methods to obtain official government recognition. Syd was furious that there were still so many charlatans pretending to be detectives, without licences. There was no law to stop them; any old Tom, Dick or Harry could set themselves up as a private detective. Zena mused that there was one Harry who she knew for sure was a charlatan.

Madge, Dave and Marion came down for the formal banquet that evening. It was such a special moment in Syd's career. Madge and Marion stuck to Zena like glue most of the night, as Syd was off being congratulated.

'I've not danced with you all night,' Zena grumbled as she whirled in a waltz with Dave. 'Mum is being impossible, and Marion is worse than a wallflower. Why do *I* have to baby sit them?'

'Because you're you, and your father would expect it of you.' Dave looked down at Zena, and she was lost. He was right.

'One, two, three!' They heard a shout, and looked around, to see Syd lifted high by a group of young men surrounding him. He wasn't keen on the time-honoured custom of the president being bumped by colleagues, but endured it, nonetheless. He was swung up high and dropped down again. Three times as it set off a dreadful coughing fit. They stopped, a shocked look on their faces and lifted him onto his feet. Spluttering, Syd said, 'That's one tradition I would like to see the back of during my term.' Everyone laughed and clapped him on the back.

The party continued into the small hours. At the end, when the last dancer had left, Dave and Zena fell exhausted into the feather bed of one of the Waldorf's finest rooms.

'Did you think Dad looked peaky?' she asked him the next morning. They breakfasted in their room, stealing more precious time alone before the journey home. Travelling with the whole family was never easy.

'That daft tradition didn't help him, for sure,' Dave replied. 'He'll be fine once he's home.'

Reassured, Zena bathed and dressed. It was too cold for the red shirtdress she'd brought. She'd hoped for warmer weather in London. She chose her navy wool dress, and jazzed it up with a lemon silk scarf, pearl-drop earrings and a pearl cluster brooch. There would be many goodbyes to the ABD colleagues, and Zena was anxious to impress. As the new president's business partner, she wanted to look the part.

Syd coughed all the way back to Liverpool. Dave had bought some more linctus at a chemist on the Strand. Madge was tetchy and unsympathetic.

'Get some air, Syd. Or at least give us some peace from your coughing,' she snapped.

Syd heaved himself up and left the compartment. Zena followed him and they headed for the dining car. She ordered him a hot toddy. Maybe that would perk him up.

'She doesn't mean it, love. She's a good sort really. She's gone through a lot over the years. You look after her,' he said. He looked tired and ill. Zena was worried, but she knew better than to suggest he see a doctor.

Syd was a little better after a weekend of bed rest. They all heaved a sigh of relief, thinking he was on the mend. Madge made copious quantities of chicken broth, and Syd made clucking noises every time she entered or left the room.

'Look, Dad. We're in the *Daily Post*!' Zena had bought

up all the local and national newspapers. Sometimes they covered the meetings. She was not disappointed.

'Listen, Dad. They mention you, and then me. ...*the retiring president was called away to pursue a new clue in a case he is trailing. His place was taken by Mr S. J. Scott, proprietor of a detective agency in Liverpool, who later was selected as the new president. Mr Scott, who was in the North West Mounted Police in the tough days from 1906-1912, and wears with pride a jemmy mark on his chin, is a great believer in Sherlock Holmes. "The greatest of them all," he said. "Any detective can learn a lot from the Holmes stories, even today." Partnered by his daughter Mrs Zena Archer, Mr Scott finds like most private sleuths that divorce investigation occupies about 55 per cent of his time, with the remainder distributed among inquiries on security, insurance and blackmail. "Do you," I asked eagerly, "ever use a magnifying glass?" "Of course," said this ex- Scotland Yard sergeant. "We often find it very useful."*

'Daft reporter. Why everyone is so obsessed with magnifying glasses is beyond me,' Syd coughed.

'It's just a bit of fun Dad. If it gets us known...'

*

Syd battled into the office on Monday, determined to help Zena interview the secretaries due to arrive that morning. Zena tried to persuade him that she could do it on her own, but he was having none of it.

'No, love. I want to make sure I can work with her too.'

'But it'll be me who is picking up the pieces after her. Look at the last one you hired.'

'I promise we won't get a scatterbrain like the last one. I know you can't manage it all on your own. I've agreed, but it is still my business,' he said, with that hard-edged stare that shut down conversation.

The first girl, Miss Downham, was a twenty-three-year-old disaster. She giggled throughout the interview, crossing and uncrossing her legs. Syd had already lost his patience with her during the first question.

'Tell me Miss Downham, what made you apply for this job?'

Her reply, 'Me dad told me I had to come.'

'Can you type?'

'Nah, but I can learn.'

They settled on Mrs Noble, and when Zena rang to tell her she had got the job, she said, 'I'm made up.' She was to start the following week. In advance of her coming, Zena rearranged the office to make room. It was a tight squeeze. Joe and Harry had to share a desk. Zena took one of their desks. Syd was still in his cubbyhole behind the filing cabinets, and Mrs Noble would have Zena's old desk moved to the reception area facing the door. That way she could field cold callers as well as type reports and answer the phone.

'What do you think, Dad?' Zena was pleased with her handiwork, but her father wasn't forthcoming. The rattle in his chest had got worse, and he was finding it tough to stay at work. Even the interviewing had taken it out of him.

After some persuasion he agreed to stay home for the next few days, wheezing but still cracking jokes.

'The best one, Zena love, was one day the other week,

when I was in court. The judge says to me, "Are you an enquiry agent, Mr Scott?" "No, m'lud," I says. "What are you then?" he says. "A private investigator, m'lud," says I.

'The judge comes back, quick as a whip. "What's the difference?"

"Two guineas per day, my lord," I said, and winked at him.'

Syd sank back into his pillows, exhausted by his own laughter. Zena laughed with him and kissed his forehead.

'Good one, Dad. See you later. I'm off to do that observation on Mr Hinkley.' She smiled back at him and threw a little wave behind her as she left.

17

DECISIONS

March 1953. Zena arrived back from Birkenhead Market late Saturday afternoon. She'd stopped on her way back from Mr Hinkley's and bought some pretty Pat Albeck grapevine fabric. It would make a perfect summer dress. She was delighted. Until she saw the ambulance. Zena flew into the house. Her mother was in the kitchen, wiping her hands over and over again on her apron. Tears flooded her eyes when she saw Zena.

'It's pneumonia. Worse than ever. He's unconscious, Zena. They want to take him to hospital, but they fear the worst. He'd want to be here though. I don't know what to do,' she cried.

'Maybe they can help him, Mum,' Zena said, starting to cry herself. 'Let them take him. Look, he's pulled through before and he will do again. Come on, Mum, he wouldn't want to see us like this. Let's go.'

Zena wasn't sure of her own words, but she had to keep her mother's spirits up. Maybe they could work miracles for a second time. Madge went in the ambulance with Syd to the hospital, and Zena followed in the car.

Zena parked in the old workhouse courtyard,

which was now the hospital car park. She sat in the car summoning up the courage to face what was coming next.

Syd had already been taken to Mersey Ward. It was a converted military hut used during the war, and now part of the new cancer unit. Zena was terrified; did her father have cancer? No one had mentioned it before.

'Mum, what's going on?' Tears streamed down Zena's cheeks, and she was panicking. Her beloved father had pulled through pneumonia, but could he fight cancer? He was so weak.

'Mum! What has the doctor said? Mum!' Zena stood in front of her mother, but Madge stared back, her eyes blank. Frozen. Zena felt like slapping her mother out of it. She stopped, hearing her father's voice in her ear, 'You look after her.' Her father lay in the metal-framed bed, grey and sunken. His cheeks were hollowed, and the waxen look of death shrouded his face. Zena swung around – searching for a doctor – anyone who could make her beloved father come to life.

'Zena, Zena. Stop. Stop now. He's gone. Stop,' Madge said, broken from her silence. 'Come here.' In a gesture of uncharacteristic warmth, she held out her hand.

'I didn't get to say goodbye,' Zena sobbed.

'We none of us did, love. It was all over before we knew it,' Madge said.

A doctor appeared.

'We think it might have been lung cancer, but without an autopsy, we will never know,' the doctor explained.

'Never. He wouldn't have wanted that. He hates being messed with. Hated…' Madge's voice trailed as she realised her mistake.

They drove home. Their thoughts echoed in the silence. Only nine days after drinking champagne and toasting his presidency, Zena's darling father was dead.

*

Even the birds stayed silent. It was as if the world knew of their loss. Dishes of junket, hot pot, shepherd's pie, arrived as if by magic. Were left and never eaten. Neighbours and friends were a rotating queue, all demanding attention. Marion, home from Wilmslow, retreated upstairs, away from the sympathy kisses. Zena wished she could do the same. She and her mother agonised over funeral arrangements and the obituary notice. They settled on: *Scott – Sydney, J., March 14, 1953. Died peacefully aged 65. Beloved husband of Madge, and a much-loved father to Zena and Marion. Funeral service and cremation at Landican Crematorium chapel on Thursday 19th March at 1pm. All enquiries to Kepple and Townsend, Funeral Directors, Wallasey.*

It appeared in the *Liverpool Echo* and the *Evening Standard*. A dozen of Syd's old colleagues from the Met came up the day before the funeral. Detective Sergeant Collins, grizzled and handsome in his uniform, called at the house to see Madge. Zena held onto her mother's hand all the while. It was rare that Madge would allow herself to be touched.

'We are sorry for your loss, Mrs Scott. Syd was a great bloke. One of the best. He never let us down.'

'You're very kind, D.S. Collins,' Madge said wiping her eyes.

'No not at all. He was the best, old Syd.'

'He often talked about you, you know. He missed you all.'

'Really? We thought he'd forgotten us up here.'

'No, no never. He always says the detectives he hires nowadays are not a patch on you lads. Oh no, oh I mean hired. I keep forgetting. I keep expecting him to come through the door at any minute.'

'Don't worry, Mrs Scott. It's hard on all of us. Syd was such a card.'

'He was wasn't he? Everyone loved him.'

'We were wondering, the lads and me. Would it… would it be ok to pay tribute to him? At the funeral?'

'How do you mean?' Zena interjected, worried that the carefully prepared plans might go awry.

'A dozen of the lads could stand at arms as the coffin goes past. And maybe some of us could help carry the coffin if you would allow us?'

Madge looked at Zena, who nodded. It was agreed that three of them, along with Dave, Joe, and Syd's brother John, would carry the coffin.

*

It was the day of the funeral, and tensions were running high.

'The hearse is here and there's not enough room in the mourners' car for Nana,' shouted Madge.

'Joe shouldn't be in there,' Zena said.

'I can't very well turf him out now, and anyway, Joe's carrying the coffin with John and Dave. He deserves a place. He was your Daddy's best friend.'

A small voice from the kitchen called out, 'Nana can take my place.' Marion had been weeping all morning. It had hit her hard, not being there when he died. Madge had put her on preparing the funeral tea to distract her.

'Are you sure, Marion?' Zena said. 'Don't you want to say goodbye to Daddy?'

'I'm sure. I'll finish up here. I'm better on my own anyway, and Nana won't want to miss out,' Marion replied, sniffing into her handkerchief.

They followed the hearse through Wallasey Village in the slow tradition. The top-hatted and tail-coated funeral director walked in front of the hearse with his cane. Passers-by stopped, lowered their heads, and took off their hats out of respect. In the back of the mourners' car, Madge stared blankly out of the window. Dave squeezed Zena's hand. Once out of the village, the hearse increased its speed and within twenty minutes they were at the Landican Crematorium in Arrowe Park. Such an enormous place. Bleak.

A dozen policemen's whistles piped long and hard as Syd's coffin was carried from the hearse into the chapel. His uniformed colleagues stood to attention and saluted him as he passed. The simple service in the crematorium chapel lasted half an hour. Thirty minutes for a lifetime. It didn't seem fair. Syd was not religious, so there was very little of that. John read the eulogy, and made everyone laugh with anecdotes of Syd as a boy. D.S. Collins regaled the congregation with stories of Syd's exploits in the Flying Squad.

'I recall one occasion when I was a young constable,' he said. Zena's heart sank. She thought he was going to read it as if he was in court.

'Syd was my guv'nor,' he continued. 'We were chasing a stolen car at seventy miles an hour through West London. We heard a screech and blow me, the thieves had slammed on the brakes and leapt from the car. Road works. "Come on, fella-me-lad, after them," said Syd. As you all know, he was never too fast on his pins. Between us we managed to catch three out of the four of them. But it's like fishing. There's always one that'll get away.'

It was not such a bad speech after all, Zena had to admit.

They sang a final hymn, *Abide with me*, which Syd had always liked. That set Madge off, and she sobbed as the coffin disappeared behind the deep red velvet curtain. It was all over.

*

Marion had done the family proud. Everything they needed was there: finger sandwiches, sausage rolls, scones and cakes, all presented on the best china. She was nowhere to be seen, and Zena found her upstairs on her bed, exhausted and still crying.

'Come on, love.' Zena handed her a dry handkerchief and patted her hand. 'Time for the toast. You can't miss that.' She stood by as Marion wiped her face and followed Zena downstairs.

Madge pushed Zena to do the toast. 'I can't do it, Zena, and you haven't said anything yet. Your father would expect it. You'll be taking over now.'

Zena looked on unsure what to say as Dave handed out the sherry, measured in his meticulous way. Ever the chemist.

'Ladies and gentlemen. Please be upstanding.' Those Association dinners had taught Zena well. 'What to say about my father,' Zena started, but her throat tightened, shutting her down. 'I'm sorry...sorry...I can't...Sorry I meant to say, in honour of a wonderful husband, father, brother and friend, please raise your glasses. To Sydney Scott. You will be very much missed.' Zena raised her glass with a sense of dread, not just for her own loss, but with foreboding at what was to come.

*

As if their own grief wasn't enough that month, less than a week later the whole nation was in mourning. Queen Mary died on the 24th of March, and all the anguish over Syd's death came flooding back to Zena and the household. Marion had returned to Wilmslow. Lucky escape. Her mother and Nana were at constant loggerheads. Nana would flounce off and take to her bed at any opportunity. Dave and Zena retreated to their back room, he to work on his books, and she to her needlework. Zena had no heart to go to the office and face the gap where her father's bulk had been. It was too much for her. She even missed his cough.

The telephone rang. The smell of cigarette smoke hit Zena as she answered it in the hallway. It was as if her father was standing over her, listening. Must be his coat. Madge had left all his things as though he had left for the office. Zena shook herself and listened to Joe's panicked voice shouting down the telephone.

'Zena! You have to come in. The place is falling apart.

273

Harry's hardly here and Mrs Noble doesn't know what to say to potential clients. Are we open for business or not?'

'I can't talk now, Joe, it's a bad time. I'll call you later,' Zena said, putting the telephone back on its cradle.

Syd had left Zena the business in his will, with her mother as a sleeping partner. Did she even want the business? Maybe she'd be better off selling stockings, or asking MJ if she could model at the fashion house. Syd had been a fabulous detective, but his accounting skills were atrocious. The business was in a mess. It would take a lot of sorting, and Zena wasn't sure she had the energy for investigating without her father's guidance. She needed time to think.

The next day was a mad March hare kind of a day as the wind whipped around Ripon Road. Zena had slept badly. She fretted and worried over Joe's plea. If she decided to sell the business everything had to be in order. She would sort it all out and then see how she felt. It was a relief to have a plan.

Walking through the office door that afternoon was like walking into Bedlam. The noise stopped Zena from thinking about her father. Joe and Harry were at the point of fisticuffs, shouting and roaring at each other, and diminutive Mrs Noble was dancing around them, trying but failing to intervene. It was rather comical, and Zena fought back a laugh. She was now the boss.

'What an earth is going on?' Zena said in a loud but calm voice. There was an immediate hush. They all tried to speak at once, and Zena held up her hand. Silence fell again, and they all looked at her in anticipation.

'Listen. I don't know what's going to happen with

the business, but until I decide, we must crack on and get things under control. That means Joe and Harry, you must work together without fighting. Mrs Noble, it means that we are still open for business. Please state that clearly when any clients telephone in future.'

'Yes, Mrs Archer,' said Mrs Noble. She moved to her desk and started sorting out the reports to type.

*

'First of all, I would like the filing cabinets moved,' Zena said, pointing at Harry and Joe. She didn't want to take her father's cubbyhole. That was his place. She would have a desk at right angles to the far end arched window, overlooking Cook Street. That way she could both look out of the window and see what was going on in the office. It might also help to keep some order between Harry and Joe.

Zena started on the accounts. If she was to sell, they needed to be straightened. Mrs Noble brought her a cup of tea, and a slip of paper with a request to return the call of a client. The man had refused to give his name to Mrs Noble and said he would only speak to Mrs Archer. Very mysterious.

'Oh, Mrs Archer, thank goodness you've called. It's a matter of life and death, and I mean that in the most literal sense of the word. Can I come and see you in person? It is most urgent. It's not a matter for the telephone.' The voice on the other end of the phone sounded professional. Zena was intrigued. It was arranged that he would come to the office at 11 am the following day.

The voice nagged at Zena during the evening. She had heard it before, but couldn't place it. Her mother's chatter was background noise to Zena's internal conversation, and she ignored it. She was too anxious to discover the identity of the mystery caller.

18

A CASE OF MANSLAUGHTER

April 1953. Dave opened the curtains to a pearly blue cloud-flecked sky. A hush lay over the garden. No wind. Bulbs had started to bloom. The weather would be kind for the Easter break. It was the first time Zena felt a glimmer of lightness since her father had died. She rose, still intrigued by the call of the previous day.

At 11 am sharp, a fine-looking silver haired man arrived at the office. He was dressed formally in a double-breasted dark blue pin-stripe suit, and maroon tie. Ah, that's who it was. Zena knew she had recognised the voice. It was Mr McKinnon, the barrister. She greeted him with genuine pleasure. He had been very kind to her during her court appearance in the House of Joseph case. He acknowledged or spoke to her each time he saw her in court. Few others of his standing did the same.

'I won't beat about the bush, Mrs Archer. I know your time is precious. I'm the barrister in a rather notorious murder case. You'll probably have read about it in the papers. My client Stanley Lister was charged with stabbing his brother-in-law Reginald Gibson to death.'

'Yes I saw it in the *Liverpool Echo*,' Zena replied.

'It's a dreadful case. The chap had beaten my client's sister. Badly. She ended up in hospital half dead,' McKinnon said, fiddling with his cufflinks. Zena noted the minute diamond set in chased gold. A man of rare taste.

'You remember Mr McKinnon that I said I would not get involved with murder cases.'

'Yes, I know, Mrs Archer, and under normal circumstances I wouldn't ask. But Stanley Lister will hang.' McKinnon paused for effect.

'Go on, Mr McKinnon.'

'He will hang, Mrs Archer, unless we find a witness who saw the whole thing.'

'You have a witness?'

'We know there is one, but we don't have her. The defence needs to prove that my client was defending his sister. I need you to trace this witness, Mrs Archer.'

'If I'm to take on the case, and I'm not promising, mind you, I need all the information you have on this witness.'

'That's why I've come to you. If anyone can find her, you can.'

'You have far too much faith in me Mr McKinnon,' Zena said. She was secretly flattered that he thought so highly of her.

'I have every confidence in you I assure you. We have so little to go on. Mrs Gibson, my client's sister has just come out of hospital.'

'Poor thing. She's gone through the mill.'

'She has, and to think that her brother might hang for defending her, is unbearable to her.'

'What does she remember?'

'Not much. All she could say was that the witness was wearing carpet slippers.'

'Carpet slippers? Is that all?'

'Yes that's it. I'll give you the address of where the attack took place. I know it's not much.'

His head dropped, and the defeated look on his face clinched it for Zena. She told him she would take the case, but couldn't promise a result. She would need a retainer. He agreed. Her father had often taken clients on trust, and when the result was not what the client wanted to hear, they sometimes refused to pay him. That had to change.

*

The next morning. Zena thought over her strategy to find the witness for Mr McKinnon's client. Obviously the first stop was to interview the defendant's sister, Mrs Gibson. Zena went the same afternoon. The court case was the following week.

'Oh, missus. Me fella Reg, he were a right batterer. He was always on the bevvie,' the woman said when Zena gently started questioning her. She painted a bleak picture of her abusive and drunken husband.

'Me brother Stan, he…' she hesitated.

'Sorry to interrupt, Mrs Gibson, but that's Stanley Lister, your brother?'

'Yes Stan, he…he was trying to get the beggar off me. He didn't mean to kill Reg. Mind you, I'm not sorry that Reg is dead.'

'It must have been awful Mrs Gibson.'

'It was. Stan was just trying to protect me. He's my big brother you see. He'd always protect me, even as a kid.'

'Tell me about the woman you saw before you blacked out. Can you remember anything about her? Anything at all. Even the smallest of details might help.'

'Saw her fat legs I did. As I were lying on the pavement. She had these horrid carpet slippers on her.'

Mrs Gibson started crying. After several bouts of questioning, Zena managed to get out of her that the witness was very overweight or suffered from severe oedema in her legs, that she wore no stockings, and her carpet slippers were red fur-lined numbers with a bobble on the top. Like those a child might wear.

Zena had no idea how she was to find this person, but determined not to be defeated, she set off down the street, knocking on doors. McKinnon had said the police had already done this, but Zena knew how people in this neighbourhood would react to any police enquiry. She recalled her Paris job, and the ruse she used to get people talking.

'Excuse me, I'm a journalist with the *Echo*, and I was enquiring as to whether you had anything to say about the Gibson murder?' Nosy neighbours loved talking to the papers. 'Did you see anything? Or know anyone who might have seen something?' Zena drew a blank. Everyone was delighted to give an opinion about the murder. How he should be 'strung up' or how his poor wife was 'well shot of him,' but nobody had spotted anything of use.

Zena was about to go home. She had covered all the houses in the street where the murder took place. She knocked on a few more doors in the next street. There was a newsagent on the corner; someone coming out of there might have seen something. The owner knew nothing, and was more interested in packing the leftover newspapers than talking to Zena. She started her door-knocking again. She would give it another half-hour. Her mother would be cross if she was late for dinner.

Bingo. The third house down from the newsagent was opened by a large woman in her early forties, dressed in a housecoat. Her long greasy hair was drawn back into a ponytail, and she wore no make-up or stockings. But she *was* wearing red fur-lined carpet slippers. It had to be her. Zena couldn't believe her luck. McKinnon would be delighted. It was not Zena's job to persuade this woman to give a statement, but just to find her. All that was needed was her address and description. And her name. After Zena had given her spiel about the *Echo*, the woman said she would be interested in telling her story. For a fee. Zena told her somebody would be in touch. McKinnon could deal with that.

Elated with her success, Zena was in a good mood driving home. She stopped off to buy carrots to go with the fish her mother was cooking for the Good Friday meal the following day. Everyone was on good form when she got home; Marion was back for a summer break, full of tales of her ever more eccentric, orchid-growing boss. Apparently he was so scared of being poisoned, that even though he and his wife ate at the most expensive restaurants, he would only eat egg and chips. Daft as a brush.

Zena telephoned McKinnon and apologised for calling so late in the evening, but he was grateful for her news. He said he would send someone round immediately. With luck he could persuade the woman to make a statement and appear in court.

*

The following week Zena was to appear in court on the Gibson murder case. The prosecution was calling her to explain how she had found the star witness. She arrived to a barrage of reporters gaggling around the door of No. 1 court. Zena ignored their jostling and thrust of microphones. McKinnon was waiting for her, and whisked her off to a bare interview room with two hard-backed wooden chairs the only furniture. He had briefed her over the phone on what to say, but he wanted to be sure she would not be swayed.

'Are you sure you know what to say, Mrs Archer? It's vital that you don't reveal how you lied to the witness about being a journalist. The prosecution will leap on that. It could destroy our case.' McKinnon's right eye twitched in a nervous tic. Zena was tempted to lift her hand and smooth it out.

Instead, she said, 'I have it all worked out Mr McKinnon. Don't fret.'

The court room was packed. Word had got around that the infamous Judge Morris was presiding. He was not known as the modern-day hanging judge for nothing. Four out of his previous five murder trials had resulted in the death sentence. It would be tough to convince both the jury and him that this was not murder.

For some reason he had always had a soft spot for Zena. As she stood in the witness box waiting to swear her oath, Judge Morris winked at her. 'Ah, Mrs Archer! As glamorous as ever, I see. Today's hat is very fetching.' Zena had dressed to look smart, not to impress. Her midnight-blue suit was set off by a royal blue cloche hat with tiny red poppies sewn into the rim.

'Thank you, your honour, that is very kind of you,' she replied. He was not a judge who would look favourably on a smart retort.

Zena read her statement as requested by Mr McKinnon, and was surprised when the prosecutor didn't look up and instead said, 'No questions, m'lud.' From what McKinnon had told her she was expecting a grilling from the prosecution. But no she was dismissed. Easy. She left the court room lighter than when she entered. She had done the best she could for the poor chap and his sister.

McKinnon phoned Zena the next week with the verdict. 'Stanley Lister got five years for manslaughter.' McKinnon was cock-a-hoop. 'Thank you, Mrs Archer. He was looking at the rope. That witness clinched it for us.' His rich, mellow voice warmed Zena. She felt she had done something worthwhile. Lister was not a bad man. He had defended his sister, and should not have to die for that.

19

MOVING ON

May 1953. A time of apple blossom and maypoles. And hope. Standing in the garden Zena drank in the rich pepper and honey smell of hawthorn blossom. April had been a washout, and the May warmth brought out the dappled fresh greens of trees and shrubs. It was one of her favourite times of the year, made even better by the fact that the family's first television set was about to arrive. Madge used some of the money Syd had left her in his will. They wouldn't have to crowd around the next-door neighbours' set with the rest of the street. The Queen's Coronation was to be televised on 2nd June, and the new television would arrive the week before. Madge was to hold a party as a memorial to Syd.

At the office on a Friday in mid-May Zena asked everyone to leave early.

'Take the afternoon off and enjoy your weekend,' she said. Joe and Harry didn't need telling twice and grabbing their coats whooped as they left for an afternoon pint. Mrs Noble however was more circumspect.

'Is anything wrong Mrs Archer?'

'No nothing wrong Mrs Noble. I just thought everyone deserved an afternoon off after the week we've had.'

'Well if you're sure there's nothing else you need from me?' Mrs Noble said.

'No nothing at all. Now you get on and enjoy your weekend,' Zena said as she handed Mrs Noble her coat and ushered her out of the office.

Zena watched Mrs Noble look back with a puzzled expression on her face. She smiled at her and waved goodbye. It was with a sigh of relief that she closed the door and looked at her watch. Five minutes. She sat at her desk, feet on the table and lit a cigarette. Bliss. A few minutes later a knock at the door heralded the person she had been waiting for.

*

A man not much older than Zena in his mid-thirties stepped into the office. Zena was uncharacteristically nervous as he approached – his hand stretched out.

'Mr Boult. Thank you for coming at such short notice,' Zena said shaking his hand.

'Please call me Frank. It's a pleasure Mrs Archer. It's not often such an interesting business is put up for sale.'

'As I told your father, Frank, I'm just exploring at this stage. This is confidential and I don't want anyone to know that I might be selling. Do you understand?'

'Perfectly Mrs Archer. At Boult, Son and Maples we pride ourselves in discretion.'

'Thank you Frank for the reassurance. Let me show you around.'

That night Zena was in a quandary.

'Dave, how can I tell her?' Zena asked.

'It's up to you, Zena. But I think your mother has a right to know.'

'I know, but she would be so upset that Daddy gave me this opportunity and I'm even considering selling it.'

'That's even more reason for her to know.'

'But there's no point upsetting her unnecessarily. You know what she's like. I'll tell her if I do decide to sell.'

'On your head be it if she finds out. You're the one who's always saying the truth will out.'

'She'll never know if you don't tell her.' Zena kissed him.

The following morning she went into the office to prepare for a new case. While she waited for her client, Frank Boult telephoned with the valuation of the business. He said the business was in a prime location, and there would be no problem selling it as a going concern. The sum he estimated was tempting. It would give Zena and Dave a chance to get a place of their own, and she could try her hand at dressmaking. Or modelling for MJ part-time. But what about her mother? Would she be OK on her own? Zena told Frank she would get back to him.

The new case was from the landlord of The Globe on Cases Street, who asked to meet Zena in person. Zena took an immediate dislike to him as he walked through the door. His slicked quiff reminded her of the spivs dealing in the black market during the war.

'Someone's stealing from me,' he said. 'I could probably find out myself who it is, but I'm too busy to keep an eye on everything. The pub's doing very well. Ever been to The Globe, Zena? I can call you Zena?' He leaned towards her in an over-familiar manner.

'Mrs Archer will do, thank you.'

'Oh. OK, *Mrs Archer*,' he said. He over-emphasised the *Mrs*.

'I've noticed the takings going down,' he went on. 'I'd like you to come into the pub and watch.'

'Watch how Mr Peabody? I can hardly pose as a customer now can I?'

'How about you come as a temporary barmaid? We can say my wife is going on holiday. I could do with her out of my hair anyway.'

'And why's that? Can't she keep watch for you?'

'Nah, she's useless that one.'

'I suspect that's not the case, but please go on.'

'I'm done. I'll expect you Monday. But one last thing. If you find that it's Nancy I don't want to know. She's the one that brings in the punters.'

Zena arrived at The Globe on Monday lunchtime. A few sad-faced Irishmen stared into their pints of Guinness. No conversation just the odd click of dominoes. Zena was able to get the lie of the land before the busy period when the dockers finished work at six. Nancy came in for the after-work rush, her pneumatic bosoms preceding her. No wonder the landlord didn't want to know if she was light-fingered; she would bring in far more than she stole. Zena could tell immediately that Nancy was not the thief. Syd's phrase came to her mind, 'as dim as a Toc-H lamp'. Nice girl, though: artless, and sweet with the customers. They all loved her. She wouldn't need to steal. She made enough in tips.

Ken the pot man looked the likelier candidate, a tall, whey-faced young man with unfortunate acne, who smelt as bad as he looked. His unwashed sock smell made Zena feel nauseous, and she said she would clear the tables to avoid him. She could watch the bar at the same time.

Several days later, Zena had discovered nothing. No money had gone missing and she was certain that neither of the two members of staff was stealing. The landlord's wife was still away. Could it possibly be her? But why would she steal from her own pub? Zena told the landlord she would come back as a customer when his wife was back behind the bar.

On Wednesday evening the following week, Zena brought Win with her as a cover, and they sat in the snug.

'Let's hope the wife comes in to serve us,' Zena said.

'Why? Do you really think it's the wife?'

'I can't see who else it can be.'

'Not the barmaid then?'

'No she's so dim, and besides she's making enough in tips. She doesn't need the money.'

'But the wife? Why would she steal from her own husband?'

'Don't forget your own situation. Cyril doesn't give *you* much housekeeping now does he?'

'True, but I wouldn't steal from him.'

'No but maybe you're not desperate enough. Look here she comes. Shhh.'

A downtrodden slip of a thing with a drooping mouth to match her cardigan, stepped into the snug. She was a complete contrast to the hail-fellow-well-met Mr Peabody.

'Please stay and have a drink with us,' Zena asked.

'Oh I'm not sure about that. My husband doesn't like me chatting too long with the customers.'

'Go on. He won't know. Just tell him you've been to the bathroom. We won't keep you long. We just want to know a bit more about this place is all,' Zena said, not wanting to scare off the poor woman before she'd had a chance to talk to her.

The wife came back with a tray of three drinks, Campari for Zena, gin and tonic for Win and a whisky for herself. Dust motes swirled in the lamplight as Zena sipped her drink and mulled over how to approach her. Honesty.

'I'm sorry Mrs Peabody, but I'm afraid we told you a bit of a fib just now. Your husband has employed us to find out why money has been going missing.'

The wife put her head in her hands and burst into tears. Zena was shocked; there was no need to say any more. They waited.

'Please don't say anything,' Mrs Peabody said. She sat up wiping her eyes. 'He never gives me any money.'

Zena looked across at Win with a raised eyebrow. See? They both nodded at Mrs Peabody sympathetically.

'He gives me a pittance for the housekeeping,' Mrs Peabody continued. 'Nothing for clothes, or for my hair. It's not like I treat myself with much, but sometimes if my stockings are laddered, or I need new underwear, I have no choice. He hits me if I ask for anything more.' She took a large gulp of whisky and looked down.

'It's OK Mrs Peabody. We'll sort it out with your husband. Don't worry.'

'Really? You can? Are you sure? Please don't tell him will you?' Mrs Peabody started to cry again. Retching sobs which were not just for fear of being caught.

'Please Mrs Peabody, it's OK. I promise. Your husband will not need to know a thing.'

The next day Zena presented the landlord with her report. Inconclusive.

'Sorry I wasn't able to discover who's stealing from you. Perhaps your calculations are incorrect?'

'What do you mean incorrect?' The landlord didn't like Zena's insinuation.

'I noticed that frequently during the evenings, when you had taken some drinks yourself, you gave out a lot of free drinks. Perhaps that's where things are going short?'

'But…but…it can't just be that. I don't believe you!' Mr Peabody blustered, but Zena didn't care. That poor wife of his deserved a bit of extra cash, and he was never going to give it to her. No pockets in a shroud she thought as she counted her blessings. Dave did not have a mean bone in his body.

There were positives to this job, Zena realised. Sometimes you could make a difference to people's lives. It made her think of her father with a mixture of sadness and pride over what he had achieved, and never would again.

*

Madge was frantic. It was June 2nd and the day of the party for the Queen's coronation.

'Get up, Zena. I need your help. Come on. Hurry up. Zena!' She had been shouting up the stairs since 6 am.

'I don't know what all the fuss is about. It will be repeated on television anyway,' Zena moaned to Dave, who was trying to keep the peace.

He had a day off from the shop and was on fine form. Unlike Zena, who had been up half the night trying to finish her blue silk dress. It had proved to be very fiddly.

Downstairs in the kitchen, Zena said, 'All right Mum. What do you need me to do? Can't Marion help?'

'No. She telephoned to say she's not coming back after all. She's still at that wretched place in Wilmslow.' Lucky Marion Zena thought.

Madge was in a panic. 'The neighbours are arriving at ten and I can't get the sponges to rise. You'll need to make some more. And scones. I need to get on with the sandwiches.'

Zena would have refused, but the gathering was to celebrate her father as well as the Queen. Her mother was at her worst when she was in a fluster. She had polished the television set to an inch of its life and put it on as soon as the broadcast started at 9.15 – just to make sure it was tuned correctly. It was only the test-card, but she stood there staring at the black and white lines and squares, as though the Queen would appear by magic.

When the bells rang to welcome the Queen to Westminster Abbey, even Zena was mesmerised. The close-up shot of the coronation dress made them all gasp. Richard Dimbleby, the BBC commentator, said that Norman Hartnell had designed the dress. Not a surprise after the wedding, but Zena had had a secret hope that the Queen would have given someone else the role. She wished that MJ could have been chosen. That was not to be, but Zena couldn't deny the beauty of the dress. Rich, bejewelled silk was adorned with hand-embroidered floral emblems of the countries of the Commonwealth. That pleased Dave, who recalled that India's national flower was the lotus.

They all knew the national flowers of the United Kingdom and shouted out the names: the Tudor rose of England, the Scottish thistle, the Welsh leek and the lucky shamrock for Northern Ireland.

'God Save the Queen!' shouted the gathering of friends and neighbours in the drawing room. They were all a bit tipsy; three hours of exclaiming over the spectacle had been accompanied by copious quantities of sherry for the ladies and beer for the men.

'And God save Sydney Scott!' Zena raised her glass and nodded for everyone to follow her. She was not going to let her beloved father be forgotten. He would have loved the sense of occasion and friendship. Zena missed him more than ever.

They took the sandwiches, scones and cake left from their own gathering to the street party in Ripon Road that same afternoon. Everyone in the street had crowded around the television sets of their neighbours before setting out trestle tables and chairs for the party. Zena had baked a three-tiered iced sponge the day before. She placed it in the centre of the red-checked tablecloths covering the trestles. Jelly and ice cream, blancmange, sandwiches and sausage rolls loaded the rest of the tables. The children played tig and Grandmother's Footsteps, while the adults talked of the dress, and how cute Prince Charles looked, peeping out from behind the Queen Mother. It was a miserable day weather-wise, cold and damp, but no one cared. Joy and celebration continued the day long.

The following day Zena felt deflated and depressed as she returned to Cook Street and Harry's beer-breath. He sat idle at his desk, reading the *Daily Mail*. Joe was nowhere to be seen. Mrs Noble diligent as ever was typing out invoices. The outfits of the guests at Westminster Abbey had made Zena hanker for more of the female camaraderie of MJs, or even L.J. Hart's. Did she have the energy to deal with the likes of Harry and Joe? Syd didn't have to put up with the constant battle with authority that Zena endured. Just because she was a woman.

Gazing down Cook Street, Zena stroked the cheese plant, its waxy creaminess comforting. It needed cutting back. It had grown into a monster since her first days at Scott's all those years ago. The June light flooded in, low and bright, scattering geometric shadows across her desk. She would miss this if she sold up.

A loud knock at the door jolted Zena awake, and Mrs Noble asked John Kenner, the solicitor from across the hall, to take a seat.

'How can I help, Mr Kenner?' Zena had never taken to John Kenner. There was a porcine arrogance to him that irritated her. Her father had always done his bidding and appeared somewhat in awe of him. Zena could never understand why.

'We were all sorry to hear about Syd, so I wanted to express my condolences,' he said, licking his lips. Liar. He never even came to the funeral.

'Thank you, Mr Kenner. That's very thoughtful of you. Is there anything else? I am rather busy.' She wasn't, but he needn't know.

'Your father used to help us with typing up letters

to clients. We don't have a full-time secretary, as you know.'

Zena knew very well. She'd been the one to type the letters. She recalled the envelope her father had stuffed in Kenner's letterbox.

'I was wondering if we could prevail on you to continue this service for us, as a neighbour, of course,' he continued with a knowing smile.

'Of course we can continue the service, Mr Kenner,' Zena said. 'For a fee. Shall we say half a crown a letter?'

Kenner's face turned puce and he looked like thunder. 'I might have known things would change when Mercenary Bloody Mary took over,' he exploded.

Zena waited until he had stormed out of the office before she burst into laughter.

'Did you hear what he called me, Mrs Noble? How wonderful. I shall enjoy using that nickname. Mercenary Bloody Mary. Dad was far too soft with him.'

'What arrogance,' Mrs Noble said in her gentle way. She looked down and carried on typing.

*

The jobs came in thick and fast. There was no let-up, and even less time for Zena to think about her next move. She resolved to be tough on Harry Jones, and he didn't like it.

'Why am I going out on this case again? Why can't Joe do it?'

'Because I said you should do it.'

He stared at Zena and sulked off, slamming the heavy glass door behind him. She sent him out on as many cases as she could to avoid dealing with his moody presence in the office. She was frustrated that she needed him. There was no time to train up another detective.

Kendrick and Associates phoned with an urgent case. The job was to serve divorce papers on Mr Thomas Evans when he appeared at the register office on the following day. Evans was from a well-known gangster family and his forthcoming marriage to a young model had been in all the local papers. Extortion was his game. He called it protection, but everyone knew what that meant.

The next morning there was a sudden turn in the weather, and a cold dampness hung in the air. Zena was exhausted. She could hardly move her leaden legs and wanted to curl up and sleep, but she had to get to Kendrick's by 9.15 to collect the papers she was to serve.

'Tommy Evans is getting married at noon today at the register office. It's the only place you'll catch him to serve those papers,' Alistair Kendrick Jnr said when she arrived. His round-cheeked baby face with a button dimple in his chin was the image of his father's. Zena took the papers with a heavy heart and went back to the office and fiddled around with some invoices until it was time to leave again. She was rarely afraid of taking on a job, but this time it was different. The Evans' family were notorious and a bully like him could easily turn nasty.

At eleven thirty Zena set off. Outside the register office she briefed Janet Evans, the first wife. She bore the hallmarks of a woman run down by life and her husband.

'Now, Mrs Evans, don't worry. There's nothing he can do to you in public. Identify him and then I can serve the papers. You don't need to speak to him, or have anything to do with him. Is that clear?'

Mrs Evans nodded, although Zena knew she'd be terrified of her ex-husband. Evans thought he was above the law – not surprising, considering the family he came from. He was loaded yet still refused to pay maintenance for his seven children. Janet Evans was at her wits' end and Zena was determined to get her the justice she deserved.

At half past twelve the heavy oak door of the register office burst open and out tripped a typical happy couple on their wedding day. The applause of their guests followed them as they laughed and kissed in the doorway, the wedding photographer clicking away as they did so. Janet nodded at Zena and whispered, 'That's him.'

Zena felt a pinch of meanness at spoiling their day. There was no choice. Her heart clenched as previous nightmares of hatchet-wielding henchman resurfaced. Most of the groom's guests were probably members of his villainous family. Zena hoped that the presence of the registrar would ensure there was no trouble.

Zena pushed through the crowd of guests; the papers clutched tightly in her hand.

'Oi, who you pushing missus?' A hefty looking man with a bull neck yanked her arm back.

'Sorry, I was just trying to get a better view.' Zena smiled at him in apology and he backed down.

'Well mind who you're stepping on,' he grumbled.

She edged closer to the couple and Evans looked her straight in the eye. She almost turned tail and ran. Maybe she should have sent Harry. No, she could do this.

Straightening herself up to her full height she marched straight up to Evans holding out the papers.

'Mr Evans, you have been served.' Zena held out her hand with the papers and looked him back in the eye.

His new bride screamed.

'What have you done, Tommy?' Her high-pitched, nasal bray echoed off the marble steps of the register office. It was in stark contrast to the beauty of her ivory silk dress and the delicacy of the rose and freesia bouquet in her hand.

'Shut up, Maisie. Leave it.' Evans glowered at her and glared at Zena, who flinched, expecting something to hit her. But to her surprise Evans took the papers like a lamb. Zena stood still for a second, unsure. Had he accepted them?

Zena whirled around, grabbed Janet Evans by the hand, and ran down the street before he or any of the guests could do anything.

'Oh Mrs Archer, I can't thank you enough. It will make such a difference to me and the kiddies,' Janet cried as they came to a shuddering halt.

'It's OK, Janet. It's my job, and you're in the right. With luck, the court will uphold the maintenance order, and he'll have to pay everything he owes you for the children's upkeep from now on. You deserve it.' Zena felt sorry for the poor woman.

*

Pleased with her day's work, Zena stopped at the butcher's in Wallasey Village on the way home. She would give Dave a treat and make some brawn. Bloodied sawdust slipped

297

under her feet as she pushed at the door. The ching of the bell summoned Mr Harrison from the cold store out the back.

'Good afternoon, Mrs Archer. A pleasure to see you, and may I say what a beautiful dress you have on today. What can I get you?' Mr Harrison looked at Zena and waited. She was a good customer, and he always flattered her into buying one sausage too many.

'Thank you. Have you a pig's head today, Mr Harrison?'

'No, it's the way I do my hair.'

Zena couldn't stop laughing as she looked at Mr Harrison's head, which was bald, pink, and bristly.

'I shall have to tell that to Mum. She'll love it.' It was moments like these when Zena missed her father. He adored a good joke. How was she going to carry on the bureau without him? Or should she even try?

20

WHAT NEXT?

July 1953. Adding the gold details on the wedding carriage calmed Zena's nerves. The sampler to commemorate the Coronation was close to being finished. Zena's mind was in a constant whirl. To sell or not to sell? If she decided to sell, what else would she do? Frank Boult was on her case. Word had got out about the potential sale. They had received an offer without even putting it on the market, and higher than their original estimate. The irresponsibility annoyed Zena. How dare they leak the information? She couldn't help wondering who wanted to buy it. Perhaps a rival firm?

Madge had been rattling on about how the business should be run, and Zena felt guilty that she hadn't mentioned anything to her mother about selling. Madge was still upset that Syd hadn't left it all to her. But he had known what would happen, which was why he had made her a sleeping partner. Fat chance of her sleeping.

Zena had discussed the dilemma repeatedly with Dave. That night in bed, she broached the subject again.

'It's Harry. I can't deal with his flagrant disregard for anything I say. I can't sack him, we've too much work on.

Maybe it's better to sell and do something else. A new profession. Or let Mum run the business and pay my wages.'

'Do you really believe that you'd be able to take orders from your mother?'

'Are you saying I can't take instructions from anyone? That's unfair, Dave, and you know it. There was never any question before. Dad was in charge. I took my instructions from him willingly.'

'Now then, love, don't get yourself all het up. All I'm saying is that taking instructions from your mother is an entirely different thing. There are other options that might be better.'

'What kind of options?'

'How about staying at home? Would that be such a terrible thing? We don't need the money. It would mean I'd see more of you.'

'What? That's no option. Stay home with Mum all day? I'd kill her, or she'd kill me!'

'There, what did I say.'

'It's all very well for you. Wait until you get *your* own business.'

'All right, all right. Look, you know I'll support you, no matter what you decide. All I want is for you to make the right decision. There's no need to rush into it.'

'OK then, my decision is to make no decision. You're right. There's no rush. I'll just have to be firmer with Harry. I can do it.'

*

The next morning, her mother was telling Dave off for burning the toast and grumbling because Nana had used all the hot water in the copper.

'Don't touch that kettle!' she shouted at Zena as she was about to lift it off the range to make some tea.

'Goodness me. Someone got out of bed the wrong side today,' Zena said, dropping the kettle back on the range and laughing. It made Madge angrier still.

Zena heard her father's voice in her ear. 'Come on then, Zena love, we've got work to do.' He was still present in everything she did. He wouldn't have given her an hour off, let alone a day.

Resigned, Zena put on her hat and coat, and headed out into the bluster of the day.

Standing at the doorway of the office, Zena was thunderstruck as she listened to Harry's voice through the door.

'Maybe we should buy the business and set up on our own. That would show that stuck-up girl of Syd's a thing or two.'

Harry hadn't heard Zena come into the office. He was a lazy good-for-nothing, but to stoop to this level of treachery. And how did he know she was thinking of selling? Zena needed a word with Frank Boult. He had ignored her letter demanding they keep quiet until she'd made her decision. He must have told Harry. The last person Zena would ever sell to. Her father would turn in his grave.

'Harry…' Joe, embarrassed, nodded in Zena's direction.

Harry whipped around, slid his eyes away from her, and charged out of the office. He shoved Zena hard as he pushed past.

'Joe, what is this? What does Harry mean? How could he buy the business?'

Joe could be slapdash, but deep down he was honest, and he loved Scott's. Syd had been a good friend to him. Joe would want to fulfil Syd's wishes. Zena was sure of it.

'Take no notice of him. Where would he get the cash anyway? And I'm near retirement anyhow.'

'But you know the business inside out Joe.' Zena had to agree with her father who had always said, "Joe gets there in the end."

'No, it's of no interest to me. I like to keep me hand in with the odd job as you know, but me and Iris, we want to see a bit of the world while we can.'

'You're not that old Joe. Retirement is a long way off yet.'

'Well Iris has always wanted to go to Australia. She's a sister out there. Now we've saved a bob or two, when I do retire we can take a cruise liner there. Spend the year travelling. Iris would love that.'

'That's all very well, Joe, but what am I to do about Harry?'

'He's hot-headed. He doesn't mean it. Give him another chance. Your daddy would.'

Zena was in two minds. Joe was right. Her father was too soft with his lads, as he called them. Zena had been determined to stand up to them, but it was easier said than done. She went for a walk to clear her head. Would she let Harry get the better of her?

What would Win say? Win was her go to when she needed advice. Dave would give in no matter what she decided. But Win would tell her the truth. She went to the telephone box and after speaking to the operator, she pushed the A button to connect the call.

'Win? Win?'

'Zena? What is it? You sound all in a fluster.'

'I am. I don't know what to do.'

'What about? What's wrong?'

'It's about the business. Should I sell up or should I stick it out? I heard Harry asking Joe if he wanted to buy the business and go in as partners. I can't let the business go to Harry, now can I?'

'What would you do if you did sell up? You'd need to find something else wouldn't you?'

'Dave wants me to stay at home, but it would drive me mad.'

'What about modelling? You loved that job at the House of Joseph.'

'But I'm too old. Who would want me now?'

'Oh come now Zena. You have so many skills. You could set up as a dressmaker even.'

'Yes I suppose so, but would I want to be making all those clothes for other people? Win I just don't know. What should I do?'

'If you're still not sure, then why don't you give it one more go with Harry and then take it from there.'

'I don't know. He riles me so. How can I…?'

'You can and you know you can. You are your father's daughter. Keep remembering what he would do.'

'You're right Win. Joe said more or less the same. Daddy would have given Harry another chance. I knew you'd have the answer.'

'Well I can't say it's an answer. Just a delay.'

Zena had the full intention of trying again with Harry. But returning to the office, she found Harry back at his desk, wide-legged and belligerent. No manners, and no hint of an apology.

The phone rang.

'Scott's Detective Bureau,' Zena said.

'Good afternoon, miss. Can I speak to the Principal, please?'

'I am the Principal.'

'No, I mean Mr Jones. Harry Jones, the Principal.'

'Mr Jones is not the Principal. I own this business, and Mr Jones is in my employ. Do you still wish to continue with your enquiry?'

The phone clicked. The client had rung off.

'You see, Zena. That's why I said I was the Principal. If they knew that a woman was running the business, they would take their enquiries elsewhere. I was doing it to help you.'

Harry wasn't even apologetic. Zena was furious. He had gone another step too far.

'For a start, I am Mrs Archer to you. You've done nothing but undermine me since I took over.'

'Now hold your horses…' Harry spluttered.

'No I won't. I kept you on because my father hired you. I don't know what he saw in you. You're a lazy good-for-nothing, and you're fired.'

'What? What do you mean fired? You can't do that.'

'Yes, I can. *I* am the Principal. Now pack up your things and get out.'

'You'll never get any clients now. They'll all come to me. I've been meaning to set up on my own anyway. Like

Charlie. You're doing me a favour.' Harry grabbed the few belongings he possessed and marched out. He shouted back over his shoulder, 'It's a two-bit operation, this, and you'll never survive. Good riddance to you.'

Zena sat down shaking. Maybe he was right.

'You're worth a hundred of him, Mrs Archer. Don't worry, we'll manage just fine without him,' Mrs Noble said in her quiet voice, as she placed a cup of tea on Zena's desk.

Maybe Mrs Noble was right. Against all the odds, she had succeeded in many if not most of her cases. She was proud of her skill and determination. Her father would be proud of her too. She picked up the telephone.

'Hello is that Frank Boult? Frank this is Mrs Archer of 3 Cook Street. I have decided not to sell.' Zena put the telephone back on its cradle, and immediately it rang. She picked it up, still trembling from her encounter with Harry.

'Scott's Detective Bureau, Zena Scott Archer, Principal speaking. How may I help?'

Zena and Marion

*Zena in the back
garden, Ripon Rd*

*Left to right Dave, Zena,
Syd, Marion and Madge*

*Zena and Dave on
their wedding day*

Zena Syd and Madge   *A family portrait*

*Zena in the Cook Street
Detective Bureau*

Zena at work 1953

AUTHOR'S NOTE

If you have read the preface, you'll know that Zena was a real life detective in 1940s Liverpool. One line, or a paragraph described in Zena's diaries or newspaper articles inspired the fully-fledged cases and anecdotes narrated in this novel. The detective cases featured are all based on fact. However most of the details and the characters (apart from Zena's family) have been fictionalised.

It was difficult to establish the exact dates of the cases covered in the novel, as Zena often retold stories many times over to the press – some with different names and details. But I have tried to capture the spirit of Zena and how she undertook her cases.

If you want to know more of Zena's real life, you can read about her and other female private investigators in Caitlin Davies' book *Private Inquiries: The Secret History of Female Sleuths* (The History Press, 2023).

ACKNOWLEDGEMENTS

The first person I must thank is Marion Smith and her husband Bill. Without those packets of diaries, newspapers and photos, writing this novel would never have come about. Marion and Bill have become dearly valued members of my family.

I would also like to thank Eric and Ann Shelmerdine, members of the Association of British Investigators, and Zena's long-time friends, who I hope to also call mine. They have been wonderful supporters of my venture into the world of private investigation. Thanks also to the other members of the ABI who agreed to be interviewed by me, George Devlin – may he rest in peace, Tony Imossi, Barbara Macy, and Stuart Price among them. It was a privilege to meet you and to be invited into your world. Thanks also to Mike Wright for introducing me to Barbara Macy, and to Joe Mercer for his advice on the circus and fairground cases. Barbara Macy took over the detective agency when Zena retired and was very generous with her time and stories.

I wouldn't have got this far without the earlier mentorship of Cressida Downing from the Bloomsbury Writers' and Artists' mentorship programme. She made me believe in myself, and that there was a story to tell. She convinced me it was ok to write Zena's story as fiction. Robert Peett of Holland House was kind enough to give me excellent feedback and put me in touch with Debi Alper of Jericho Writers. She helped me edit the novel and encouraged me not to give up.

In wonderful happenstance, Caitlin Davies contacted me as she too wanted to write about Zena in her book *Private Inquiries: The Secret History of Female Sleuths* (The History Press, 2023). Her enthusiasm and encouragement to collaborate has spurred me on to finish this novel and I hope our collaboration continues for years to come.

Lastly I would like to thank all my dear friends and family who believed I could do this, and supported me all the way. Some of you read bits of the novel and gave good advice along the way. You all know who you are. Jacqui Mair my sister, deserves a special mention, as she is the fantastic illustrator for the cover of this book. As does Jan Penrose, who proofread the final version. Thank you all.